Dust Girl

To the memories of
Woody Guthrie and Huddie "Lead Belly" Ledbetter:
I never did see you, see you
I never did get to meet you
I just heard your story, story
And I just want to sing your name.

THE AMERICAN FAIRY TRILOGY

~ BOOK ONE ~

Dust Girl

SARAH ZETTEL

RANDOM HOUSE 🏠 NEW YORK

Text copyright © 2012 by Sarah Zettel
Jacket art copyright © 2012 by Juliana Kolesova

Visit us on the Web! randomhouse.com/teens

Educators and librarians, for a variety of teaching tools,
visit us at randomhouse.com/teachers

Library of Congress Cataloging-in-Publication Data
Zettel, Sarah.
Dust girl / Sarah Zettel. — 1st ed.
p. cm. — (The American fairy trilogy ; bk. 1)
Summary: On the day in 1935 when her mother vanishes during the worst dust storm ever recorded in Kansas, Callie learns that she is not actually a human being.
ISBN 978-0-375-86938-9 (trade) — ISBN 978-0-375-96938-6 (lib. bdg.) —
ISBN 978-0-375-87381-2 (pbk.) — ISBN 978-0-375-98318-4 (ebook)
[1. Fairies—Fiction. 2. Magic—Fiction.] I. Title.
PZ7.Z448Dus 2012 [Fic]—dc23 2011043310

Printed in the United States of America
10 9 8 7 6 5 4 3 2 1

First Edition

Contents

1

In a Month Called April, a County Called Gray

Once upon a time, I was a girl called Callie. That, however, ended on Sunday, April 14, 1935. That was the day the worst dust storm ever recorded blew across Kansas. That was the day Mama vanished.

That was the day I found out I wasn't actually a human being.

Now, mind, I didn't know any of this when my cough woke me up that morning. Hot, still air, damp with my own breath, pressed against my face, and my tongue felt as stiff and strange as the sole of somebody else's shoe inside my mouth. Unwinding the muslin scarf, which Mama made me wear over my mouth and nose when I slept, didn't help much. It was already too hot and too dusty to breathe easy. Through the layers of sackcloth and muslin that we used for curtains, I could see the sun hovering like a rotten orange over the straight black Kansas horizon. Dust carried by the wind scratched and pattered against the windowpane, trying to get inside.

I lived with my mama in the Imperial Hotel in Slow Run, Kansas. Once, it was the finest hotel in the county, with its Moonlight Room, and the smoking lounge all decked out in red velveteen and gold fringe, and a ladies' parlor sporting an Italian marble fireplace so big I could stand up in it. Even empty, it was the biggest, grandest home imaginable.

Slow Run itself was not a place you ever heard of, unless you had to live there or stop overnight on your way somewhere else. Used to be a lot of people did stay overnight. A lot of things used to happen in Slow Run. The trains used to bring in travelers and take out carloads of wheat from the grain elevator. Mama used to make plenty of money running the hotel her parents started.

It used to rain. But now Kansas was part of the Dust Bowl, along with Oklahoma, Texas, Arkansas, and Indiana, and had been for five, maybe six years. I could just about remember the time when I looked out my window to see the green wheat rippling all around the straight lines of clapboard buildings that made up Slow Run. Now there was nothing but the blowing dirt under that rotten orange sun.

I jumped off my brass bed, ran to the bathroom, and switched on the tap. Water came out in a thin gray stream, but at least it came. It didn't always. I drank a little to rinse my mouth. It tasted like old tin. I plugged the basin drain and ran about an inch of water into the sink so I could scrub my face and hands with the little piece of store-bought soap. I wiped myself down with the washrag so the soap wouldn't get into the basin water. I got store-bought soap because of my good skin, Mama said. My skin was cream-colored and soft with not too many freckles. But that meant I had to take special care of it, and always wear a hat and gloves when I went outdoors so I wouldn't turn brown. I had good eyes too, she said, a stormy blue-gray color that people said turned steel gray when I got mad. My hair was another story. My black hair was my mother's worst enemy. "So coarse," she'd mutter while she combed the tangles out. She'd wash it in lye water and lemon juice, when we could get them. But even when we couldn't, it had to be brushed a hundred strokes every night and kept done up in tight braids so it would be nicely wavy.

"When you're older, Callie, we'll put it up in a proper chignon," Mama told me. "It'll be so pretty. Until then, we'll just have to do our best."

Doing our best meant a lot of things to Mama. It meant keeping ourselves and the hotel clean, and minding our manners even when there was no one to see or care. It meant being patient, even on the worst days when my lungs felt so heavy from breathing in the blow dust all the time that they dragged my whole body down.

My workday dress used to be yellow, but wash soap and dust had turned it a kind of pale brown. I looped my scarf over my arm and carefully carried my wash water down the short, narrow hallway. Our staff quarters at the back of the hotel had two bedrooms, the kitchen, and a little sitting room. As expected, the kitchen was empty. Mama would be somewhere in the main part of the hotel, trying to chase Gray County back outside.

I scooped one cup of water out of my basin and poured slow drips onto the tomatoes growing in soup cans on the windowsill. The rest went into the tin bucket by the door for the chickens. Before opening the door, though, I pulled on my canvas work hat and gloves and tied my scarf securely over my face.

As soon as I stepped off the porch, sweat prickled on the back of my neck and at the edges of my scarf. The stems from our dead garden rattled in the hot wind. A brown grasshopper clung to one broken twig, waiting for a chance to get into the house and between my sheets.

I tried not to hate the hoppers, even when they got into the water basin or my shoes. The only reason we still had chickens was that the birds could live on hoppers and the little green worms that crawled out of the sunbaked fence posts.

The hens fought each other over the water while I helped myself at the nesting boxes. We were lucky today. Six warm brown eggs went into my pockets. My mouth watered. Maybe we could sell a few at the store for flour, or milk, or even butter, if there was any at Van Iykes's Mercantile. The mercantile was the last store in town. There used to be a choice between Van Iykes's and Schweitzer's Emporium. But last week, Mr. and Mrs. Schweitzer locked their doors, tossed the key in the dust, climbed into their truck with their babies, Sophie and Todd, and drove away. Mama and I stood out on the porch and watched them leave.

"Cowards," I muttered, because I didn't want to think about how much I wanted to leave with them.

As if that thought was a signal, my cough started up again, in sharp little bursts. It hurt, but not as much as knowing Mama would never leave Slow Run.

The truth was, Mama was kind of crazy, and had been for years, but there was nothing anybody could do about it. Especially not me. She acted normal about most things. About everything, really, except my papa. My papa, Daniel LeRoux, had run out on Mama before I was born. He'd promised he would come back, and she'd promised she would wait for him. That promise kept us both pegged to this place while the state of Kansas dried up and blew away.

The wind swirled dust across the tops of my shoes and tugged at my skirts.

Look shhhhaaaarrrrp, said a slow, soft voice. *Look shhhhaaaarrrrp. Shhhheeee's nearrrr. . . .*

"Who's that!" I spun around. But there was nobody there.

Shhhheeee's nearrrr . . . shhhheeee'ssss clossse. . . .

"Casey Wilkes, if that's you . . ." I ran around the corner of the hotel.

From here, the whole of Slow Run spread out stark and

plain: the square clapboard and brick buildings marking out the straight, dust-filled streets; the four church steeples weathered a pale gray; the dusty tumbleweeds leaning lazily against the walls. Farther out, sagging barbed-wire fences ran alongside the black lines of the railroad tracks all the way to the hazy outline of the grain elevator, with the spindly windmills standing sentry in between.

What there wasn't was any person close enough to whisper in my ear. Except I could still hear the soft, deep, strangely beautiful voice.

Clossser, clossser. Look shhhhaaaarrrrp. . . .

I turned and ran for the kitchen door.

2

I Got the Dust Pneumonia in My Lungs

"Calliope! What on earth . . . ?" cried Mama.

I shoved the kitchen door shut behind me and leaned against it, wheezing hard, pain clamping down on my lungs and stomach with each breath.

"What's the matter, Callie honey?" Mama shook out the match she'd been using to light the stove and came over to undo my scarf.

Mama had never been a big woman, and work and heat had worn her thin and bled the color from her golden hair. Nothing had touched her eyes, though. Those were still big and blue with dark lashes, the eyes of a little girl in an old woman's face.

"Snake," I croaked as Mama pulled my scarf off. "Rattler . . . in the yard. Startled me."

"Good heavens, that's all we need." Mama stepped around me and opened the door, peering out into the haze. "Well, I can't see anything now. We'll just have to hope it stays out there." She shut the door firmly and put the latch on it, as if that would make a difference. "Did you get anything from the hens?"

"Six eggs." I set my pretty brown prizes on the counter. Fortunately, they'd survived all my charging around.

"Well done!" She clapped her long hands, and her blue eyes sparkled. "We'll save three for supper." Mama selected the eggs with care and laid them in a bowl in the icebox. There was no ice, of course, but it made a good pantry because the dust had a hard time weaseling its way through the sealed door. "See if there's any bread left in the box, Callie."

There was, a hard brown heel wrapped in layers of cheesecloth and newspaper. I sliced it carefully so it wouldn't crumble. Humming "The Midnight Special" under her breath, Mama dropped the bread into the cast-iron skillet, where it could fry in the grease alongside the other three eggs. Reverend Schauenbergh said it wasn't a decent song, but it was her favorite. She used to sing it to me as a lullaby when I was a baby, and just hearing it could make me feel better, especially when it came with the smell of Mama's cooking.

Mama was an amazing cook. Everything she put her hand to turned out delicious. Back when the hotel was open, she'd fixed whole banquets: roast beef and roast turkey with heaps of creamy mashed potatoes, and all kinds of breads and puddings and congealed salads. She could trim up a wedding cake with sugar flowers you'd swear were just picked in the garden. When she brought her pies to the county fair, the other ladies just gave up and went home. Grandma once said it had been Mama's cooking that really caught my father's attention. It was one of the few times Grandma mentioned him at all.

The smell of Mama's good cooking filled the kitchen, and my stomach squeezed so tight it forced a fresh barking cough out of my lungs.

"Oh, honey!" Mama dropped her fork and ran to me, rubbing my back firmly. "Let it go, Callie."

I tried. My lungs strained and coughed, and strained and coughed, but there wasn't any room to get the air in. Mother whacked me hard between my shoulders. A spill of bitter brown goop splatted onto the table.

Now I could breathe, long, harsh gasps. Mama took me in her arms and held me tight. Her embrace was hot and she smelled like sweat, dust, and grease, but I wanted her. I wanted to crawl inside her mind to find that place that let her smile and sing through the worst dust storms. If I had to be crazy, I wanted my mama's kind of crazy, because she was never afraid.

"It's all right now, Callie," she murmured, sitting me down at the table. She put a cup with an inch of water in front of me.

"Sip it slow, honey. You'll feel better in a minute."

My cheeks and eyes burned with shame for having spit up all over the table where we had to eat. Mama said nothing, just wiped up my mess with one of her cleaning rags. The water was warm and tasted stale, but it felt good sliding down my raw throat.

Mama forked our breakfast onto clean plates and set them on the table. She'd given me two whole eggs and most of the bread. My throat hurt at the thought of trying to swallow the hard bread.

"I'm not that hungry, Mama."

"Nonsense." She sliced her fried bread into tiny, ladylike bits with her tarnished knife. "You're a growing girl. When your father gets back, I don't want him thinking I've starved you."

Mention of my father took away what was left of my appetite, but I picked up my fork and knife and cut through my eggs. Golden yolk ran across the white china and leached into the fried bread. If I didn't look up, I wouldn't have to see how Mama's eyes emptied out like they always did when she thought about my papa.

Daniel LeRoux had been a piano player. He didn't come through Slow Run on the train like most people, or even in a Model T Ford. He drove up to the front door in a brand-new buggy pulled by a team of matched horses. He said he was out of Kansas City and looking for work. He could play all the new dances, so my grandparents let him stay.

Mama said he had a wonderful smile, that he could

sing like an angel and play like the devil. "But you don't need to tell anybody else that," she whispered to me. "We'll just let people go on thinking their fool thoughts. We'll just keep your papa our secret, all right?"

I'd promised, and I kept that promise, not because Papa was a jazz musician, which was bad enough, or because he'd never married Mama, which was worse. But because of the thing we never, ever talked about.

My papa was a black man. That made me a black girl. That meant there was a whole world of things I couldn't do, and places I couldn't go. I couldn't sit in the Moonlight Room, or go to the white school, or try on clothes at the emporium, or ride in a Pullman car on the train, if we ever went anywhere. If anybody knew about Papa, and I got caught doing any of those things, I could end up in jail. Or dead.

That was the real reason Mama just let people go on thinking my father had been an Irish traveling salesman named Mike McGinty, and called me Callie McGinty to anybody official. But it was Daniel LeRoux's ring she never took off, and Daniel LeRoux she insisted was coming back.

A knock sounded at the door. Mama wiped her mouth and folded her napkin neatly before she got up to answer it.

"Mornin', Maggie." Dr. Kenny shook the dust off the brim of his Stetson hat before he stepped inside. He was a big gray man with cheeks that sagged loose around his face.

"Good morning, Doctor," Mama said, as polite as if welcoming in a king. "Won't you sit down? I'm sorry, the coffee's not done yet. . . ." There was no coffee, not even chicory. A glance at the stove with its single pan would tell Dr. Kenny as much.

"Nothing for me, thank you," he said. "I just came by to say . . ." He cleared his throat. "I wanted to tell you we're leaving."

"Oh?" Mama raised her eyebrows, as if she couldn't think of a single reason why someone would do such an odd thing.

"I hoped we'd be able to stick it out, but . . . well, it's been five years since the county's seen a drop of rain, and there's the children to think of, and Mrs. Kenny's got cousins in Chicago. So . . ."

He was talking to me. I put my fork down quietly, even while egg and bread tried to come back up my sore throat.

"Well. Chicago." Mama's voice wavered just the tiniest bit. "I do hope you'll write to us. I'd love to hear about Chicago, and I'm sure Callie would too. Wouldn't you, Callie?"

"Yes, please." But inside I was thinking, *The doctor's going. That's got to be the last straw. There can't be anything left if even he's going.*

He looked at me like there was a whole lot he wanted to say, starting with "I'm sorry." He cleared his throat again. "I wanted to give Callie's lungs one more listen before we left."

"That's very kind, Dr. Kenny. Thank you."

He put his black bag down on the table and got out his

stethoscope. He polished its steel bell carefully with a huge white handkerchief before he laid it against my chest.

"Breathe deep, Callie."

It hurt, and I coughed, which hurt worse, and I coughed again. Dr. Kenny sat back, pulling the stems out of his ears and shaking his head.

"Maggie . . ." He looked Mama straight in the eye. "I'm telling you for the last time, you've got to get this girl out of here."

"We'll manage fine, Doctor. Callie wears her scarf every night and when she goes outside. . . ."

"This is the dust pneumonia, Maggie. Scarf or no scarf, her lungs are filling up with dirt, and pretty soon she won't be able to breathe at all."

"Her father will be back soon and we'll all go together." Mama laid the words down like bricks, one on top of the other, blocking off the only door.

The doctor's sagging face twisted tight. "If it's money, Maggie, I can loan you the train fare. You pay us back when you get settled someplace, maybe in St. Louis, or Atlanta. . . ."

"That's very kind of you, but we'll be perfectly all right."

Dr. Kenny bowed his head. "I do hope so, Maggie. I do." He dug a bottle of soothing syrup out of his bag and handed it to Mama. She nodded her thanks, and he gathered up his things.

"You be a good girl and mind your mother, Callie."

His eyes met mine once more. He was sorry. Maybe even real sorry. But we both knew that wasn't going to change anything.

The door closed hard behind him.

Mama sat back down at her place. "Don't you worry, Callie." She sliced up the last of her toast and dipped it neatly into the drying egg yolk. "We'll be fine."

My stomach heaved. Maybe she'd be fine, but I wouldn't. I had the dust pneumonia. The dust was going to keep right on filling up my lungs until I smothered and died. Then my crazy mama would bury me next to my grandparents in the Methodist churchyard and keep right on waiting for a man who ran out on her. On us.

I jumped up and ran after Dr. Kenny, kicking up clouds of dust.

3

She Blowed Away

Dr. Kenny was just climbing into his car. He saw me running across the dead, dirty yard, though, and stopped with one foot on the running board.

"Please." I panted. "Please. Take me . . . us with you."

The doctor hunched in on himself. I saw how tightly his belt cinched his waist, and how wrinkled and sunburned the skin on his hands was. *He's drying up.* "I wish I could, Callie, but . . ."

But your mother won't go. He didn't say that, but I could hear the words anyway.

"Please."

"We've only got the Model T, and there's five of us as it is." His gaze drifted to the flat horizon, as if there was a magnet pulling everything over its edge. "You've got to talk to her, Callie. She does love you." He laid one big, hairy hand on my shoulder. "She'll do whatever it takes to keep you safe."

So that was that. I turned away and trudged back across the yard. The car's engine coughed and I coughed back. Its tires ground against the dust and the doctor drove away.

Look shhhhaaaarrrrp. The wind gusted hard around my ears, and the dust scraped like hot fingernails against my cheeks. *Wheeeerrrre? Wheeeerrrre issss shhhheeee?*

I lifted my head. "Who are you?"

Clossse, the wind and dust answered. *Weeee knoooow shhhheeee's clossse. . . .* And it was gone again.

Maybe I should've told Dr. Kenny about the voice. If he'd known I was starting to hear things, maybe he would've taken me with him. Maybe I was better off never having to watch him make that choice.

Shaking, I walked back inside.

Mama wasn't in the kitchen. A clean napkin covered my plate. The Maxwell House coffee can where we kept the ready cash sat on the table, with the bills and coins laid out neatly beside it: a five, two ones, and six pennies. Not enough for train fare for even one person as far as Topeka, never mind Georgia or California.

The bankbook lay there too, but that was useless. Slow Run's bank had crashed and closed all the way back in '29. The farmers went out to Constantinople to pay their mortgages, the ones who could still pay, that is. The rest of us didn't bother with banks anymore.

I took the deepest breath I could and tried to think. There had to be some way to get money, someone we could still sell out to. My bodiless dust voice and Mama's empty-headed dreams couldn't be all we had left.

There was only one place Mama went when the news got bad. The Moonlight Room. It was her favorite place in the whole world. Once upon a time it had been mine too. The Moonlight Room had served as the Sunday parlor for everybody within fifty miles of Slow Run. The Moonlight held weddings, dances, and political banquets. We even had a movie projector and a screen we could pull down at the back of the little stage.

It also had my father's piano.

I'd never actually seen the instrument. Under its starched sheet, it hovered like a ghost at the edge of the Moonlight Room's half-circle stage. I'd tried to lift the corner of the sheet once to creep under during a game of hide-and-seek, but Mama caught me and slapped my hands so hard I cried.

"Nobody touches the piano!" she shouted. "Nobody but your papa!"

The Moonlight Room was always dark now. Cobwebs streaked its velvet curtains. Netting covered the gilt and crystal chandelier. I walked down the exact center of the red carpet runner, down the broad front hall that ran from the hotel lobby to the Moonlight. If I moved slowly enough, maybe an idea would find me before I got to the door.

There has to be something I can say, I prayed with every part of me. *Something I can do. I'll do anything. Please . . .*

"Please." Mama's voice drifted into the hall, a perfect echo to my own frightened prayer. Except she wasn't praying to Heaven. "Please, Daniel. You promised. You *swore* to me. . . ."

I eased the door open. The tables and chairs stood like half-carved headstones under their dustcovers. Mama was on the stage, doubled over like me when the coughing got bad. Both her hands clutched the white sheet that shrouded my father's piano.

"I've tried, Daniel. I waited as long as I could. . . ."

I swallowed a cough. "Mama?"

"Callie!" Mama straightened up fast, yanking her manners and deportment over her. "Good. Come here, honey."

I didn't like the light tone to her voice. It didn't match her eyes. They held a wildness I'd never seen before.

I inched forward. It was wrong to be afraid of my own mother, but fear choked me like the dust in my lungs.

"Help me with this." Mama lifted the edge of the sheet and tugged.

I gasped. She never uncovered the piano. No one was allowed to touch it, not ever.

"Close your mouth, Callie, you'll catch flies." My jaw snapped shut. "Now help me, there's a good girl."

It was like she'd asked me to unwind an Egyptian mummy. I'd come in here thinking to beg her to leave, or maybe yell at her, or get down on my knees like in a melodrama. Never in a million years did I expect her to ask me to uncover the piano. But she just stood there, and I didn't know what else to do. So I climbed the three steps to the stage, grasped the dust-stiffened cloth, and helped her lift it aside.

My first sight of my father's piano was sort of disappointing. It was the same kind of upright piano you could see in any parlor in town. The only remarkable thing was that its pale wood was absolutely clean. Not a speck of dust marred the curlicue and thistle flower carving across its front. The white keys all but glowed in the dark.

"Now, Callie, I want you to play," said Mama.

"Play?" I shifted my weight uneasily.

"Yes. Sit down, and play the piano."

This is it. She's gone right round the bend this time. "I can't play piano, Mama," I reminded her. "You never let me learn."

"Well, you'll just have to do your best."

"But why?"

"So your father will hear you." Her knuckles turned white as her hands clutched at each other. "I've tried and I've tried, but he won't listen to me."

Disbelief slackened my jaw again. "That's because he's *gone,* Mama! He left us!"

"He just doesn't know what kind of trouble we're in." Her demeanor remained terribly calm. "But he'll know it's you playing his piano and he'll have to answer you."

"That's crazy, Mama!" I screamed. "You're crazy!"

The slap was so sudden, I didn't even know why my cheek hurt, or why the world spun. But there was Mama, rearing up over me as angry as I'd ever seen her, hand raised high.

"Calliope Margaret LeRoux, you will do as you are told!"

My knees buckled, sitting me down hard on the bench. Dazed, I scooted around to face the piano. The keys were smooth white and pure black, reflecting what little light oozed between the velveteen drapes.

Waiting for me. The thought popped into my spinning mind as I stared at those shiny keys. *They've been waiting a long time.*

I touched a black key with a tentative finger. One thin note lifted into the stuffy room. My heart fluttered in my chest, and my blood went still in my veins.

Mama nodded. "Louder, honey. He's got to hear you."

I fit the fingers of my left hand to the white keys, the ones on my right to the black. Something rose inside me. It pushed against my heart and crowded my dust-filled lungs.

"Mama . . ." The thing was trying to get down to my hands, and there was no telling what it would do once it did.

"Play, Callie!"

I pressed down on the keys. A chord, a full, clear moment of music rang through the room. Its vibration resonated through the keys, through my skin, and into my finger bones. It caught hold of that thing inside and pulled.

My wrists lifted. My fingers rearranged themselves on the keys. My left hand started to rock and jump back and forth on the low, deep keys, making a steady beat. At the same time, my right hand danced up and down across the high, bright keys, setting a lively melody free to soar through the room.

Boogie. I was playing boogie-woogie, joyous, infectious, dangerous music. Music that made Reverend Schauenbergh slam the pulpit and bellow about the end of the world. But Reverend Schauenbergh was long gone, and here at the end of the world this music had blown into my head, and into my suddenly nimble hands.

"That's it, Callie!" cried Mama. "Play loud!"

Mama. Mama, who'd let her mind trickle away waiting for a man who would never come back. Mama, who'd kept us here while the dust crawled into my lungs. She should have gone, she should be gone. . . .

"No, Callie. Oh, no. I know you're angry, but you mustn't play for me, not like that. Play for your papa, honey. Play him back to us."

Anger burned at the base of my throat. It swelled in my dust-filled lungs and surged down my hands. Papa was the last person to sit at this piano. My fingers touched the keys like his did. Papa had gone off and left us, left *me* to choke and die in the dust. . . . The beat under my left hand grew harder; the dance in my right grew faster. I was going to die. The man who had played this piano, he broke my mama's heart so hard her mind broke with it, and he didn't even know I was alive. I breathed in music the way I breathed in the dust. Breathed it in and poured it out again, loud and wild and sick and angry.

"No, Callie!" cried Mama. "Not like that!"

But Mama seemed a long way away. Mama was already gone. And I was here. For just this little while, I was still alive and my papa was going to know about it. Just this once, wherever he was, whoever he'd left us for, he was going to hear me. The whole world was going to hear.

There she issss! cried a voice, low and wild as the wind rattling the shingles. *There! THERE!*

"Calliope, *stop!*"

The world spun like when Mama had slapped me, and something hard slammed against my shoulder. I gasped, coughed, and shuddered. I was on the floor of the stage with Mama standing over me, trembling. She must have knocked me off the bench. I was stunned and furious, but only for a minute.

The music had stopped, but the other sound, the roaring sound, hadn't. Mama went white. She ran to the windows and yanked back the curtains.

"No," whispered Mama.

On the edge of the flat Kansas prairie, a range of midnight-black mountains loomed over Slow Run. But they weren't standing still like mountains should. Those mountains surged and boiled, and they lumbered slowly forward.

Heeeerrrre! the mountains roared. *Sheeee'ssss heeeerrrre!*

"Dust." I struggled to my feet, coughing the whole way. "Mama, it's a duster!"

Mama ran out of the Moonlight Room without looking back. Weak as a kitten, I staggered down the stage steps and into the hallway after her.

A door slammed.

Oh, no. No, please, no.

I stumbled into the kitchen, and a gust of wind almost knocked me over. The door swung free on its hinges.

"Mama!" Dust slammed into my eyes and nose and filled my open mouth. Reeling, I snatched the napkin off the remains of my breakfast and pressed it over my face.

"Go away!" Mama screamed from outside. "Go away! She didn't mean it! She's just a child! She didn't mean it!"

Yes, she did, laughed the voice. *Yessss, she did! Weeee sssseeeee you noooow! Weeee got you now!*

"No!" I hollered into the cloth. "Leave her alone!" My flailing hand hit the threshold, and the mountains tumbled down over me.

A burning, roaring darkness swallowed me, like I was Hansel and Gretel's witch shoved headfirst into the stove. I shrieked and swallowed dust. The floor hit my knees, my chest, my chin. I lay there, blind, deaf, and burning. Grit scraped every inch of my skin, and the storm wind drove it in like needles. My head went dizzy, and a dozen different pictures flashed in front of my blind eyes—Reverend Schauenbergh shouting that this was the end of the world; Dr. Kenny's rattletrap Model T rolling down the road; my hands on the gleaming piano keys; people dancing in an arena with a crowd cheering them on; a huge, ugly man striding grimly through the dust with a sawed-off shotgun tucked under his arm; a skinny, mangy dog staggering through the storm; Mama stretching her arms out as the mountains poured down.

Mama. Have to find Mama.

I fumbled with the corners of my napkin and got it knotted around my face. I found the door frame and hauled myself up. Hanging on tight, I made myself open my eyes, just a crack.

Lightning flashed overhead, and for a heartbeat, I could see the wind. Red, beige, and black, it billowed and moaned past the door. The steps had already vanished under drifts of dust. So had the path to the henhouse. So had the henhouse.

"Mama!" *What if she's fallen? What if the dust already buried her?*

Lightning flickered again, showing a black shadow against the whirling red dust, a human shape staggering through the storm. I made to rush forward, but I stopped. I could barely see, and all the landmarks were gone. What if I got out there and couldn't find the way back? It happened in blizzards. We could both be lost a few feet from our back door.

The thought of blizzards gave me an idea. Mama kept a clothesline on a shelf in the canning room. I ran for it and threw the coil over my shoulder. My hands wouldn't stop shaking, but I gritted my teeth until they hurt and I managed to get one end of the rope knotted around the doorknob.

With the other end tied around my waist, I stepped off the back porch and sank right up to my knees in hot dust.

Each step forward wrenched another cough out of me.

Each step brought the silhouette in the dust a little closer, but behind that thickening screen of dust, it kept changing its shape. First it was a person. Then it was a skinny dog. Then it was a person again.

The silhouette crumpled. I screamed and lunged forward, scrabbling in the dust. A hand grabbed mine. I heaved myself backward so hard I almost fell.

But it wasn't Mama who staggered upright in front of me.

It was a man.

4

It Dusted Us Over, and It Covered Us Under

Dust sluiced off the stranger's shoulders and was whipped away by the wind. He was tall and skinny and dark. His eyes flashed beneath a wide-brimmed, high-crowned hat. But all I could really see was that he wasn't my mother.

"Mama!" I screamed past the man. Dust poured straight down my throat. I gagged and heaved. A big, rough hand clamped across my mouth, shoving my scarf back into place.

The wind gusted hard, driving dust into my eyes, and the hand slithered away as the man fell to his knees again. Dust filled up the whole world, and my lifeline was stretched taut. No matter how bad I wanted to, I couldn't go any farther. The stranger slumped down lower, his hands digging into the hot dust, looking for solid ground to hold him up.

I didn't know who or what he was, but I couldn't leave him out here.

Hanging on tight to the rope with one hand, I tugged on the man's shirtsleeve until he staggered to his feet again. I pressed his hand to my shoulder so he could hold on to me. His grip tightened, signaling he understood.

I found the rope with my fingers, and hand over hand, I followed it. There was nothing to hear but the roaring wind. Nothing to see but the rolling red-tinted darkness. That bony hand clamped tight to my shoulder was the only way I knew the stranger stayed with me.

After what felt like a year in that roaring dark, my toes hit the back steps. I kept one hand on the rope and groped with the other until my fingertips found the kitchen door. Fumbling, I gripped the handle and yanked it open. The man fell inside behind me, sprawling full length on the floor.

"Mister!"

The man didn't move. He lay there, still as death among the dust drifts on the yellow linoleum.

Water. Had to get water. There was water in the icebox. I gulped a swallow straight from the pitcher, and coughed and choked and spat red mud into the sink. Even with the door shut, the dust hung in the air, as thick as coal smoke. The wind howled all around, and the dust scrabbled at the windowpanes, prying at the seams, looking for the weak spots. My throat was still choked half full with dust but I could breathe, and think.

I got down on hands and knees and tugged against the fallen man's shoulders until he rolled onto his back.

"Mister, wake up!" I splashed water onto his face. "We can't stay here! Wake up!"

The stranger's eyelids snapped open. For a second, I saw two black holes where his eyes should have been. But then he blinked, and they were just eyes.

"Get up!" I hollered over my shoulder as I ran to grab the clean dish towels off the shelf by the stove. "We gotta get in the parlor!"

The man said nothing, just followed me as I staggered through to the ladies' parlor carrying the water jug and towels. The chandelier had only one bulb left, but it lit when I flipped the switch. Dust turned the light hazy and pink. So it was red dust. Kansas dust is gray. It's Oklahoma dust that's red. This was Oklahoma blowing over us.

I kicked the door shut and stuffed the dish towels into the water jug to wet them down.

"Here, get the windowsills." I shoved a wet towel at the man. He stared at it like he'd never seen such a thing before. But as I jammed my own roll of damp cloth beneath the door, he seemed to get the idea.

All around us the Imperial groaned long and slow, complaining as it leaned into the wind. We kept stuffing towels around the edges of the doors and the one window behind its velveteen draperies until they were all used up. Then we both kind of backed into the middle of the room and stood there, panting. Finally, I had a chance to take a good long look at the stranger I'd pulled out of the storm. He was an Indian—Apache, maybe, or Shawnee. He had copper-red skin, a long face, and a long mouth to go with it. His skin hung loose around his bones and dragged the corners of his mouth down, making him look like the saddest thing in the world. He wore his black hair in two club-shaped pigtails tied with leather thongs and blue beads. Somehow he'd kept hold of his hat. It was as black as his eyes, with a couple of feathers stuck into a furry band that had a loose end dangling over the brim like a tail. His bright red shirt and blue jeans were stiff with dust.

"Did you see a woman out there?" I asked. "My mother?"

His black eyes emptied right out, the way Mama's did when she talked about Papa. My heart froze.

"I saw a white woman, dressed all in sorrow." He had a deep, rumbling voice, like he was pulling it right out of the ground. "She called for her lover."

"Where'd she go?"

Light and shadow shifted in his black eyes. He blinked and shook his head. "Sorry. Can't see that far."

I felt light, like my feet didn't touch the floor. I couldn't hear anything right. I thought maybe I had gone deaf from the pounding the wind had given my ears. I drifted over to the window and shoved the red velveteen back with both hands.

Outside was gone. There was only a wall of shifting dirt

pressed up against the window. I'd have thought we were buried, but the wind rattled the glass in its frame as if it was a burglar checking the latch.

Mama was out there.

"It's my fault," I whispered.

"How your fault?" asked the man.

Weeee sssseeeee you noooow! Weeee got you now! The voice swirled through the memories in the back of my head.

"I played the piano and the storm came. Now it's got her. It's all my fault!"

I shook. The tremors loosened a cough, and another, and a dozen more, and I couldn't stop them. My lungs were on fire. I was burning to ash, to dust. Brown Callie dust to mix with the red Oklahoma dust and then blow away.

I kind of passed out after that.

When I came to, I was lying on the couch and staring up at the ceiling. My throat hurt bad. My mouth tasted like dust, but I could breathe. I sat up. The stranger sat in front of the marble fireplace, his huge hands dangling on his knees.

"You're back." He climbed to his feet. He was big too. From where I lay, it looked like his hat almost brushed the chandelier. "That's good."

The pitcher sat on the coffee table. The man poured clean water into a glass I didn't remember bringing in. I didn't think there was any water left. He could have gone out and gotten some, except it looked like the towels were all still in place around the door.

While I drank the sweet, clean water and tried to get my head back together, the man paced around the edges of the room. His dusty cowboy boots made no sound at all on the carpet. His steps were long, but he moved carefully, gracefully. In fact, he seemed to kind of flow around the furniture.

"That was you making the music?" he asked.

I nodded, and he grunted. "Thought I heard something new. 'Swhy I came. Too curious for my own damn good, like always." He sighed. "You're not strong enough to do this, though." He flicked his eyes toward the curtains that hid us from the storm. "This is somebody else."

"Who?"

"If I knew, you think I'd let them on my land?" he snapped.

"Your land?"

But he wasn't listening to me. "Stupid white people. Stupid yellow people, or stupid brown people. Bringing in all kinds of ghosts and little spirits. Can't even tell who's in the game anymore." He shivered and coughed and spat on the floor.

"Hey!"

"Sorry. No manners. Me dirty injun." He grinned, big and stupid. His teeth were all brown, and he smelled like tobacco and whiskey. His tail waved back and forth.

Tail? I ground my knuckles into my eyes. The tail was gone. When I blinked again, he wasn't taking up so much space. I'd thought he was big, but he was a little old man, with a million wrinkles around his black eyes and sagging skin on his bony hands. I could've taken one of the droopy feathers out of his hatband and knocked him over with it.

Except he hadn't been like that a minute ago. Except he'd always been like that. I knuckled my eyes again.

"Who are you?"

"Who are *you*?" he shot back.

"Callie McGinty."

He grunted. "That's what you're called. Who are you?"

I didn't mean to answer. I never told anybody about my real last name. But he looked at me so steady, and he'd seen Mama in the storm. I wanted to know what he knew. To do that, I had to answer him.

"Calliope LeRoux."

He considered that. "Closer. Try again. Who are you?"

"I don't know," I whispered.

He blinked. "Me neither. Well, Calliope LeRoux, you can call me Baya."

I wrinkled my nose. "I thought injuns all had names like Crazy Horse or Sitting Bull and stuff."

"You need to be real careful, Dust Girl, before saying you know the right names for what walks this world. It'll get you into even more trouble."

I almost said I wasn't in any trouble, but you know

what? I was alone here with a strange red man, and outside, Oklahoma was rolling over the top of Kansas. I was in huge trouble.

I had only one question left in me. It was a stupid, nutty question. But because of how the storm started, because of my music and what Mama said before the storm came down, I had to ask.

"Are you my father?"

Baya looked at me for a long moment. He didn't seem quite so old and wrinkled anymore. His eyes went from midnight black to autumn brown.

"No," he said at last. "I don't think so."

I collapsed back on the sofa, which just made me start coughing again. Baya settled back down cross-legged in front of the fireplace, like he was waiting for something. I didn't want to look at him anymore. I didn't want to think about him. I got up, switched on the radio, and spun the dial, searching for a voice, any voice, just so I'd know there was somebody else left alive in the world. There had to be somebody out there, saying what was going on, how big the storm was, and when it was going to be over. But there was just the crackling static that rose and fell with the wind. I shivered and shut it off. I looked at Baya again. He just sat there, saying nothing, doing nothing.

"Do you . . ." I found myself wondering desperately what Mama would do with a stranger in the parlor. "Do you want something to eat?"

"You got food?"

The clock on the mantel said it was only just going on eleven. But cooking us up lunch would mean I could think about something besides the storm and Mama being gone.

"Put the towels back under the door as soon as I'm out," I told him. I eased the door back, squeezed through, and shut it tight behind me.

It wasn't too bad in the kitchen. The windows were still taped over from the last duster, but an inch-deep drift had already sifted under the back door. I put on the lights, and they flickered hard but stayed lit.

The stove was working too, and that was something. I pulled a bowl down from the cupboard and wiped it out. There was one can of condensed milk left in the pantry, and one can of stewed tomatoes. I thought about holding those back, but then I got reckless. If this was the end of the world, why save anything?

I dumped the tomatoes in a pot and put them on the back burner to heat. There were two potatoes left in the root bin. I peeled and sliced them up and tossed them into the skillet and got them cooking, making sure I put the skillet lid on tight. I wiped the bowl out again, cracked the eggs, and whisked in some of the condensed milk. When the potatoes were tender, I pushed them to the side with the fork and poured in the eggs. The whole mass sizzled and steamed. I couldn't smell anything, though. My nose was too filled with dust.

While I worked, I was sure I was being watched. It

was that feeling right in the back of your neck that gets tighter and tighter the harder you try to ignore it. I knew they were right outside the window, hands and faces pressed up against the glass. But it didn't matter how many times I looked over my shoulder; I couldn't see anything except the dust. But I knew they were out there. I *knew* it.

I fixed up a tray with the food, laid a towel over it, and carried it all back to the parlor. Baya pulled the door open when I kicked it.

We ate at the coffee table. He sat on the floor. I sat on the couch. The water pitcher was still full, and there was an extra glass I didn't remember bringing in. We had plates of eggs and potatoes, and I put the tomatoes in a bowl between us so we could help ourselves. I couldn't taste much of anything except more dust. Despite my being careful, the dust got into the food, and it ground in my teeth and grated against my throat.

But the food felt good in my stomach, so I guessed I was hungry. Baya polished off his portion while I was still working on mine, and he stared at the bowl with the tomatoes. I pushed it toward him. He poured them onto his plate and ate them all.

At last, the food was gone, including the rest of the condensed milk, which we drank as a kind of dessert.

Baya rested his arms on his knees and looked up at me.

"Time was Baya would have married you for this," he said. "Last girl, though, she had these teeth . . . well, never

mind. You're a good girl, Calliope LeRoux, and you saved
old Baya. What can he do for you?"

I almost laughed at him. "What? Are you going to give
me three wishes or something?"

He considered this. "Three wishes, hey? Could do
that. What would you wish for?"

I didn't even have to think about it. "I wish the dust
couldn't get me."

He nodded. "Easy enough. What else?"

"I wish I knew where Mama is." My heart thumped
once. "And Papa too."

He gave another one of those grunts. "Mama and
Papa too, hey?" His eyes narrowed, as if he was squinting
into the sun. "There's a spirit man, tall and fine. He's full
of love and mischief. He's promised to a spirit woman of
his enemies, but he doesn't want her. He wants his other
woman. She's fair and fine, and she's got his baby. He
stands up in the council tent and he says he won't stay with
his tribe anymore. He runs for that other woman, but he
can't run fast enough. The Shining Ones capture him and
lock him away, but he still won't marry their woman. They
tie him up tight, in the golden mountains of the west,
above the valley of smoke. Now both tribes go looking for
his other woman and his baby. They look for years but
they don't find her, because he won't tell them her name.
They set their wisewomen out on a vision quest, and still
they cannot find her.

"Then they hear music. Music of magic and power and

spirit heart, and they find the woman. They take her to the house of St. Simon, where no saint's ever been, and they hold her there." Baya shook himself and came back into his skin. "That's where they are."

I was silent for a minute. The long, strange, terrible day washed over me.

"But . . . I don't understand," I said finally. "Spirit man? How can my papa be a spirit?"

Baya shrugged. "There are all kinds of spirits, Dust Girl."

"But if my papa's a spirit . . . what does that make me?"

"Different."

"Thanks a lot."

He shrugged again. "Hey, even old Baya only knows so much at once."

My eyes burned. Tears leaked out the corners. Baya tucked his rough hand under my chin and lifted my face so I had to look into his eyes. Those eyes were old and young; there was dawn light in them and starlight. I hadn't seen the stars since the dust came, years ago now, and I hadn't realized until that moment how much I missed them.

"I wish I knew who I am," I whispered to the stars in Baya's eyes.

Slowly, Baya shook his head. "Oh, Dust Girl, that's the hardest wish of all. Not even Baya can give you that one. That one you earn."

"Then I wish I could find out."

Baya put a hand on my head and he started to talk. I

couldn't understand the words, but his voice rose and fell like the song of the wind. Not the hot dust-storm wind, but the gentle summer wind that piled up the clouds overhead and smelled like rain. I forgot to be afraid. I forgot to be careful. I looked deep into his eyes, because I wanted to stay with the stars. Then I was falling into pure, empty darkness.

5

Got the Do-Re-Mi

When I woke up, Baya was gone. It wasn't just that he'd left the room; he was gone away a whole lot farther than that. I could feel it, like I'd felt someone watching me through the kitchen window before.

This made me feel about as easy as smelling smoke and not knowing where the fire was.

I sucked in a deep breath. That was when I knew something else was gone. The pain—the burning and the weight like stones on my ribs—was all gone. I took another breath, in and out. I didn't cough. I laughed, pressing my hands against my chest, and gulped air, and it went down smooth and clean. I had so much air I got dizzy. I tore open the parlor door and ran straight out the Imperial's double front doors.

"Thank you!" I shouted to Baya, wherever he'd gone. "Thank you!"

No one answered. The hot wind whipped at my dress, and the grit scraped across my skin. Slowly, it sank in that the dust storm hadn't let up yet. Dust still rolled in black clouds across the sky. The strange, silent green lightning that we'd been told came from static electricity in the blow dirt flickered overhead. Tumbleweeds rode the roaring, dusty wind like the biggest-ever crows and piled themselves up against the walls of houses and churches. The streets were already gone beneath the drifts of sepia dirt. All that was left were some houses sticking out of piles of blowing sand. Out beyond the passenger depot, windmills marked where fields used to be. Their spindly towers swayed back and forth. The static electricity had gotten into them too, and they lit up with the same spooky green color as they swayed back and forth.

Maybe I should have just been happy. I could breathe. I'd spent a year wishing I could breathe again. I wasn't going to die now. I could feel it in my bones, and in the way I'd run out the front door without coughing. But being able to see through all the dust . . . that was something else. It was like the music that had poured through my hands when I'd touched Papa's piano. A thought got into my head that if I could see through the dust, maybe other things in this dust could see me.

I went back inside and shut the door. That didn't help any, because as I stood in the big, empty lobby, the quiet filled my head, reminding me that I was all alone. I sat on the bottom step of the grand staircase and hugged my knees.

What do I do? What do I do?

The clock on the registration desk said quarter after six. I didn't even know if it was six in the morning or six at night.

Mama, what do I do?

I pressed my forehead against my knees. I had to find her. I knew that much. But how? Where would I even start? Baya—whoever or whatever he was—had talked about the golden mountains of the west. That could only mean California. Never mind that it was impossible for Mama to be in California when she'd been here in Slow Run, Kansas, just a few hours ago. Everything about this day had become impossible, me included.

So, California. How was I supposed to get to California? The only money I had was the seven dollars from the coffee can. Maybe I could hop a freight. Plenty of people did, kids included. I saw them every time a train went past, riding on the tops of the coal cars, or sitting in the open-sided boxcars. Sometimes they came to the Imperial's doors, and Mama would trade them food and a night in one of the empty rooms if they would spend a few hours helping her clean.

But even supposing I could get out to California by going on the bum, how would I find the "valley of smoke"? Or the "house of St. Simon"? Somehow I didn't think those would show up on one of Rand McNally's maps.

Then I thought, what if while I was wandering around trying to find Mama, Mama came back here? Or sent word?

If she was in California, she might send a telegram or a letter, and I wouldn't be here to get it.

Which was almost funny, because that must have been exactly how Mama thought about Papa all that time.

One thing was certain: I wasn't going to get any answers just sitting here. I got to my feet. First things first. I'd go back to our part of the house and take stock of just what I had that might be useful, and then . . .

A car horn cut through the sound of the wind outside. I froze.

Can't be, I thought. *Nobody could drive in this.*

But it sounded again, a double beat, high and sharp and demanding.

I pulled the front doors open again. Dust whirled all around me. In the patch of rippling sand where the front drive used to be sat a car, but not just any car. It was huge, heavy, and shiny, with a burgundy and cream paint job, chrome bumpers, huge headlights, and a hood ornament big enough for the prow of an old-fashioned sailing ship. It was a Duesy—a Duesenberg—the kind of car the boys sighed over in the auto magazines.

While I stood there with my jaw hanging loose, the driver's-side door opened and a man climbed out. He was a match for the car—big, solid, and expensive, with white skin turning red from the heat, a cream-colored suit, and two-tone wingtip shoes that sank into the dust. He wore a pair of round spectacles thick enough to make his dark eyes look blurred and bulgy.

"Is this the Imperial?" the man bawled, clapping one big hand down on his straw boater hat to keep it from blowing away.

I swallowed. "Yes, sir!"

"Very good. I'll be requiring rooms for the night!"

"I . . ."

"Come, come, girl, what's the difficulty?" The diamond on his pinkie ring flashed as he waved the beefy hand that wasn't holding his hat. "This infernal dust has blocked the roads, and my family needs a place to wait out the storm. This is a hotel, is it not?"

"Yes, sir, but . . ."

"But what?"

I cleared my throat. "I'm sorry, sir. We're not open for business."

The window on the Duesy rolled down and a woman stuck her head out. Like the man, she wore thick spectacles, but hers were round and tinted blue for the sun. Which meant she must have been about blind right then, because there was no sun. Her perfectly curled gold hair waved in the dusty wind under the drooping brim of her white hat, which was pinned with a brooch set with stones the exact color of the scarlet lipstick on her perfectly shaped mouth.

"What's happening, Desmond? Is there a problem?"

"The girl says they're not open for business, Irma."

"What? Nonsense. Have you told her we can pay?"

"Well? What of it?" the man snapped at me. "We're not a passel of Okies, as you can see. How much for your best rooms?" With that, he yanked a roll of bills bigger than my fist out of his pocket. "Will this be sufficient?" Those thick fingers peeled off a fifty.

"I . . ."

He peeled off a second bill and slapped both down onto my palm. "That should be more than enough."

A hundred dollars. My fingers curled over the bills to protect them from the wind. That was a hundred dollars in my hand. I'd never seen that much money, let alone touched it, not even when I was a little kid back before the Crash.

What I did next was about the hardest thing I've ever done in my life.

"Sir, I'm sorry. There's only me here. I couldn't give you the kind of service you expect for a hundred dollars." I held the bills out. Can your hand feel like it's going to cry? 'Cause I swear mine did. "But you're welcome to stay till the storm's over." You didn't send anybody away in a duster, not strange Indians, not rich folks in big cars.

"Hmph!" He took those fifties back. "I'll have you know, girl, I'm a businessman and I don't take charity. I'm giving you a chance to make something. You give us the best you've got for one night, food and rooms complete, and you'll get not one hundred, not one-twenty, but one hundred and fifty dollars." He held up the bills. "What do you say?"

What did I say? A hundred and fifty dollars could get me to California and back again and keep me fine while I was out there. Maybe I could even hire a detective like in the movies, to help find Mama.

My shoulders squared. If this man didn't want charity, he wouldn't get it. "I'll need fifty up front so I can lay in supplies for the night."

"That's the spirit!" The man slapped a fifty into my palm and shook my hand doing it. The bill was new and crisp. It crackled as my fist closed around it.

"Irma!" He opened the front passenger-side door of that shiny car. "Children! Come, my dears! We're staying."

The entire family piled out, every last one of them done up as fine as could be. There was a tall, fair-haired boy in a white suit and straw hat, just like his father. After him came a thin, willowy girl, wearing a summer dress with a bright green sash and a pleated skirt. Her hat and shoes matched the sash. The next-in-line boy wasn't out of short pants yet. His blond curls peeked out from under his flat-brimmed cap, and he had freckles all across his stubby nose. The youngest girl held tight to her sister with one hand. In the other, she clutched a blue-eyed doll in an emerald satin dress nicer than anything I'd ever owned. Every last one of them wore the same kind of thick, round spectacles that made their eyes too big and too dark for their sharp faces.

The man's chest swelled with pride at the sight of them. "Now, young lady, you see before you the proud Hopper clan. My wife, Irma. My heir apparent, Hunter. That fine strapping lad with him is William. This lovely lady is Letitia, and this is our little Clarinda." Mr. Hopper waved his hand at me. "My own, this plucky young lady is offering us the run of her fine establishment for the night, and hot, home-cooked meals in the bargain."

I looked at the Hopper kids, and the kids looked back at me, their spectacles glittering even in the dust-filtered light. I saw their tidy white-and-green clothing and tried not to tug at my own too-small, dirt-smeared, used-to-be-yellow dress.

"Won't you come in?" I led the Hopper family into the lobby and shut the door tight behind them. I hoped they didn't notice how the dust had already drifted up against the registration desk and the foot of the stairs.

But it looked like I didn't have to worry. "Well, this will be charming. Just charming." Mrs. Hopper smiled at the carpet and the curving staircase and the chandelier under its cloth cover. "We certainly didn't expect to find such a lovely hotel. We were getting ready to sleep in a hay barn, weren't we, Desmond?"

"Exactly!" he cried. I tried to picture these clean, rich folks bedding down like hobos and couldn't do it. It wasn't right. I mean, it was okay for people who were used to it, but not folks like this. "But we are all rescued. Now . . . Miss . . . ?"

"Callie." I ran around the desk, opened the registration book, and rummaged in the drawer for the fountain pen. If I was going to do this, I was going to do it right. Mama would expect it. "If you'll just sign in, Mr. Hopper?"

"Excellent!" Mr. Hopper signed the book with a flourish.

Little Clarinda was staring all around at the stairs and the lobby and the covered chandelier, inching closer and closer to her sister the whole time. "I'm hungry!" she announced in a high, piping voice.

"Yes, honey pie." Her mama smoothed her yellow corkscrew curls and idly straightened her big green hair bow. "We'll be eating soon. I promise."

I swallowed, wondering how I was going to feed the Hopper tribe, and tried to keep my brain on the job right in front of me.

"If you'll follow me? You can wait in the parlor while I get your rooms ready."

All six Hoppers followed me down the carpeted hallway, with Mrs. Hopper murmuring "Charming, charming" every few feet. I pushed open the door to the ladies' parlor.

"Please, make yourselves at home." I hurried around, pulling dustcovers off the furniture and piling the dishes from my lunch with Baya on the tray. It felt like he'd left a million years ago. The Hoppers filling the parlor seemed to wipe out all sense of him, like the sun wipes out a dream. "I'll go see about those rooms."

Mrs. Hopper looked around with bright eyes, taking in all the details. "Charming," she said again, and gave me her warm smile. I'd never seen a lady like her, not in real life anyway. She was so neat and pretty, like a movie star. She carried herself as if she'd never had to worry about anything and didn't want you to have to either. "So unexpected and so charming."

I blushed and hurried out.

It was a kind of relief to have my head fill up with

details of taking care of guests. It pushed out all the weird things that had happened and made everything real and everyday again. Even the rattling windows and the groaning walls were familiar. It was the season for high winds, after all.

The best suites were on the second floor. Those had their own sitting rooms and baths. Mr. and Mrs. Hopper could have one room and share the bath and sitter with the girls, while the boys could have the suite across the hall. I pulled tape off doors and the heavy dust cloths off furniture. I had to run to the linen cupboard to get the big laundry bag to stuff the cloths in. None of the beds were made, so it was back to the linen cupboard for pillows, sheets, and blankets. Perspiration poured off me by the time I finished with the last bed, and I had to keep wiping my face on the maid's apron I'd wrapped around me, to keep from dripping on everything. It must have been almost nighttime, but the air wasn't getting any cooler, and I didn't dare open a window for the breeze because it would bring the dust in.

As I tucked in the last hospital corner on what I figured would be the boys' beds, I heard a scraping noise and whirled around. Clarinda Hopper peered in the door from the sitting room. She'd tilted her head all the way sideways like little kids can, so I could just see her spectacles, nose, and upper lip around the door frame.

"Can I get you something, Miss Clarinda?"

Her upper lip twitched, like she was maybe trying to

smile. Then she was gone except for the sound of her patent-leather shoes thudding on the carpet.

Probably shy. I smoothed down the bedcovers. The Hoppers would want to wash up, I realized. So they needed towels. I started out again, thinking about what we had left in the linen cupboard, but something caught my eye and I stopped.

The Imperial's thresholds and doors all had a dark walnut varnish that was still smooth despite being nearly fifty years old. On the doorjamb, though, right at waist height, a pale crescent had been gouged out of the wood.

I straightened up and hurried down the hall. I tried hard not to think about how that fresh crescent-shaped, splintery gouge was at the same height as little Clarinda Hopper's twitchy upper lip.

6

Layin' in That Hard Rock Jail

Mrs. Hopper, of course, found the rooms charming. She strutted about the sitting room with its old-fashioned mahogany and burgundy velvet furniture as if she was in the Waldorf-Astoria. I opened the doors off the sitter to show the two bedrooms and the private bath. The smile on her perfectly-done-up mouth never once wavered. Of course, she also hadn't taken off her tinted spectacles, so I couldn't exactly be sure how much she really saw.

Mr. Hopper only seemed to notice the brass, cannon-shaped lighter on the mantel. He lit himself a cigarette and blew a fat cloud of smoke at the ceiling, his whole frame relaxing instantly.

The older girl, Letitia, seemed less enthusiastic. She prodded suspiciously at the sofa cushion before she sat down. Clarinda, on the other hand, saw the big bed in the master bedroom. She made a beeline for it, climbed aboard, and started bouncing up and down. I grinned. It was the most normal thing I'd seen any of those kids do.

William came charging in from across the hall. "Pa, I'm hungry!" he shouted as he barreled through the sitting room to join his sister in jumping on the bed.

"Me too!" cried little Clarinda. "I'm hungry!"

"Hungry, hungry!" chanted both kids, bouncing hard enough now to make the brass headboard bang against the wall.

"Yeah, Pop." Hunter strolled in and flopped down on the sofa next to his sister. "It's about time for something, isn't it?"

"I have to say, I'm famished as well." Letitia looked over the rims of her spectacles at me. Her eyes looked big and black in the dim room. "There must be *something* here."

Mr. Hopper blew out another big cloud of smoke. "Well, Miss Callie, what about it?"

"Yes, sir." I tried to sound brisk, but I was tired. Hauling all the big sheets and blankets and making up all the beds in the thick heat had already been a lot of work. My arms felt like lead. I had a hundred and fifty dollars to earn, though, and I'd known it wasn't going to be easy. "I'll have to get to the store, but I'll be back shortly. If you'd like to wash up . . . ?" I gestured toward the bath and the stack of clean towels.

"Fine idea. Be off with you then." He waved his cigarette toward the door and I was off with me.

I tried to tell myself I didn't have to hurry *that* much. It wasn't like they could up and leave. They were stuck here until the roads got dug out. With a big duster, that could take days. But something inside me didn't think getting the Hoppers mad would be any kind of good idea.

Outside, I squinted into the wind and got my bearings down the line of dust that had been Front Street. What few people still lived in town must have sealed themselves into their shuddering houses. Alone, I waded through sand up to my ankles, and I passed drifts that would have been up to my knees. I could breathe and see just fine, but that wasn't a comfort anymore, because it wasn't right. There was no way I should be able to walk through this. Nothing human could.

I gritted my teeth and bent double into the wind. I couldn't think like that. I had to keep moving.

I hadn't forgotten the voices from this morning. My ears strained, waiting for them. I wanted to hear them. If I heard them, maybe I could follow them, find out who they belonged to.

But it wasn't those dusty wind voices I heard.

"Take this hammer . . ."

I stopped and immediately sank halfway up my shins. Somewhere, a muffled, distant, draggy voice was singing.

"Take this hammer, carry it to the captain!" THUMP! The line ended in a crash like somebody kicking a door.

"Take this hammer, carry it to the captain!" THUMP!

"Tell him I'm gone, tell him I'm gone." THUMP!

The verse dissolved into a bout of coughing. I turned slowly, trying to pick out where the voice was coming from.

"If he ask you, was I running?" THUMP!

It was hard to tell over the wind, but it started to sound like the jailhouse.

"If he ask you, was I running?" THUMP!

It sure didn't sound like Sheriff Davis making all that noise, not that I'd ever heard him sing.

"If he ask you, was I running?" THUMP!

So if it wasn't the sheriff singing in the jailhouse, who was it?

"Tell him I was flyin', tell him I was flyin'." THUMP!

The jail was the only building on Front Street besides the post office that was made of actual brick. It was small, just a box big enough to hold two desks and a cell with two cots.

"Hello?" I kicked a tumbleweed back from the jailhouse door. The front room with its two desks was empty. Nobody had sealed it up. Dust had made a desert out of the floor and piled itself high in all the corners.

"Hello?" called a boy's voice from the back. "Is somebody there? Help!"

The Slow Run cell didn't have barred walls like the ones in the movies. The solid steel door had just one little window at the top. Right now, the window also had the top of a boy's tousled head and two blue eyes peering through.

"Help! Please! I can't get out!"

Which kinda seemed like the point of being in jail. "How'd you get in?"

"I was too slow hopping a reefer and they locked me up." I didn't know for sure what a reefer was, but I guessed it had something to do with train cars. Sheriff Davis didn't like hobos and bindle stiffs in his town any more than he liked Indians or Negroes or Mexicans. Everybody knew if he caught a vagrant, no matter how young, he shipped them out to work off the fines by chopping cotton or digging ditches.

"This fella ran in and yelled something about a God Almighty big duster kicking up out there, and the sheriff took off. I don't think he's coming back. Please, let me out."

It was hard to tell from just the top of his head, but the boy didn't look much older than me. Still, he might have been a thief, or worse. Some of them were. Then I thought how there wasn't a window in there. I thought about being locked up alone in the hot dark, with the storm going on, and about being on the other side of that door having some-body turn around and walk out.

I didn't know what this kid had done, but right then I knew it wasn't enough to deserve that.

The big iron key still hung on a hook behind Sheriff Davis's desk, so I had the door open in a few seconds. The boy tumbled out, kicking through the dust drifts.

"Thank you," he mumbled, then ducked past me to the little sink. He drank down a tin cup full of water, gasped, and drank down another. It must have been an oven in there. His face was flushed under all the dirt, and he was shaking. He didn't smell so good either. I didn't look in the cell to see if they had a toilet in there, 'cause I had a feeling I didn't want to know.

"You okay?" I asked.

He nodded, but then his face kind of twisted up and he coughed hard and spat brown into the sink. He stayed there, hanging on tight to the sides of the basin, until he wasn't shaking so much. Then he straightened up so I could get a better look.

He was a tall, skinny white kid with big blue eyes, his ears sticking out beneath a bird's nest of brown hair, the kind of boy who gets nicknamed Beanpole. His knobby knees pressed against his worn knickerbockers, and the wrists above his too-big hands stuck out from the too-short sleeves of his dirty shirt. His hands and face were streaked with storm dust and coal dust mixed together. His shoes had split at the toes, and one black stocking had a big hole in it.

He started trying to smooth his shirt down but gave it up pretty quick. "Have you got anything to eat? I'm sorry to ask, but I haven't had a single bite since yesterday and . . . I'd work for it, you know, if you had a job. . . ."

I thought about the Hoppers back at the Imperial. But truth to tell, this boy didn't look like he could do anything right now, and I sure didn't want a hobo in the hotel while I had paying guests, even a kid. Kids off the road could be hard and mean. One little boy Mama had put up for the night stole two of our chickens when he lit out. Some of the girls had done a whole lot worse when they were supposed to be cleaning rooms in exchange for meals. All the chickens were gone now, and I didn't have anything else worth stealing, but the Hoppers sure did.

I bit my lip. The storm was still going on, and there was no telling how long it would be before it let up. This boy would fill up with dust if he walked out there now. Maybe get the fever and the dust pneumonia, and I didn't think Baya would be around to help him any.

"You ever wash dishes?" I asked him. "I mean in a real kitchen?"

"Sure." He cracked a big grin. Somehow he didn't look so knobby and skinny when he was smiling. "I been a pearl diver in roadhouses, and worked the flat top, and swept up." Pearl diver, that was a dishwasher, and the flat top was the grill. So he'd been a cook too.

"Okay, then. I got a load of guests at the hotel. I need help in the kitchen and with fetching and carrying. You gotta be able to give 'em the yes, sir and yes, ma'am, and do what I say."

He nodded immediately. "Sure. I can do that."

"Okay, then . . ." I remembered something important. "What's your name?"

"Jack. Jack Holland, Miss . . . ?"

"Callie . . . Callie LeRoux." I don't know why I said it. It was like since I'd told Baya the truth, I didn't have to bother with hiding behind the "McGinty" that had never really fooled anyone anyway.

"Pleased to meet you, Callie LeRoux." Jack Holland stuck out his hand.

"Pleased to meet you, Jack Holland." His palm was hard, and his fingernails were stained black. He'd worked a lot with those hands, and they felt strong and warm. My insides gave a little squirm and I let go. I didn't need anything else strange to think about.

"I heard you singing," I said. "That's how I found you."

"I was hoping that'd happen." He pulled a battered newsboy cap out of his back pocket. "I been singing since the sheriff left. Kept me from going crazy. Shall we?" He bowed and swept his cap like a hotel doorman in the movies.

I giggled. "Let's do." I held out my skirt hem and put my nose in the air and tried to mince out the door. He chuckled, and that made me feel kind of good. At the same time, I thought to myself Jack Holland was a boy who could make people do what he wanted. He had the kind of face that could look all sweet while hiding a world of secrets. I'd have to watch him close while he was in the Imperial.

My insides did that squirmy thing again. Maybe this wasn't such a good idea, but I couldn't go back on my word.

"God Almighty," Jack whispered.

I stopped. He'd been stuck in that cell and hadn't seen the storm. He was getting his first look at what it had done.

"I seen dusters before, but not like this. . . ."

"Don't think there's ever been one like this." And it was my fault. No matter what Baya said. I knew, somehow, I'd done this. Now I was standing around instead of working for the money I needed to go find Mama. "Come on. We gotta get to the store."

We waded through the dust to Van Iykes's Mercantile.

The sky still boiled black, and the dust tried to needle its way into my skin. Jack kept his nose pressed to his sleeve. I kept one eye on the street out of town, looking for cars or people. There was nothing, just the houses hunkering down under the storm. There had to be people behind the curtains, all sealed into their rooms. The town only looked empty; it wasn't really.

The dust swirled around and chuckled in my ears.

The mercantile door was unlocked. The bell rang when I pushed it open.

"Mr. Van Iykes?" I called. "Mrs. Van Iykes?"

No answer. Fresh dust snaked inside around our ankles. I blinked hard while my eyes adjusted to the twilight filling the store's front room.

Then I wished they hadn't.

"God Almighty," croaked Jack, just like he had when he saw the storm.

The mercantile was an old-time general store—one big room with the groceries on the left side, dry goods on the right, and hardware at the back. Right then, it looked like it had been hit by a cyclone. The racks of dime novels and magazines were flopped on their sides next to empty barrels. The butcher's case was busted open, and sharp bits of glass lay glittering on the dusty floorboards. Heaps of cans lay behind the counter on one side, and shredded bolts of cloth on the other. The fridge door flapped open, and the smashed milk bottles lay in stinking white pools. A green trail leaked down from the icebox, where the pistachio ice cream had melted. Flies had gotten trapped in the sticky green puddle on the floorboards and died.

"Mr. Van Iykes?" I called again. "Mrs. Van Iykes?"

"I'll go look upstairs." Jack vanished up the back steps. I heard him clumping around over my head. I just kept turning in a circle, trying to understand. Then I noticed the books were torn like the cloth was. No. Not torn, chewed. They had holes right through them, and big crescent-shaped chunks taken out of the spines—just like the chunk taken out of the door frame where little Clarinda Hopper had been spying on me.

That was when I saw how the bones lay on top of the broken glass—pork bones, beef bones, lamb bones, all picked as clean and white as if they'd been in the desert for years.

Staring at those bones, I barely heard Jack Holland thumping back down the stairs.

"There's nobody up there," he said. "Doesn't look like it's been robbed or anything. . . ."

"What am I gonna do?" I tore my eyes away from the bones. I couldn't understand what I was seeing. No, I didn't *want* to understand it. So I told myself, all I really understood was that the Hoppers were back at the hotel, hungry and impatient, and I had their fifty in my pocket. "They're expecting me to feed them. What am I gonna do?"

"Whoa. Wait." Jack held up both too-big hands. "Who's expecting you?"

I told him about the Hoppers, and the hundred and fifty dollars. "We need the money," I said. "I can't not feed them. They'll leave and I'll have nothing." I knew what I must sound like, worrying about money when it was plain the Van Iykeses had been wiped out by . . . by something. Wild coyotes, maybe, or crazy people. People went crazy in dust storms sometimes. But I needed that money if I was going to find Mama.

"Okay." Jack wiped his hands on his pants. "Okay. Look. There's still the cans, right? You can make plenty out of cans."

I rubbed my eyes. "Yeah. Yeah."

"So you see what you can find. I'll go look for a wheel-barrow or something we can load up."

I didn't want him to leave me alone in that ruined place, but I nodded. There were a couple of crates behind the grocery counter. I knocked the dust out and started sorting cans. All the boxes had been torn open. Heaps of cornflakes, shredded wheat, and Jell-O powder were vanishing under a coat of dust. I picked out cans of beans and creamed corn and tomato soup and condensed milk and set them on the counter. I added tins of deviled ham, tuna fish, sardines, and Ovaltine. There were even some tinned clams.

The battered metal bread box on the counter held treasure: two long, squared-off Pullman loaves, still mostly fresh and only a little dusty. I wrapped them in brown paper from the big roll bolted to the counter and added the bread to my rows of salvaged canned goods. For a wonder, the ham and salami hanging over the busted-up meat case were untouched.

They only took the fresh, my brain said.

Shut up, I said back to my brain.

But the barrel of salt pork hadn't been touched either. I wrapped up some slabs of that too and tried not to feel my hands shaking. I pulled my nerve together and headed down into the cellar. More luck. There was homemade jam on the shelf, and potatoes, onions, and carrots in the bins. Maybe Mr. Van Iykes had been able to chase off whoever robbed the place before they made it to the cellar. Maybe he and Sheriff Davis had gone to round up the robbers and were caught out by the storm and they'd be back soon. They'd be glad to see the money then.

That idea made me feel better as I helped myself to what I could carry of vegetables and preserves and took it all back upstairs.

Jack dragged a wheelbarrow inside and started loading groceries. He must have been dog-tired, but he'd said he would work and he was. That spoke better for him than any easy smile. Maybe this would be all right after all.

While Jack tied a tarp over the barrow, I grabbed the pad of order blanks from the drawer under the cash register and added up the prices for all we'd taken, making guesses on the jam and vegetables. The total was fifteen dollars and eleven cents. I punched the keys on the register. The bells chimed, and the cash drawer shot open.

I stared.

There was all of fifteen cents in the drawer, along with a stack of IOUs.

I'd always thought the Van Iykeses had plenty of

money. After all, they ran the only store left in Slow Run. But nobody in the whole town had money to buy anything, so I guess Mr. Van Iykes did what the rest of us did, take the promises and hope.

I felt bad about leaving another IOU, but I didn't know what else to do. So at the bottom of the order blank I wrote:

> Mr. Van Iykes:
>
>   I needed some groceries for guests at the Imperial. I will come by tomorrow and pay you for what I took and bring your barrow back.
>
> Callie

Writing that down helped me believe the Van Iykeses would be back tomorrow to see my promise bundled with all the others. I shut the order blank in the drawer so it wouldn't blow away. The register chimed as if for an actual sale. It didn't know the difference.

"Let's go," I said to Jack. I didn't want to stay there with the bones and broken glass a minute longer. I wanted to be back in my own home, where there was still a chance I could do something to make a difference.

Jack looked at me like he understood, grabbed up the handles of the wheelbarrow, and followed me out the back door into the storm.

7

All the Hungry Little Children

"Ah, there you are, Callie! We were beginning to wonder."

Mrs. Hopper sailed into the Imperial's main kitchen while Jack and I were unloading the last of the groceries. We were both streaked with sweat and grime. It had been impossible to push the barrow through the blow dust. We'd had to drag it behind us like a couple of mules hitched to a plow.

"Why, who's this?" Mrs. Hopper tilted her chin down so we could just see the green flash of her eyes above the rims of her tinted glasses.

"Jack Holland, ma'am," I told her. "He's here to help out while you stay." Which was true as far as it went. The Hoppers didn't need to know where or how I'd found him.

"Charming!" She held out her hand and smiled. Her teeth were very straight and very white. Jack blushed and shook her hand. "Mr. Hopper will be pleased. He believes in rewarding hard work. Now"—she grew brisk—"as my children made clear before you left, I'm afraid we're all just a tiny bit hungry. Callie, you'll put together some tea for us, won't you?"

Tea? I hadn't thought about tea. It was going to be hard enough to pull together a dinner for so many, even with Jack's help.

"No hurry, of course," Mrs. Hopper said in a tone that meant just the opposite. "But as soon as you can."

"Yes, ma'am."

She beamed at me and sailed out through the swinging doors.

Tea. I looked at the heap of groceries salvaged from Van Iykes's. How was I going to make them tea?

"She's pretty." Jack hooked a tall stool out from under the counter and sat down a little too hard.

That woke me up. I planted my hands on my hips and glared at him. "She's a guest. So don't go making a fool out of yourself." Then I realized he wouldn't do me any good starved and thirsty, so I filled a glass from the sink and shoved it at him.

"Who are you calling a fool?" Jack gulped the water down.

"You, if you go making eyes at married guests." I plucked the salami out of the crate and a sharp knife out of a drawer and passed him both.

"I wasn't making eyes!" He snatched up the salami and swiped a slice off the end.

"You were! You're red as a beet."

"I am not," he muttered around his mouthful of hard sausage.

"Suit yourself." I shrugged and turned to face the kitchen.

Except for the Moonlight Room, the kitchen was the biggest room in the Imperial. The two cast-iron stoves sat solidly in the middle of it all, with the bake ovens underneath and the warming ovens on the side. In the corner, the housekeeper's desk sat under the hook board where we hung the spare keys.

I started filling the kettle and a couple of big pots. "First thing to do when you're cooking is get the water boiling," Mama had told me. "It saves time and you'll always find a use for it."

I remembered playing with pots and pans in here when I was really little, while Mama and the cooks worked, filling the air with the best smells. Gradually, the cooks drifted away and it was just Mama, and then even that ended. Now it was just me. Well, and Jack, but he was just wolfing salami, and I couldn't really count him yet.

"You'll get a stomachache," I said, shaking out the match I'd used to light one of the burners on the right-hand stove.

"Already got one," he told me around another mouthful. "You can pick 'em up for free on the road. Thought I'd see if store-bought is better quality."

I peeked in the tin box labeled TEA and found there was actually some tea in it. That was something. "How long you been on the bum?"

He shrugged. "Not so long. I'm headed to Los Angeles."

"Everybody's headed to California." I laid out the vegetables on one of the marble counters and wiped a bread knife clean with a dish towel. I threw the towel over my shoulder to keep it handy. "The place must be full up by now."

"Of people going to work the crops, sure. But that's not me. I'm going to be a newspaper writer."

"You are?"

"Sure." He sat up straighter. "I worked the paper at school. Won a prize for it and everything. They take boys on at newspapers in big cities. Let 'em work as copyboys and learn the trade. Sometimes even for pay, but I wouldn't mind doing it for free. I could get another job in a city like that. I can do anything. You'll see."

I looked at him, sitting on that stool, in clothes that were too small and all tore up, cutting hunks off a salami he got as charity, and at the same time talking about how he could do anything, like nothing bad had ever happened to him. Jack Holland was either really brave or completely cracked.

That seemed too big a question to try to answer right then, so I wiped the dust off another section of counter and started slicing up the Pullman loaf instead. Jam sandwiches sounded like something you'd have with tea, didn't it? And deviled ham.

Jack wiped his hands on his trousers, found the apron

on the clothes hook, and started filling the double sink. "Which dishes you want to use?"

I pointed to the cabinet where the afternoon china was, plain white with a black border and gold rim. He got it down and started washing it.

"What was that song?" I asked while smearing jam on bread. "The one you were singing in the jail?"

"Work song. I heard it from some fellas on a chain gang."

I decided not to ask if he'd been on the gang with them. "Sounded pretty good."

"Thanks. You figured out what you're gonna make them folks for dinner?"

"Manhattan clam chowder. I'll cook up the carrots and potatoes, and put the clams in the tomato soup with their juice, and season it up. They can have that for a first, with bread. Then ham and beans and biscuits." We had flour in our little kitchen in the staff quarters, and I'd found an untouched can of Crisco at the mercantile. "Then bread pudding for dessert."

"You're really good at this."

"Mama showed me." I cut the crusts off the bread— they could go into the pudding—and sliced the sandwiches into little triangles to pile onto plates.

"Where is your mama?" Jack asked.

"She's gone." I grabbed up the tray of tea things and was out the door before he could ask where to. It was heavy and awkward to carry, piled with the towel-covered dishes, the teapot, and the sandwiches, and my hands were tired from all the work I'd already done. I was terrified I'd drop the whole thing on the way to the parlor. I kept my mind on the hundred-and-fifty and gripped the tray tight.

"Your tea, sir, ma'am," I said as I backed through the parlor door.

"There now!" exclaimed Mr. Hopper. I set the loaded tray down on the table and started lifting the towels to show the heaps of sandwiches. "I told you Callie wouldn't let you all go hungry! Dig in, my own! Dig in!"

The way those Hoppers fell on my sandwiches, you'd think they were half starved. But then, folks this rich wouldn't be used to waiting to eat. They probably had servants and everything back home to bring them snacks whenever they rang a bell. It hit me that I'd forgotten the napkins. As I headed off to the downstairs linen cupboard to fetch some, I thought about how Mama used to smile with satisfaction when she fed people dinner, even if it was just salt pork and beans. Now I understood why. It felt good, seeing people enjoy something I'd made like that.

I'm coming to find you, Mama, I swear, I thought as I took up a big stack of white napkins from the cupboard. *I'm leaving just as soon as I've got that money.*

I knocked on the parlor door and went in. "I thought you'd need some . . ."

I stopped. I stared.

The sandwich plates weren't just empty; they were pol-

---

ished clean. I thought the Hopper kids must be playing some kind of trick on me, until Mr. Hopper flicked a bit of deviled ham off his sleeve and burped.

"Pardon me! That was excellent, Callie!"

There'd been a dozen sandwiches when I left. I'd been gone less than a minute. I lifted the lid on the teapot. That was empty too.

"I'm afraid Hunter here's still a bit hungry," Mr. Hopper went on. "He is a growing boy after all!" Mr. Hopper laughed heartily, but Hunter just licked his lips. His tongue was bright pink against his white face.

"I'd better make up some more sandwiches," I heard myself whisper. I didn't want to be in that room anymore. Not with all those Hoppers looking at me with their big white smiles and their identical dark eyes behind their spectacles.

"Whatever you have on hand will be fine, I'm certain." Mr. Hopper clasped his hands across his broad stomach and leaned back on the sofa.

"But do hurry, Callie," said Mrs. Hopper. "It's not just Hunter who still has an appetite. We've all had such a long journey today."

"Yes, ma'am." I grabbed up the tray and ran back to the kitchen.

"What's the matter?" Jack had been busy while I was gone, slicing carrots and onions. He already had a good pile.

"They ate them." I set the tray down on the counter. "The sandwiches. They're gone."

"That ain't possible! Not even if they was starving!"

"I know." In my mind I saw the white bones lying in the broken glass on the mercantile floor. I would have given anything not to have that picture in my head just then. "They want more."

"More!" cried Jack. "What are you going to do?"

I forced myself to straighten up. I had to give them what they wanted, or Mr. Hopper might change his mind about the money.

I told Jack to keep going on the vegetables for the chowder. I sliced up the rest of the Pullman loaf and made a bunch more sandwiches. I still had the other one for the bread pudding. I drained two cans of peaches and forked some sardines into a bowl for good measure.

"There. This'll hold 'em awhile."

I toted the heavy tray back into the parlor. All the Hoppers looked up and smiled as soon as I pushed through the door.

"Now then!" Mr. Hopper clapped his meaty hands. "See what you can do with just a little motivation, Callie? Dig in, my own! Dig in!"

I barely had time to get clear of the table before they were on it. All the Hoppers, all at once, crowded over the tray. I backed off until I bumped up against the door. Those rich people in their white clothes slurped and smacked and slobbered as they grabbed at the food. Mrs. Hopper snatched up the bowl of sardines, opened her mouth wide, and poured them all in. Her cheeks bulged like a squirrel's, but only for a minute before she swallowed. She didn't even chew. She tossed the bowl aside, swatted Clarinda's hand back, and grabbed up a fistful of yellow peaches, squishing them between her fingers as she crammed them into her bright red mouth.

Under all the slobber was a clicking, buzzing sound I felt sure I should recognize. But I was seeing those white bones on the mercantile floor again, and all I could think was, *Got to get out, get out before they remember about me. . . .*

I backed up, but too fast. My heel caught the footstool, and I toppled hard onto the carpet. A big cloud of dust puffed up around me. I shook my head and blinked.

Through the rosy cloud of dust, I saw the Hoppers elbowing each other around my tray. Only they weren't people anymore. I saw the horsey faces and huge eyes made up of a million shining facets, waving antennae, hard black skins, and delicate legs with saw-sharp ridges.

The Hoppers were locusts. Black locusts the size of people.

I screamed. The chomping and buzzing stopped, and all those bug heads tilted to look at me. The dust was settling, and they were the Hoppers again, except not quite. Because now I could see how their eyes behind those thick glasses stayed round and lidless. Bug eyes.

"Why, whatever is the matter with Callie?" asked Mrs. Hopper.

"Poor girl's fallen down." Mr. Hopper reached out his big, meaty hand to me. This close, I could see through him, like Mr. Hopper was a chantilly lace curtain draped over the insect underneath. I could see hooked feet and skinny legs and the way its curved mouth parts moved back and forth. "Let me help you."

"No thank you, sir." I pushed myself up against the footstool. "I'm all right."

"That's good." He grinned, way too wide for his face. "Because I'm afraid my family has eaten all those excellent sandwiches."

It was true. The plates and bowls were empty. Hunter had peach juice and crumbs all over his face, and he grinned at me, exactly like his daddy.

"They're hungry, Callie." Mr. Hopper's voice buzzed and rattled. "A man can't let his family go hungry, now can he?"

"N-n-no, sir."

He clapped his hand on my shoulder. It was heavy. It was light. It had fingers. It had a hook. I could feel it both ways, just like I could see the man and the locust. "You'll bring us something else, won't you? Whatever you have on hand will do fine."

"Y-yes, sir."

I backed the rest of the way out of the parlor. I stood in the hallway, panting hard. I'd gone stone cold despite the fact that I was still sweating.

Every nerve I used to have snapped in two, and I ran.

"Jack!" I hollered as I slammed back into the kitchen. "We gotta get outta here!"

"What?" He looked up, knife in one hand and half-peeled carrot in the other. "Why?"

"They're not people! They're bugs! Giant bugs!"

"What're you, crazy?"

"I swear! They're locusts! That's why they can eat like that! They . . ."

"Callie! Is that any way to talk about paying guests?"

It was Mrs. Hopper. Her hat had come off somewhere, and two black antennae stuck out of her yellow curls. They both pointed right at me. Jack must have seen them too, because he turned white and green, and backed away, just like I had.

"What *would* your mother say?" Mrs. Hopper's antennae curled and opened again, like fingers. But her words blew all the fear right out of me.

"What do you know about my mama?"

"More than you could begin to guess." Mrs. Hopper stepped forward. Jack made a little noise in his throat and tried to back up again, but between one blink and the next, Mrs. Hopper was beside him with her hand, her hook, around his wrist.

"I'll just take this sweet boy here, so you don't have any distractions while you're getting our supper ready."

Whatever happened later, I will say this about Jack Holland—he had nerve. With that giant Hopper holding his wrist, he kept his head. "But I've got to get back to the store, ma'am," he said, his voice tight as he tried to keep it from shaking. "There's some stuff Callie needs."

"That's right!" I yelped. *If he gets out of here, he can go for help. . . .*

"How thoughtful!" Mrs. Hopper patted his cheek. I thought Jack might faint. I sure wanted to. "But I know Callie can handle all of that sort of thing. You come along with me. I want to introduce you to my sons."

The helpless look Jack threw me over his shoulder as she dragged him out sank straight into my stomach. The door flapped back and forth behind them, and I couldn't move. The Hoppers had him and they were still hungry.

I squeezed my eyes shut so hard I saw red and gold inside my lids. I had to think. I had to see what I had and use it. I had to, because otherwise . . . otherwise . . .

I couldn't think about otherwise. I opened my eyes.

The first thing I saw was the heap of vegetables Jack had cut up. Ridiculously I thought I'd better get the potatoes in the pan before they turned brown. Past the counter, I saw the housekeeper's desk, and the hook board with the spare keys.

The keys.

They weren't just room keys; they were all the downstairs keys too. Including the key to the ladies' parlor.

I'd seen how the Hoppers ate. They hadn't paid attention to anything else while they were stuffing their faces. I'd make a pile of food. A whole great big mess of food. Then, while they were eating, Jack and I could sneak out and I'd lock them in and we'd run.

I felt better with a plan. Not a lot, but better enough that I could start moving and keep ahead of the part of me that wouldn't stop screaming.

I sizzled up the salt pork in the old cast-iron Dutch oven, poured in the beans, and put that on the back burner to heat slowly. I made up the biscuits and got them in the oven. I cut bread into cubes, mixed in sugar and condensed milk, and put that in one of the other ovens. I cooked down the onions, carrots, and potatoes Jack had cut up in one of the big soup pots. I dumped in the clams and juice, got all that hot, and then poured in tomato soup and water. I lost track of time. Sweat ran in rivers down my face. I was close to worn out from heavy work and heat, but I didn't dare stop. If I stopped, the fear would catch back up with me and I wouldn't be able to do anything at all, even run. I sliced off thick ham steaks and put them in a pan and poured one of the nickel Cokes over them to make the glaze. I brewed coffee and used some of it for redeye gravy.

I could have fed the entire population of Slow Run with all this. I just had to hope it would hold the Hoppers long enough for me and Jack to get away.

"Oh, Callie!"

I jumped. The spoon shot out of my hand and hit the ceiling, then the floor, spattering gravy everywhere.

"I'm sorry, Callie, I didn't mean to startle you." Mrs. Hopper's antennae waved in two directions at once, tracking the slick brown splatters. "I just wanted to let you know we've moved over to the main dining room. So comfortable and charming."

The Moonlight Room. The Hoppers were in the Moonlight Room. My favorite place, the last place I'd seen Mama, and now it was full of Hoppers. . . .

"Is that a problem, Callie?" She tilted her head, waiting patiently. Waiting to see if I'd do something stupid.

"No, ma'am." Fear dug in, urging me to take a chance with my plan. "Could you . . . could Jack come and help me, please? There's going to be a lot to carry, and I don't want the food to get cold."

"But sweet, sweet Jack's looking so tired. I'll send Letitia in to help, how's that?" She didn't wait for an answer. I didn't see her go, she moved so fast. There was just the door flapping.

It didn't matter. My heart sank right through the floor. I'd ruined my whole plan. I'd have Letitia right behind me while I was serving. She wouldn't be joining the others at the table if she was keeping an eye on me. What was I going to do now?

"I hope you eat yourselves sick," I muttered, clutching the spoon tight. "I hope you choke, you . . ."

I stopped. *Eat yourselves sick.* The words repeated in my brain. *Eat yourselves sick.*

I had to be fast. I ran out the back door, into the narrow side hall that led to the bathroom. In the bathroom was a medicine cabinet. Mama kept a stock of useful stuff in that cabinet for guests with emergencies. There were bandages and aspirin, but also bottles of milk of magnesia and Pepto-Bismol, in case you needed to hold something down, and syrup of ipecac, in case you needed to bring something back up.

I stuffed the ipecac into my apron pocket and ran back to the kitchen.

"There you are." Letitia folded her arms. I didn't think it was just the breeze from the door that made her sash ends wave. I didn't look too hard. "I thought maybe you ran out on us and your little friend."

"Just had to use the water closet," I muttered, going around the far side of the counter to get back to the stove.

Letitia made a delicate face. Then she leaned over the stove and sniffed at my gravy. "This better be good. My parents are *very* particular, and I think Clarinda's starting to take a liking to your friend."

The back of my brain tried to tell me what that meant. I told it to be quiet. "It'll only be another minute." I picked up the wooden spoon, stirred the chowder, and tasted. "You can go tell them."

She wrinkled up her borrowed nose. "Nice try, but I'm staying right here." She stomped her foot. "My parents think you won't light out on that skinny little boy, but I'm not so sure."

"Then can you get the tureen off the shelf?" I pointed. "This is ready."

She snorted, but she did it. As soon as her back was

turned, I yanked the stopper out of the ipecac bottle and emptied the whole thing into the bubbling pot.

"Anything else, *Miss* Callie?" Letitia banged the tureen on the counter.

"Thank you." I poured the chowder in, careful not to spill a single drop. "That should do fine."

8

No Home in
This World Anymore

With Letitia Hopper marching behind me, I carried that tureen full of ipecac-laced chowder into the dim and dusty Moonlight Room.

The Hoppers ringed a table in the exact center of the room. They'd stuffed Jack between Mr. Hopper and the oldest boy, Hunter. Hunter's jaws moved like he was chewing a wad of gum, and he had one arm draped around Jack's shoulders. Jack had turned a nasty shade of green, but he clenched his jaw and tried to swallow his panic as I set the tureen down. I shook my head just a little as I lifted the tureen lid, releasing the salt-and-tomato smell of my improvised chowder.

"Excellent!" Mr. Hopper inhaled deeply. Hunter smacked his lips. William burped, and little Clarinda giggled.

That was when I realized the dust cloths that had covered the tables and chairs were gone. All of them. Even the dust sheet we'd dropped beside Papa's piano had vanished.

Mrs. Hopper glared at her children as she shook out her napkin and smoothed it daintily over her lap. None of the others seemed to have saved theirs. "Is it going to be enough, Desmond?"

"This is just for starters," I made myself say. "There's more food in the back." I looked at Jack over the Hoppers' heads. *Don't eat it,* I tried to think toward him. *Even if they offer, don't eat it.* But there was no way to tell if his attempt at a grim smile meant he understood.

"Well, if there's more, let's have it," said Mr. Hopper. "Letitia, help her."

This did not sit well with Miss Letitia. "Pa! I'm hungry too!"

"Do as you're told, Letitia." Mrs. Hopper leaned over the tureen, a thin river of spit running down her chin.

Letitia grimaced, and her mouth parts clacked under her false face. I walked away. Behind me, the buzzing and humming noise of the Hoppers settling down to their feast rose up, and I didn't dare look back. But as I heard Letitia's angry clacking, a new plan formed in my head.

"It's not fair they won't let you sit down with them," I said to Letitia once we were both in the kitchen. "You gotta be starved."

"We're always starved." Her voice sounded different when she said that, light and thin but more . . . *real.* "There's never enough for all of us."

"Then what could you want out this way? There's not much left to eat since the dusters started." I took up a side towel and pulled the bread pudding from the oven. It had come out perfect, all golden brown and shimmery with the milk custard. The rich, sweet smell mixed with the scents of the ham, beans, and gravy still bubbling away on the stove top. It set my mouth watering, but Letitia . . . she looked at that bread pudding like it was the most beautiful thing she'd ever seen.

"Now that we've found you, we'll be fed." She took two steps toward the pudding. "The Seelie King will reward us all."

I couldn't have heard that right. "King? Who the heck is Seelie King?"

"*The* Seelie King." Letitia snickered and took a step closer to the pudding, like it pulled her on a string. "And he's offered a reward to the first of us to bring you to him. You're famous, Miss Callie. There's a whole prophecy about you."

The words dropped like stones into the middle of my confusion, but I just adjusted the pudding on the counter a little. "Prophecy?"

Letitia's bug eyes misted over. I could see my pudding's reflection in her spectacles. *See her now, daughter of three worlds. See her now, three roads to choose. Where she goes, where she stays, where she stands, there shall the gates be closed.*

Those words went straight down into my blood and bones. They twisted around in there, looking for the way to my heart. She was telling me the truth, and I knew it. The problem was, I had no idea what the heck that truth *meant.*

It didn't matter. I could work it out later. Right now, I had to take care of Miss Letitia and the rest of the proud Hopper clan.

"You know," I said slowly. "It's not fair that they're all out there stuffing their faces and you're in here doing the work. Why don't you have this?" I slid the pan toward her.

Letitia opened her mouth wide, but she didn't move right away. She shifted her bug eyes sideways to me, and back to the pudding.

I made myself smile. "It'd serve 'em right."

"Serve 'em right." Letitia dug in with both hooks and stuffed a big, boiling-hot heap of pudding into her mouth. She bent down over the pan, chewing and buzzing, and not looking at me at all.

So I whacked her a good one with Mama's best silver tray.

Letitia fell *splat* into the pudding, and I hit her again, hard enough to dent the tray. She slid to the floor, but she didn't stay down.

"You little brat!" Letitia bounced to her feet. Her spectacles hung crooked and custard-spattered from one ear, and her faceted bug eyes glittered hard and dry. I had one short second to get good and scared before Letitia leapt into the air. Her green sash unwound from her waist, turning into a pair of iridescent green-veined wings.

Half-bug, half-human Letitia swooped down. I dove

across the tiles like I was sliding into second base, and banged hard against the stove. Letitia laughed and circled tight, lining up for another run. I scrambled to my feet and—still thinking baseball—grabbed the cast-iron frying pan off the stove with both hands. Letitia dove, and I swung. Momentum carried me in a full circle. I felt the thud and heard the scream before I could see straight.

"What *is* all this commotion?"

Mrs. Hopper came through the door in time to get hit by a gob of flying ham and to see her girl knocked smack against the wall.

"Oh, *dear.*" Mrs. Hopper's antennae waved toward her daughter, who was sprawled on the tiles and did not get up, but her eyes stayed fixed on me. "Callie, I am very much afraid we're going to have to dock your pay for this."

"Come on, you big bug!" I hefted the frying pan, dripping sticky Coca-Cola glaze. "You wanna take a bite outta me? Come on and try it!"

Which was a stupid thing to say, because Mrs. Hopper did come on. For a minute, I saw the locust plainly. Taller and heavier than I was, it scuttled on four of its legs, its hooked feet held out in front. Its mandibles snapped, looking for something all covered in sticky cola to chew.

Fear blanked my mind. I backed up, clutching the frying pan in front of me.

The bug shivered and became Mrs. Hopper again. She pressed a hand against her stomach.

"What . . ." Mrs. Hopper covered her mouth, and her

eyes rolled. With a groan, she reeled sideways. Vomit splattered all over the floor.

It was disgusting.

Seeing no point in waiting around for her to finish, I ran headlong for the swinging doors and slammed into Jack.

We both staggered backward, clutching our noses and gawking at each other.

"The Hoppers are all being sick!" He pointed behind him. Then he saw Mrs. Hopper retching, and Letitia still out cold against the wall. "God Almighty."

"Come on!" I bolted down the corridor toward the front doors, still holding tight to the frying pan. My plan was forgotten. All I could think about was getting away. I jumped off the porch and plowed straight into the dust drifts.

"Wait!" Jack grabbed my wrist. "The car!" He waded toward the Duesenberg, which sat gleaming in the light that trickled from the Imperial's glass-fronted doors.

"We don't have the key!"

"Just get in!"

I dove through the driver's-side door, my pan banging the door frame behind me. All at once, the Duesy was gone. I sat in a rattletrap Model A truck with a cracked windshield and an open back.

Jack and I stared at each other, but only for a heartbeat. Jack folded the Model A's hood back and plunged both arms into the engine. A second later, the engine coughed and the smell of gasoline filled the passenger compartment. The whole truck shuddered, and the motor caught. That unsteady rumble was the sweetest sound I'd ever heard.

I threw myself and my frying pan sideways as Jack leapt feetfirst into the driver's seat. He worked the choke, yanked the throttle open, slammed the gears, and stomped hard on the accelerator, and we lurched off into the dark.

"Which way?" shouted Jack.

The world beyond the little space cleared by the head-lights was a wall of solid black. I squinted, and found out my ability to see through the dust didn't mean I could see in the dark.

"Just drive!"

Jack's cheek bulged as he clenched his jaw. A line of barbed wire and fence posts appeared in front of us. Jack swore and tried to swing right, but he was too late. Wire twanged and snapped around us as the truck lumbered straight ahead.

I stared and stared. Slowly, I made out the line of the hogback ridge, and then the vague shape of a windmill. With the fence, that meant we were headed east, away from town, out toward the railroad tracks. I opened my mouth to tell Jack to bear left, but the wind gusted hard, blowing dust in through the truck's open windows. Dust, and voices.

Look shhhhaaaarrrrp! Look shhhhaaaarrrrp!

"No! Oh, no, no, no, no!"

"What?" Jack demanded.

"Can't you hear it?"

"No!"

THUMP! The truck rocked under the impact of something heavy falling square on the roof.

"Heard that," Jack muttered.

A second thump shook our flimsy getaway truck.

"That too," said Jack.

A huge Hopper head, mandibles scissoring, ducked into the window. I screamed and shoved the frying pan straight into its mouth. There was a hiss and a stench like burning hay, and the bug tumbled off into the dust.

"Got it!" I shouted.

Jack hooted and pounded the steering wheel.

A black hook curled around the window frame.

"Take that!" I banged the frying pan down on the hook. The Hopper howled and the hook vanished.

Jack gripped the wheel so tight his knuckles went white. "Hang on!"

He hit the brakes and wrenched the wheel around. The engine groaned, and the rickety Ford spun in a tight circle, rocking like a ship in a storm. The Hopper flew sideways, tumbling away into the dark.

Miraculously the truck didn't stall out. I was ready to marry both Jack and Mr. Henry Ford as we went rolling over the dunes.

Then the engine coughed and the truck lurched.

"Come on, come on," Jack pleaded, working the throttle and the choke. "Not yet!"

"What's wrong?"

"Engine's taking in dust," he said grimly. "It's gonna smother."

Caaaalliiiieeee . . .

I stuck my head out the window. There was just enough light to see the big black bug leaping from dust ridge to dust ridge, right behind us.

"One of 'em's back there?"

"Yes!"

The truck coughed and staggered again.

"Okay." Jack clashed the gears and cussed a blue streak, throwing the truck into reverse. The wheels spun and I was afraid he'd dig us into the dunes. But he just swung that truck around until the Hopper glittered in the headlights.

"What're you doing?" I shrieked.

"Playing chicken!" Jack grinned like he was a Hopper himself and put all his weight onto the accelerator, almost standing up from the seat. The truck flew forward. So did the bug. I swear I heard it laughing.

"They can fly, you idiot!"

Jack said nothing. The bug jumped up and landed right on the hood with a hollow thump. It scrabbled at the glass, its mandibles and hooks digging into the spiderweb of cracks, ready to winkle us out of our tin shell.

It didn't see the windmill looming up in the headlights behind it.

"Jump!" Jack shouted.

I kicked open the door and jumped, thudding into hot dust and rolling tail over teacup down the new dune.

There was a crash and a scream and a big, juicy, buzzing squelch.

Coughing hard and spitting dust, I picked myself up.

The Model A had plowed into the windmill, and the Hopper, whichever one it was, was squashed between the twisted struts and the steaming guts of the wrecked truck. Yellow oozed out of its broken body and dripped onto the dust.

I looked at Jack. Jack looked at me. Above us, the windmill's bent frame creaked and swayed in the wind.

I grabbed Jack's free hand and dragged him behind me.

We ran until we couldn't run anymore. After that, we walked. The wind was kicking up all the new dust. It stuck to my glaze-smeared skin and itched like a whole family of fleas. Jack coughed with every step, and I was ready to be sick wondering what I'd do if he started to suffocate. So when we saw the deserted tenant farmer's shack sticking out of the sand, we didn't even think twice, just stumbled inside and collapsed in the middle of the floor. Jack threw his coat over us both and we huddled close under the worn-out cloth.

After a while, we fell asleep.

9

Dust Bowl Refugees

An arm smacked me on the ear. I shouted and sat up. Jack's coat slid off my head.

"Hannah! Hannah, stop!" Jack rolled back and forth, his eyes squeezed tight and his arms flailing in every direction.

"Wake up!" I hollered. "Jack, wake up!"

His eyes snapped open, and for a minute, it was plain he didn't know where he was, or why his arms were stretched out like that. Slowly, blinking hard, he sat up. Sweat streamed down his brow, and he wiped it away with the back of his shaking hand.

"Nightmares?" I said, and he nodded. His face was so pale under the dirt, I figured it was better to change the subject. "Thanks for getting us out of there. Where'd you learn to drive like that?"

Jack fiddled with his shoelaces for a second. "Before they repealed Prohibition, my folks were bootleggers—

bathtub gin, moonshine, stuff like that. Sometimes I had to drive the car on the deliveries." He didn't look too proud of that, which should have been a clue about how he felt about the rest of his time at home, and probably should have stopped me from asking my next question. "Who's Hannah?"

"My sister. She's dead." Jack got to his feet without looking at me.

"I'm sorry."

Jack shrugged and kept on not looking at me. Instead, he wiped his hands on his pants and walked over to the door to turn the handle. When the door didn't open, he leaned on it. It didn't budge.

"We're drifted in solid," he said.

The shack had two windows, one beside the door and one at the back. I tried squinting out the one beside the door, but it was too grimy to let me see much. From the sound of things, the wind had died down, but dust still pattered and pecked as it settled onto the shack's tin roof, a sound enough like rain to make you cry.

Jack came to stand beside me, looking through the dust-covered glass. He grunted, wrapped his coat around his fist, and punched each of those glass panes in a no-nonsense way. He swept his arm around, clearing out the glass and splintering the mullions, which were already half gone from dry rot. As soon as the window hole was clear, we both climbed out onto the drift that had piled up level with the sill. Standing on that shifting dust pile, we looked at what the storm had made of Kansas.

I was used to being alone, but never like this. Hills and ripples of red sand spread under the glare of a pink-and-white sky. Nothing broke the smoky horizon, not so much as a fence post, let alone any sign of road or railroad track.

"Let's get back in," said Jack.

I nodded. The shack was rickety and the dust was piled in every corner, but its rusted roof shut out that empty country.

"So." Jack rested his arms against his bent knees. "You gonna tell me what all that was with the Hoppers back there?"

"I don't know."

"Right, and I'm the king of England."

"I don't know! It just . . ." I flapped my hands, like I could shoo the question away. "It just *happened.*"

I told him about the voices I'd heard, and how Mama made me play Papa's piano and then vanished in the dust storm. I told him how I went looking for her but found Baya instead; how I got three wishes, then got the Hoppers. Finally, I told him what Letitia Hopper had said about the prophecy: *See her now, daughter of three worlds. See her now, with three roads to choose. Where she goes, where she stays, where she stands, there shall the gates be closed.*

Jack took off his cap, knocked the dust off, rubbed his brushy hair, and put his hat back on. Then he leaned his head against the wall and stared up at the tin roof for a long time.

"That Apache you pulled out of the dust . . . ," he said to the roof. "I think you met Coyote."

"Baya was a coyote?" I shouldn't have been surprised, but part of me just would not give up the idea that *something* still had to be impossible.

"Not *a* coyote." Jack sat up straight and folded his long legs. "*Coyote.* He's a big Indian spirit, and there's a ton of stories about him. There's one about how he hung the stars, and another about how he named all the animals, all kinds of stuff like that."

I was quiet for a little while, because I was remembering the shape I'd thought was a dog in the dust storm, and how I'd seen the stars in Baya's black eyes.

"You got any idea what the Hoppers were?" I asked. "Besides really big bugs?"

Jack's face scrunched up as he considered that one. "I think they're fairies."

Now I knew he was crazy, and I guess that showed on my face. "What else are they gonna be?" Jack demanded. "Besides big bugs?" He started ticking points off on his fingers. "They're magic. They don't like iron. . . ."

"How do you know they don't like iron?"

"You said you clobbered Letitia with the silver tray and she got right back up, but when you hit her with a cast-iron frying pan, she stayed down."

"Couldn't that just be because the pan's stone-dead heavy?" I gave him my best fish eye, but at the same time, I was thinking how the Duesenberg changed into a rickety Model A as soon as the pan banged against the door.

"Could be, but I don't think so. See, iron's poison to

fairies, so I think they're fairies." Jack took off his hat and rubbed his head again. "And I think you are too."

My train of thought screeched to a stop so hard it nearly jumped the track.

"Me?" I said, hoping I'd heard him wrong. "I'm a fairy?"

"Well, what did Baya tell you? About your pa?"

I didn't have to think about it. Every word had carved itself right into me. " 'There's a spirit man, tall and fine. He's full of love and mischief. He's promised to a spirit woman of his enemies, but he doesn't want her.' "

"See? 'Spirit man.' That could mean fairies." Jack leaned forward, his hands talking as much as his mouth. "The Irish say there're two kinds of fairies. There's the *Seelie.* They're bright and beautiful. Then there's the *Unseelie,* and they're all dark and ugly, like trolls and goblins and stuff. Each side has their own kings and their own territory, and they're always at war with each other and . . ."

Jack kept on talking, but I was hearing a very different voice.

"The Seelie King will reward us all," I whispered.

"What?" Jack frowned.

"Letitia said that, when we were in the kitchen. She said, now that they . . . the Hoppers had found me, the Seelie King would reward them."

"See! I'm right!" Jack shouted.

I felt sick anger crawl up out of my stomach to glower at him. I did not like Jack knowing more about what was going on than I did. The whole world had turned upside down and shaken us out into this lonesome place. I wanted him to be just as confused and lost as I was, though for the life of me I couldn't have said why.

"How can you know all this stuff?"

Jack shrugged. "That wasn't the first time I got took up for vagrancy. I got caught coming through Texas once, and they put me on a road crew. I spent thirty days chained to this mick kid from Brooklyn, and he told me a bunch of stories his grandma told him."

"You said iron's poison to fairies. If I'm a fairy, how come I could hold on to the frying pan?"

I figured I had him there, but not for long. "Maybe it's because you're only *part* fairy," said Jack. "Daughter of three worlds, right? Your mama's a regular human being, right? So you can handle iron and salt and stuff because of your human blood."

"I can't be a fairy. They're little girls in puffy skirts and they've got wings. . . ." *They're all white.* "I don't *feel* like a fairy."

"How do you know? If you've always felt like you, you wouldn't know if that was how a fairy felt or not."

"It doesn't matter." I was not going to talk about this anymore. I was not even going to *think* about this. There were all kinds of more important things to think about. Like how we were going to stay alive without food or water or any idea which way town was. "I still gotta get to California. That's where Baya said Mama is."

I got to my feet and went over to the broken window again. I stared and stared until I felt the veins standing out in my forehead, and I still couldn't see anything.

"I can get you to California," said Jack.

"How're you going to do that?"

He shrugged. "We can ride the rails out. I'm going that way anyhow, and two's better than one when you're bummin'." He cocked his head at me, and those big blue eyes turned all sly. "I won't do it for free, though."

"But I don't have any . . ." I stopped. "Wait! I still got . . ." I shoved my hand in my apron pocket, but when I brought it out, all I had was a single dead leaf. I opened my fist, and the tired-out wind brushed leaf crumbs across the floor. The fifty hadn't been any more real than Mrs. Hopper's pretty face. "I got nothing."

"You got your story. You tell it to me, and I can write it up and sell it to the magazines." The way Jack said it, I was sure that was what he had been thinking of all along.

"Who'd believe any of this?"

"Not like news, dopey. I'd do it up like a story. You ever read *The Wonderful Wizard of Oz?*"

As if there was a girl alive in Kansas who hadn't read that book.

"Oz made L. Frank Baum rich." Jack's face lit up like it had when he talked about getting a newspaper job in Los Angeles. "You can make a fortune with just one book, especially if Hollywood decides they want to make a movie out of it. What do you say?"

I hated the idea. But what could I say? Without Jack Holland I'd have been a Hopper supper already. "Okay, but you gotta get me to California first."

"Deal!" He stuck out his hand, and there in the middle of the biggest nowhere ever created, we shook on it. "This is gonna work out swell. I can just see it: my journey with a fairy girl to the Golden State . . ."

"Yeah, yeah," I said, just to shut him up. I wasn't a fairy, but there was no way I was going to get him to believe that. I'd have to prove it somehow, but how do you prove a thing's not so? "What do we do now?"

Jack shoved his hands into his breeches pockets and looked me over. "You sing."

"What?"

"We have to find out what you can do. From what you said, it all started when you played your father's piano. . . ."

"Played, not sang," I pointed out.

He shrugged. "So we have to find out if you need an instrument, or if you can make magic with any music."

I gawked at him. If there had been any flies around, I would have caught them. How could he be so calm?

"It's not safe," I reminded him. "Last time my mama vanished and the Hoppers found me." I was starting to like Jack less and less, but I didn't want him vanishing, and I sure as sure didn't want any more Hoppers, not when I didn't even have so much as a frying pan.

"Just try," Jack said. "You brought Hoppers last time; maybe this time you can . . . I don't know, bring us breakfast."

You know how in a cartoon when somebody's got to make a choice, they'll get a little angel on one shoulder and a little devil on the other? That was how I felt right then. Half of me was saying: *Don't do it, don't do it, something bad will happen.* The other half was saying: *Do it, do it, you gotta find out what will happen.*

But the word *breakfast* had its own magic, and the little devil won. "What do I sing?"

Jack made a face like he knew I was stalling. "How about 'I Been Workin' on the Railroad'?" he said. "Everybody knows that one. Come on." He started clapping to set the time and sang. "*I been workin' on the railroad . . .*"

"*All the live-long day . . .*" It was a kids' song. I didn't like it, but he was right, I did know it. Its tune flowed into my brain and I started clapping along. Jack and I set up a strong, steady rhythm, like a chorus of hammers, like men keeping time as they swung those hammers down on the iron spikes, pinning the great black rails to the wooden ties, binding the country together and opening it wide up at the same time.

"*Can't you hear the whistle blowin'? Rise up so early in the morn . . .*"

I forgot about being thirsty, about being lost, and about everything else except this stupid little kids' song with its driving rhythm and its memories of work gangs so long gone nobody knew what it was about anymore.

"*Can't you hear the captain shouting, 'Dinah, blow your horn . . .'*"

I felt it happen. Everything shifted, though my eyes

couldn't see what or how. The whole world just twisted as if we were inside a lock while somebody was turning the key. The feeling lasted less than a second, but when it finished, the air all around us had changed, as if a fresh breeze was blowing in.

"Dinah, won't you blow?" we sang. *"Dinah . . ."*

"Drill, ye tarriers, drill!"

A new voice cut across mine. Jack's hands froze between one clap and the next, and his mouth gaped.

"Drill, ye tarriers, drill!"

It wasn't just one voice; it was a full-throated chorus of men. Their rough and ragged singing soared in from the ruined prairie, where a minute ago there had been nothing at all.

"For it's WORK all DAY for the SUGAR in your TAY, DOWN on the OLD rail-WAY!"

Jack scrambled to his feet and ran for the window hole. I followed, slow and afraid.

"And drill, ye tarriers, drill! And BLAST! And FIRE!"

Sun-bleached grass rippled beneath a pure blue sky. It smelled sweet, sweeter than my bread pudding. Bees buzzed among the cornflowers and Queen Anne's lace. A hawk wheeled overhead, and sparrows clung nervously to the nodding grass stems. All at once I remembered being a little girl and running through grass like this, up to the hogback ridge to watch rain clouds pile up on the horizon.

A great gash had been cut in the grass for the iron rails.

Shirtless men stood carefully spaced on either side of those
black lines. Each man held a long-handled hammer. The
hammers swung up and the hammers swung down, in time
with their song.

> *"Every morning at seven o'clock*
> *There's twenty tarriers workin' on the rock!*
> *Boss comes round and yells, 'Keep still!*
> *And come down heavy on the cast-iron drill!'"*

"Look." Jack tugged at my sleeve. I turned, and he
pointed to the shanty's back window. Through that other
window, there was still the silent, empty desert.

Out front, the men laying the rails across the lush green
grassland kept right on singing. It was like something out of
a pulp magazine, *Astounding Stories* or *Weird Tales.* Jack
had punched open the glass window, but somehow I'd
punched open a . . . a *time* window.

Or maybe it wasn't a window at all. Maybe it was a gate.

Whatever it was, it was wrong. I felt that down to the
soles of my feet. It was completely wrong and I was respon-
sible. Again.

"We gotta get out of here." I started for the desert
window.

"Wait! They got a cook wagon." Jack leaned out the
broken window across the living prairie. I couldn't help
but look. A little, old-timey steam engine with a big red
cowcatcher jutting out front waited on the track that had

already been laid. That engine was hooked up to a full-fledged railcar with a trickle of smoke coming out of its chimney. The breeze blew through the window again. This time, it carried the smell of cooking bacon. My stomach growled and cramped up. Another breath and I could smell baking bread as well. My stomach didn't so much growl as roar.

"We can go bum a meal!" Jack had his foot up on the sill, but I hauled him back.

"No! We can't go out there!"

"Why?"

"Because what if we can't get back?"

That stopped him. He saw it now. If it was a gate, and if somehow I'd opened it, somebody else could shut it. Or I might accidentally shut it, because sure as sure, I didn't know what I was doing or how I was doing it.

If my gate shut while we were in that other time, we might never be able to get back.

Jack looked toward the cook car and the smoke coming out its tin chimney. "We have to try."

"We can't!"

The face he turned toward me was nothing I'd seen on him yet. Anger and desperation were knotted up together with his hunger. "You stay here if you want," he said soft and slow, so each word dropped separately between us. "I'm going after something to eat."

He was out the window and running through the grass while I was still opening my mouth to yell "No!" I grabbed the windowsill and leaned out as far as I could. I felt the strange, shifting parts of the invisible lock all around me. I felt them wobble, and I felt the key begin to turn. I tried to grab it, but it slipped free.

"Jack!" I screamed. "Jack! It's closing!"

He stopped and turned. "You're just saying that!"

"No! I'm not! I swear!" It was turning, turning. The barrel and the tumbler were shifting. The hinges were straining, and I was in the middle. I felt the pressure inside my brain and inside my heart. "Hurry!"

Jack looked at the cook car and the singing men, and at me. He cussed loud and angry and came pelting back. I shook. I didn't know where these feelings were coming from, and I didn't know how to stop that twisting I could only think of as the key.

Jack slapped both hands on the windowsill and vaulted through. I shuddered and screamed. *SNAP!* The sound rocked the shack, and even Jack reeled.

Hot, dusty wind blew across the windowsill into our faces as we stood there, panting and shaking and staring out at the unbroken Kansas desert.

Jack wiped his dusty sleeve across his mouth. "You swear to me you didn't do that on purpose?"

I shook my head. "It started to close on its own. I couldn't hold it. I tried, I promise I did."

He took off his hat and rubbed his head. "What do we do, then?"

"Start walking, I guess."

So we climbed out into our own time to trudge hungry and thirsty over the blowing dunes. We kept our eyes straight ahead so we both had something like privacy while we cried for the smell of growing grass and baking bread.

10

Going Down the Road Feelin' Bad

It took me and Jack three days to get to the town of Constantinople. And I'll tell you this—Jack was lucky to be alive by that time. Not because the walking was so hard, which it was, but because I was ready to kill him stone dead.

The whole three days we walked, Jack Holland would *not* shut up. He kept after me and after me to sing something so he could see what would happen. It was like he'd forgotten all about the Hoppers and how he'd almost gotten stuck in that railroad work camp out of the olden days. He kept trying to tell me all these stupid, baby fairy stories he'd heard from some crazy Irish guy, or some crazy Negro, and even this extra-special crazy Eye-talian. Kept trying to tell me I must be all fairy magic and everything. He thought it was so exciting. He didn't get it. It was bad enough when I had to hide being half black. Now I might not even be human at all. How was I supposed to hide *that*?

Pretty soon I found out the only way to shut him up at all was to ask what happened to his little sister, Hannah. But then we'd go maybe another mile, and he'd start right in again. And every night, before it got too dark to see, he'd pull out this little notebook and stubby pencil he carried and write stuff down. Stuff about me, I just knew it.

I lay awake nights, listening to the wind until my head hurt. But there were no more voices. That didn't make me feel any better. That could just mean whatever was out there was keeping quiet, and waiting.

Jack woke up sweating and staring every night, calling out for Hannah to stop whatever it was she was doing.

Even with my special dust eyes to see the way, it was hard to keep to the road buried under drifts of blow dirt and tumbleweeds. We passed people working their way out from under the storm. We saw a farmer hauling his wife and kids out of the second-story window to stand on the roof. The dust had buried the rest of the house. We saw another man sitting on the hood of his tractor, his head in his hands. We stopped and helped a woman and her three little kids pull their cow out of a drift. She shared their supper of fatback meat and beans, and let us sleep on their roof with them that night. We stopped again and helped a man and a pregnant woman dig out their Model T. They gave us some water from their canteens and let us ride with them toward Constantinople, until we got stopped by more drifts over the road. They said they'd wait for the plow trucks. We wished them luck and started walking again.

The third night we stayed in a cellar hole. We lit a fire from the timber pile that used to be the house overhead and took turns sleeping, in case a duster came up.

By the time we stumbled to the edge of Constantinople, I was ready to drink the Mississippi dry and then fall down and sleep for a year.

I'd been to Constantinople before, but not for a long time. It was bigger than Slow Run. They had a clothing store as well as a general store, along with five saloons, but only four churches. As if to make up for this, the churches were all built of brick, with steeples sticking high and proud into the dusty sky. There was even a real movie theater—the Bijoux—with a big, flashy marquee out front announcing they were showing *The Man Who Knew Too Much* starring Peter Lorre, along with a SECOND BRAND-NEW FEATURE.

Constantinople had people too. They came and went from those stores and churches, or stood on the board walkways talking with each other. They glanced at me and Jack as we stumbled up the street, but just as quickly looked back to their own troubles. A group of men clustered around the curving bumpers of a Packard car all leaned in so close to the radio that their hat brims touched.

"Colorado's governor has authorized the mobilization of National Guard troops to help Denver in the aftermath of what may have been the biggest dust storm ever to hit . . ."

The problem was, there we were, walking into town all filthy and hungry, our feet burning from the hot dust, and we had nothing but the crumbs of a dead leaf in our pockets. I turned to Jack. "Now what?"

But Jack didn't answer right away. He just kind of faded into the shadow beside Morrison's Hardware Store. As he surveyed the main street with its battered cars, rickety wagons, and starving mules, Jack's face changed. He tightened up. The "gosh wow" dreamer with his big grin who could believe in magic and fairies without blinking was gone. This was the hobo kid who could hot-wire a car and drive it like a bootlegger.

"Won't be no trains yet today," he said. I knew that much. On the way in, we'd skirted the rail yard and saw the men fighting the wind to get the tracks cleared. "So we're gonna need to find food, and maybe a place to bed down." His narrow gaze flickered this way and that, taking the measure of the whole town. "Callie, you just go stand in front of the window of that lunch counter and look hungry."

I'd tried to get ready for the idea we'd have to bum something, but now that I was actually faced with begging, I balked. "Why me?"

"'Cause you're a girl," Jack said, really slowly like I wasn't too bright. "Folks'll give a meal faster to a girl than a boy."

"Why?"

"Just will, that's all. Besides, you're smaller than me. That always helps."

I looked out onto the main street. Men in overalls and women in dungarees or worn dresses went in and out of stores with dusty windows. They stopped to talk with each other. A dented, lopsided truck rattled by. Away on the other side stood the lunch counter. I couldn't do this. I couldn't beg with all these people around to see.

Then the wind twisted until it was blowing straight from across the street. The smell of hot grease went right to my stomach and kicked out my pride. I could do anything if it meant I could get one mouthful of whatever was making that smell.

"So I just stand there?"

"That's about it." Jack kept his eyes on the street. I didn't know what he was looking for, but he looked for it hard. "If a customer sees you and offers to buy you a meal, you take it. If the waitress or the fry cook comes out, you offer to sweep up or do any kind of work they got. Be sure to tell 'em you been walking all day and your brother's out looking for work."

"My brother?"

"Me."

I eyed him up and down, from his bright blue eyes and brown hair to his knobby knees. "Nobody's going to believe you're my brother."

"Most people believe what you tell 'em. Oh, and one thing to remember."

"What?"

"Don't go nowhere with nobody unless you take me with you. Some people ain't safe."

"I knew that one."

"Just makin' sure. Now go on." Jack gave me a shove on the shoulder. He could smell the cooking too, and he'd been hungry longer than I had.

I didn't like it, but what was I gonna do? We weren't going to get any farther without something to eat. My throat felt like it had been sunburned, and my legs felt like rubber bands. I wasn't sure I was even going to make it across the street.

But I did, and I stood in front of the big plate-glass window with CARMODY'S APOTHECARY written across it in fancy gold letters. It was plastered over with signs for aspirin, Pepsodent toothpaste, and food: COFFEE AND PIE, TEN CENTS. HAMBURGER, FIVE CENTS. They had the radio going too, all about the duster.

". . . declaring from the floor of the United States Senate that now is the time for decisive action on the question of soil conservation and agricultural reform . . ."

Right behind the dust-dimmed window stood a couple of wooden booths and tables, and past them was the long counter with its red-and-silver stools. In one of the booths sat a windburned man with his shirtsleeves rolled up past his rough elbows. While I watched, he scooped up a big, fat hamburger from a nest of french fries and bit off a hunk of meat, cheese, bread, and onion. Juice dripped down onto the napkin tucked into his shirt. The waitress came by with a coffeepot and a slice of bright yellow pie topped with three inches of fluffy meringue balanced on a tray.

I thought I was going to faint dead away on the sidewalk boards.

The waitress poured a stream of black coffee into the man's cup. She glanced up, and our eyes met. I didn't have to try to look hungry. I felt sick just trying to stand there. The next good blast of wind would have blown me right over.

The man, still chewing, turned his head. He saw me too. He wiped his mouth with the corner of his napkin and tossed it on the table, climbed to his feet, collected some things from the seat beside him, and stumped toward the door.

The bell rang as he came out, and the smell of cooking hung all around him. The world reeled again. I'd have done anything to get some of that food. I'd have gotten down on my knees right there on Main Street.

Then I saw the gun hanging from his belt. And the nightstick. I looked around frantically for the badge, and finally saw it clipped beside the weapons. It wasn't a sheriff's star, though. It was a golden shield.

"What you want here, girlie?" The man smelled like onions and tobacco.

I looked the whole way up into his hard gray eyes. "P-p-please, sir. D-do you have a job of work I could do? I been walkin' all day with my brother, and . . ."

He crouched down so his eyes were level with mine, and he smiled all across his broad, tanned face. "Well now, girlie, I'll tell you what," he began. Hope filled the hungry parts of my insides. Then he pushed his hat back on his head and went on. "I'm gonna give you exactly thirty seconds to get off this street. If you ain't gone by then, I'm gonna take this club and crack you a good one across your backside. If you don't run fast enough after that, you're gonna find yourself on the chain gang choppin' cotton for the rest of your natural-born days. How's that sound?"

I backed up, one step, two, three. The man kept right on grinning.

"Bull Morgan don't allow no bums on his trains, girl, or in his town." He reached down and pulled that shiny brown club out of its holster beside the wooden-handled revolver.

Fear found the last of my strength, and I bolted like a scared rabbit. Jack caught hold of me as I ran past, and swung us both around behind the hardware store. All the while, I heard that big man—Bull Morgan—laughing.

I was shaking and I couldn't stand anymore. I slid down the clapboard wall until I was huddled on the ground. I could still smell the grease and the onions, and tears were starting.

"It's okay." Jack put his hand on my shoulder. "It happens sometimes. We just wait till he's gone. Then we try again. Back door this time. That waitress felt sorry for you, I could tell."

I shook my head hard. "I can't do that again."

"You're just not hungry enough yet. Give it another hour. You'll go back."

"Well," said a new voice, "I call that an awful shame."

A Negro woman was walking down the backstreet, swinging a little white handbag.

"A great big girl like you begging in the streets." She stopped right in front of us and planted a fist on her hip.

She had a pretty face, with round cheeks and a wide mouth that looked like it was holding back a smile. Her skin was the color of the earth in good times. The blue flowers on her white dress made splashes of bright color against our dust-dimmed surroundings, and a wide-brimmed white hat shaded her face, making it hard to see her eyes.

Jack was on his feet. "'S not her fault, missus," he said in a high, pathetic voice that sounded a lot younger than his own. "We been knockin' and knockin', lookin' for a job of work, but there's nothin', not with the duster, and we were so hungry. . . ."

I'd been right about Jack Holland. He had the kind of face that could make you believe. He made his eyes go all wide and puppy-dog as he twisted his cap in his hands and hunched over so he didn't look so tall.

"Tsk-tsk." The woman shook her head slowly. But she wasn't paying attention to Jack. She just kept looking at me.

"Come here, girl," she said at last.

Jack gave me a hint of a nod. So I got up and brushed myself off and walked to the woman. She was pretty, in her flower-print dress, white hat, and white gloves. Now I could see her eyes were the color of strong coffee.

She looked at me hard with those eyes, and then broke into a big smile. Unlike Bull Morgan's, this one was full of joy.

"Well, well." The woman clapped her hands together. "If I haven't gone and found myself Callie LeRoux."

"'Scuse me?" I said, forgetting my manners entirely. "I don't know you."

"No, you don't, but I know your papa, Daniel."

Just like that, I was struck as dumb as a dead stump. Jack slipped closer, but I couldn't so much as turn my head away from this lady. I couldn't have moved if the whole Hopper clan had come pouring out of the hardware store.

"You got us confused, missus," Jack said clearly and politely. Probably to keep her attention off the fact that he was also kicking my ankle. "Our daddy's name is Dennis, Dennis McClaren."

She looked down her nose at him. You could tell she'd had a lot of practice doing that. "Is this . . . boy with you, Callie?"

I licked my lips and remembered I actually had a voice. "Yes, ma'am."

"Well, all right then. You can both come with me."

"Where to?" demanded Jack.

"Why, to lunch, of course. There won't be talking sense to either of you if you're half starved."

Jack gripped my arm, and to my utter shock he said, "Thank you kindly, missus, but I don't think so."

She shrugged. "Suit yourselves."

And just like that, she walked away, swinging her handbag, switching her hips, and not looking back.

I yanked my arm away from Jack. "What're you doing?" I whispered fiercely.

"I don't trust her." Jack stuffed both hands in his pockets and looked after the woman with his hard hobo eyes. "How does she know your name?"

"She knows my papa!"

"How can she just be walking down the street and know your father?"

I pulled back and shook the question away. "He was a musician! He must've played towns all over the state. I bet we could have met somebody who knows him in Dodge, or Topeka."

"And you should think careful about what kind of people that'd be," Jack said. "Remember what Baya said about your papa."

"I remember," I snapped back. "And I remember how you've been jabbering on about how he was a fairy and I'm a fairy and how we've got to find out what that means. But when we meet somebody who might actually know, you don't want anything to do with her!" I bit down on both lips. I'd never win if I got Jack's back up.

"Look, she said she'd feed us. Do you want to eat or not?"

"We can't! The stories all say if you eat anything in Fairyland, you can never leave."

That was all I could stand and a little bit more. "We're not *in* Fairyland! We're in Kansas! Whoever she is, she knows something about my papa *and* she's got food and I am going after her!"

I pelted around the corner of the store, afraid the woman would have gotten out of sight. But no, there she was, marching down the dusty hardpan street between the backs of the shops and the fronts of the first low houses. As I ran to catch up, she disappeared into a shuttered clapboard building, not much more than a shack, really. It wasn't until I got to the porch that I saw the hand-painted cardboard sign tacked to the door that read SHIMMY'S.

Piano music trickled out around the door, a soft, wandering blues tune. I shifted my weight, and the porch boards creaked under my shoes. I knew what this was. It was a juke joint—a place where people could come and hear music and dance and drink. We'd had a place like it on the edge of Slow Run called the Turn Out. It was a big dare with the kids to sneak down there at night and try to see in the windows, or maybe watch the dice games out back.

But it was the music that made me hesitate. There'd been a lot of music in my life lately, and following it had not been getting me anyplace good. If I followed this music now and something went wrong, I didn't have anything or any-body to help me. Not even Jack.

I put my hand on the knob. I didn't bother to knock; I just pushed the door open and stepped over the threshold. As I did, I got that twisting key-in-the-lock feeling again, like I'd had when I opened that window or gate or whatever it was to the living prairie and the railroad men working. I knew I wasn't just walking into an ordinary room; I was walking into Someplace Else.

This time, though, Someplace Else didn't look like all that much. The room on the other side of that doorway was dim and hot. The smells of tobacco, dust, and beer rose up from scarred floorboards. Crooked chairs stood around bare wooden tables. As my eyes adjusted, I could make out a small stage in the far corner. The woman we'd met in the street rested her elbows on the top of an upright piano and smiled big and bright down at the player. He was a lean black man with a pencil-thin mustache and his black hair slicked down tight against his scalp. A cigarette burned in the stand ashtray at his elbow. His long hands moved slow and easy across the keys, coaxing out the tune.

"Let him go, let him go, God bless him . . . ," crooned the woman, and the player smiled into her eyes. *"He can roam this wide world over, and never find a sweet gal like me. . . ."*

I took a step. The dusty floor creaked underfoot, and the man and woman stopped.

"Well, it's about time." The man swiveled his stool

toward me. "Shimmy said you'd be coming along. Hello, Callie girl."

"Who're you?"

"Well," said the woman, "I guess I'd better perform the introductions. Callie LeRoux, meet your papa, Daniel."

11

I Seen My People

The floor tipped. My lungs closed up tighter than they ever had when they were full of dust. I was sliding sideways. I had to put my hand out to stop from falling against the wall.

"Easy now, honey." The woman—Shimmy—beamed at me, like she'd just brought home the canary for the cat.

"I'm sorry to break it to you so sudden, Callie," said the man—my papa? Really? "But seeing you there, I couldn't hold off."

"You . . . you're my papa?" I whispered.

He smiled, showing his teeth, which were straight and even and bright, bright white. He wore neat gray trousers with red suspenders over a crisp white shirt. A gold and pearl pin held his red tie in place, and a big gold ring glittered on his pinkie finger. I couldn't see his eyes. The room was too dim for that.

"I'm awful glad to finally meet you, Callie."

He held out his arms, ready for me to run right in. He was so handsome, and he sat at an upright piano that might have been the twin of the one in the Moonlight Room. But more than that, his voice was familiar. I was sure I'd heard that voice before, somewhere else, a long way away. With memory kicking my shins, I was tired, frightened, and starved enough that if this had been maybe two days ago, I just could have believed him.

But it wasn't two days ago, and my brain was going full steam ahead.

"You told Mama you'd come back for her." I didn't run forward. I walked a couple of steps, keeping my eyes wide, just like Jack had done when he was lying up a storm to Shimmy. "She said you told her, 'Always remember I'm coming back for you, Josie.' "

"I was on my way too, but I got held up in this duster. I couldn't believe it when Shimmy said she saw you on the street right here in town. But we're together now, and that's all that matters." He lifted his arms an inch.

I took another step. His eyes twinkled in the dim light. At first glance, they were a warm brown like Shimmy's, but now I was close enough to see they were gold and silver and black too, all mixed up together in a way that wasn't quite human. Close, but not quite. But even with his strange eyes, he looked so happy. It would be so easy to sink into belief, just because this man wanted me to.

"Mama said you'd know me right away when you saw me." I could feel this word game was dangerous. I was playing with something I didn't understand all the way.

"I couldn't miss you, Callie," he said. "You look just like my Josie."

That did it. I grabbed his hand and shoved it down. "My mother's name is Margaret. I don't look a thing like her, and whoever you are, you *ain't* my papa."

That bright smile fell off his face so far I could have kicked it across the floor.

Shimmy threw back her head and laughed. "Well, sir, if she ain't the clever one after all." Still chuckling, she pulled a compact, the kind with a mirror inside, out of her purse. She studied what she saw there and dabbed at the corner of her mouth for a second before she snapped it shut and tucked it away. "Don't you mind Shake, Callie LeRoux. He's just mad 'cause you're smarter than he looks. Sit down here with me." She sauntered off the stage and slipped behind one of the tables.

Truth to tell, I didn't want to get any closer to her. But I wanted her to talk to me, so I pulled out a chair and sat, trying to keep to the far edge without looking like I was. That just made her laugh again.

"You hungry, Callie?" She spread her hands out. There wasn't anything on the table in front of us. Then there was.

A huge roast turkey with corn-bread stuffing spilling out of it sat in the middle of a sea of food: three kinds of congealed salad lined up alongside green beans, sliced bread, macaroni and cheese, and a bowl of creamy white mashed potatoes. There was a bowl of soft butter, and another of rich brown gravy.

A fresh wave of dizziness made me really glad I was

sitting down. I wished I could wipe my mouth with my sleeve like Jack did. "No thank you, ma'am," I whispered. "I ain't hungry."

Shimmy rolled her big, coffee-colored eyes. "You been listening to stories, ain't you? Well, the rules ain't the same for family."

That finally got my eyes off all the magic food. "We ain't family."

"You so sure about that, Callie?" said Shake.

I took a long sideways look over at the lean man where he sat glowering by the piano.

"Oh, let go of that." Shimmy waved the man's entire existence away, just like that.

"But we *are* kin, Callie." Shake stood up and walked slowly down the steps off the stage. "And if you stop a minute, you'll feel it in your bones."

That food smelled so good. It was like an itch begging to be scratched. Every part of me wanted to reach over and grab up just one piece of bread and take a huge bite. Despite that, I knew the last thing I could trust around these folks was a feeling in my bones.

"You say we're related? You prove it."

"Yeah, go on, Shimmy. You're so smart, you prove it to the gal." Shake leaned back and folded his arms. "This oughta be good," he added to me.

"Just my luck," Shimmy muttered. "I find the girl everybody's looking for, and she turns out to be stump-stubborn." She brought her hands together, and all the food vanished. Not a sight or smell remained. My heart broke into about five hundred pieces. "You want to see how close kin we are, you go ahead and make us dinner."

"How am I supposed to do that?" But I was already looking at Shake's upright piano. He jumped back up onto the stage, pulled out a red silk handkerchief, and made a big show of dusting off the stool.

I took a U-turn back to my own good sense. "Uh-uh. No. Bad stuff happens when I make music."

"That's because you ain't had none of your own kind around to teach you." Shake smiled. "It's all about concentration. You've got to keep your mind on what you want, and only what you want. The more practice you get, the better you'll be able to put it over."

Just then, a beam of light sliced through the room. I turned in my seat. Jack had thrown open the shutters on the far side of the house and was peering in the window, hands framing his face. I waved, to try to show him I was okay. But he just frowned and went around to the next window. The shutters opened, and he pressed his face right up against the glass.

"What's the matter with him?" I waved again, but Jack just rattled the frame. After a minute, he pulled out a pocket-knife and worked it into the sash, trying to jimmy the lock.

"He can't see you," said Shimmy. "He ain't got the eyes."

I felt bad. He must have followed me after all, and was waiting for me to come out. Now he was worried, and still hungry because I didn't know how to bum. Plus, it was really starting to look like he'd been right about me all along.

An idea swam to the surface. "If I . . . if I made the food, could my friend eat it without it hurting him any?"

Shimmy held up her hands, asking for patience from the ceiling. "You make the food, you make the rules, Callie."

Outside, Jack's mouth was moving, making me think he was cussing as he tried to work his knife deeper under the sash. I tried to think about the things he'd told me while we were walking, about the kinds of tricks fairies liked to play. About how they'd kidnap human babies and put a fake in their place. A whaddayacallit . . . a changeling.

"If I let him in here, you wouldn't . . . you wouldn't try to keep him or anything?"

"I swear on my breath and bones, if he comes into my house freely, he will leave just as free," said Shimmy.

That was a lot of words to say something simple like "yes." I was starting not to like the way these people talked.

I got up and walked to the door, kind of sideways because I didn't want to take my eyes off Shimmy and Shake. They both looked smug and smiled little satisfied smiles. I put my hand on the knob. These two knew something I didn't, and I was about to let Jack into the middle of it. I thought about all those words Shimmy had used to make her promise. My hand slid back down to my side.

"Is this your house?" I asked. "You said if Jack came into your house freely, he'd be able to leave freely, but you didn't say if this place was your house."

Now it was Shake's turn to laugh, and he did, long and loud. He laughed so hard he stumbled backward and bumped into the wall, and he kept right on laughing.

"Oh, she's good, she's good!" He wiped his eyes with his hankie. "She got you on that one, Shimmy!"

"Hmph!" Shimmy glowered at me, and I swear I saw sparks in her brown eyes. "All right, all right, Miss Smarty, you bring the boy in, you take him out. Makes no difference to me."

"Okay." I pulled the door open. The turning key and shifting lock feeling shivered through me. "Jack!" I shouted.

"Callie!" He came running around the corner, his pocketknife out, like he thought he was going to need to stab somebody. "Are you okay?"

"Just fine." I stepped back so he could walk inside. "This is Shimmy, and this is Shake. They . . . they say they're kin to me."

Jack froze for a split second, and then whipped his cap off. "How do you do, Miss Shimmy? Mr. Shake?"

"Hmm." Shimmy gave him that straight-down-the-nose look and deliberately turned to me. "Well, now that your little friend's here, are you going to get supper set, or what?"

"Supper?" repeated Jack numbly. "Callie . . ."

"It's okay. If I make the food, it's all right."

You could tell Jack was torn between what he'd heard about the rules of fairy dinners and not having eaten anything decent for almost a week. I wasn't torn. I was flat-out scared and more than ready to run. But run where? To do what? We had to eat, and Bull Morgan might still be out there with his club and his gun, waiting for us to try bumming on the street again.

"So, how does this work?" I asked Shimmy.

"You wish."

"Sorry?"

"You take up the nearest source of power, and you wish." She sighed. "But you have to be very clear about what it is you're wishing for. Leave out any details and, well . . . let's just say things ain't gonna come out how you might think."

"And this nearest source of power, what would that be?"

She shrugged. "It depends. Music is always good, but anything that creates a strong feeling will do. A crowd of mortals can be a good source. Your own feelings will work, but that can make it more difficult to concentrate on shaping the wish. It can also wear you out fast. Shake." She sauntered back to the stage. "Play something for our girl here, won't you?"

"I'll do it," Jack said.

Now we were all staring at him. He ignored us and plopped down at the piano. He curled his fingers over the keys and started a halting piece of ragtime. I wondered where he'd learned, and then thought how if he'd been helping bootleggers, he would've had to hang around the honky-tonks, and maybe he learned a few tunes. It didn't matter. Jack's halting music was already winding its way around the hunger and the mystery inside me and setting it all to simmer.

"What do you want, Callie?" whispered Shake. "What do you wish for?"

What did I wish for? I squeezed my eyes shut as a thousand things flashed through my mind. What I wished for right now was dinner. A real dinner, a proper dinner that was safe for me and for Jack. A dinner that would make up for all the meals we'd missed on the road and would take the taste of hunger and dust right out of our mouths . . .

I felt that wish form inside me. I felt it twirl Jack's music around itself, and I felt it . . . leave, like a sudden push from behind. I staggered, and my eyes opened.

Food filled the table nearest the stage. But this wasn't some turkey dinner out of *Ladies' Home Journal.* This was barbeque. White platters held beef ribs with shimmering red sauce and piles of corn bread. There was a basket of biscuits with a jar of honey, a crock of baked beans, and another of potato salad. A huge sweet potato pie waited to one side.

"God Almighty," whispered Jack as he lifted his hands off the piano keys. I knew exactly how he felt.

"There, you see?" Shake smiled. "That's how our kind do things."

"But you gotta be careful, Callie LeRoux," Shimmy said seriously. "Now that you know the wishing ways, you'll feel the wishes around you. They'll make you itchy, 'cause you know you can do something about them, but that ain't always the best idea."

I nodded, but I wasn't really listening. All my attention was taken up by that magic dinner I'd made. Together, Jack and I walked down to the table with its steaming, delicious burden. Jack looked at me. He was asking if it was all right. He was trusting me. It *was* all right. I could just tell, as if I had discovered an extra sense, somewhere between scent and sight. This was the same sense that could feel the turning key and shifting lock of the world. It told me this might have come from the same place as Shimmy's dinner, but it was mine and I'd *made* it all right. So I nodded.

We attacked that dinner before our rear ends touched the chairs. I'll tell you what, I'm plenty good as a wishing cook.

Hungry as we were, though, Jack and I eventually had to slow down. Even with Shimmy and Shake digging in alongside us, we couldn't polish off half of what was on the table. I looked at all that leftover food and thought about all the people we'd seen on the road and felt guilty.

Shimmy must have seen my look, because she waved her hands and the remaining food vanished. All that was left were the crumbs on our cheeks and the stains on our napkins. Now that my belly was full, I felt ready to take on anything. Starting with Miss Shimmy.

"So how come you knew my name?" I asked. Jack nodded, to let me know he agreed this was a good place to start. "Were you looking for me?"

"All of us are looking for you, Callie," Shimmy said. "Especially now that you're finally outta that moldy-oldie hotel."

"Who's us?" asked Jack.

"*Us,*" Shake said. "The Midnight People, the deep ground people, the secret people." He looked me right in the eye, and I saw those golden sparks shine. "Your papa's people."

"Don't start up with that again," I told him. "You don't know nothing about my papa."

That just made Shake smile. "I know he fell in love with your mama even though she was just a common human woman and he was a prince of his people. I know he stood up in front of the council and said he was leaving, and they could all fight it out who would be the next king, because he was through." Shake changed as he said those words. He became more solid, like he was rooted tight to the ground. I felt the blood drain out of my face, and I remembered what Baya had told me. *He stands up in the council tent and he says he won't stay with his tribe anymore.*

"We were both there." Shake took a drag on his cigarette and puffed out a long white smoke plume toward Shimmy. "I must say, for a man doing something so stupid as turning down a kingdom, he did it up right. Broke his sword across his knee, kicked his crown across the floor."

"Swore three times he'd never sit on your granddaddy's throne." Shimmy shook her head. "Then he walked out, leavin' all of us with our jaws flappin' right down to our knees."

It took a while for these new words to settle in and make their manners with all the other impossible ideas that had set up housekeeping inside me over the past few days. But once they did, I knew they were staying for good.

"My papa's a *prince*?"

Shake examined the burning end of his cigarette. "That he is. Now ask the next question, Callie." My heart was knocking against my ribs. Jack touched my wrist, to back me up or to warn me away, I couldn't tell. It didn't matter. I had to ask.

"What does that make me?"

Shimmy looked to Shake, and Shake nodded. Shimmy smiled broad and slow, and she got to her feet.

"Never thought I'd be the first to say it." She put one foot behind the other and bent her knees, sinking low. It took a second to realize she was making a curtsy to me. "Welcome home, Your Highness."

12

They May Beg You to Go with Them

"No. No. This ain't right." I looked to Jack for some kind of help, but he was just sitting there with his jaw hanging open like it had come unhinged. "This can't be right."

"It is right." Shimmy straightened up, smoothing her skirt.

"You, Callie LeRoux, are the heir to the Midnight Throne." Shake smiled and blew another big cloud of smoke. His gold-and-silver eyes glittered on the other side of the cloud, and I shivered.

"Your grandparents have had us out looking for you for the last thirteen years," Shimmy went on.

Jack finally managed to pull himself back together a little bit. "If it's what you say . . . why'd her papa leave? Why didn't he bring her mama to the . . . her grandparents' kingdom?"

Shimmy probably would have ignored him, but I folded my arms and cocked my head, because it was a really good question. Shimmy saw my stubborn face and sighed. "Your papa was supposed to marry the Seelie princess, but he'd already fallen in love with your mama. So he decided to run off and be a mortal man with a mortal wife." Shimmy plucked Shake's cigarette out of his fingers and took a drag. "As if Their Majesties were ever gonna let *that* happen." She blew the smoke toward the ceiling and handed the cigarette back to Shake.

He runs for that other woman, but he can't run fast enough. The Shining Ones capture him and lock him away, but he still won't marry their woman. The room tried to start spinning. I knotted my fists and dug in my heels. There was no telling how much longer these two would feel like talking. I would just have to get dizzy later.

"So where is he?"

Shimmy shrugged. "If you don't know, nobody does."

"*Do* you know?" Shake looked at the glowing tip of that cigarette, but I could feel him watching me.

I shook my head and tried hard to think about the taste of the barbeque we'd just finished, instead of what Baya had told me. Just in case they could read minds or something. If they were . . . were . . . fairies, they just might.

Shimmy frowned, and I felt something bunch up tight inside her.

"Well, that's all right," said Shake. "We've got you here and that's what counts. Your grandparents are gonna be real happy when we take you to them." His eyes sparkled through the smoke again.

I was beginning to wish I hadn't eaten so much, because my stomach and heart were both flipping back and forth, not sure which way to settle. On the one hand, I did not like Shake. I did not like the way he looked at me with those glittery gold-and-silver eyes, as if he hadn't had enough dessert.

But at the same time, he'd said I had grandparents. Grandparents. Mama's parents were dead. I'd never really let myself think about my papa having family. Longing rose up in me as strong as the hunger had been. Right then I didn't care if they were a king and a queen; what mattered was that they were alive and I could talk to them.

"If her grandparents want to find her so bad, why aren't they here?" prompted Jack. It was funny: he was the one who'd wanted all this fairy stuff to be true, but now that it was, he couldn't seem to believe a word they said.

Shimmy rolled her eyes. "Since when does the king run his own errands?"

I thought that made sense, but there was no way to be sure. Too much had piled up in my mind. I needed room to breathe and clear it all out.

"I know it's tough, honey." Shimmy laid her hand over mine. It was cool and soft. Shimmy was not somebody who did a lot of work. "And we'll help you all we can."

"That's right." Shake nodded and stubbed out his

cigarette. I felt a current between them so strong that if I'd thrown a rock at it, I'd have struck sparks.

"I ain't staying with you."

"None of us is staying here. Too many of *them* around." Shake jerked his chin toward the window. "Looking for you, may I add. We gotta head for the city gates and get you safe inside."

"No." I shook my head again. "I gotta find Mama. When that's done, I'll come see my . . . whoever wants to talk to me."

"Your mama." Shake made a face like he wanted to spit. "They *got* your mama."

"Who?"

"*Them,*" snapped Shimmy. "The pretty, shiny ones. The bright, light, straight, and uptight."

"You mean the Seelie court," said Jack.

Shake tilted his head toward Jack, like he was just seeing him properly for the first time. I edged a little closer to Jack, because something way down inside me said he didn't want Shake to see him, not really. "That's right, young man. They got her but good," Shake said, all slow and thoughtful.

"Then I'll get her back," I said, trying to sound like it was no big deal.

"Ha!" laughed Shake. "You don't understand, do you? They *got* her. She won't want to leave now."

"Don't listen to him, Callie," said Jack. "He's just trying to get you all mixed up."

He was right. I shouldn't listen. They'd already tried to fool me twice that I knew about.

"You trust this boy over one of your kin?" Shake asked softly. "Callie girl, you ain't even *begun* to find out what kind of liar he is."

I was glad he said that, because it reminded me who my friends really were. "You leave Jack alone!"

"You're the one who should leave *him* alone." Shimmy leaned forward, her brown eyes shimmering, her voice low and urgent. "You come with me and Shake. We'll take you to your grandparents. They're the ones who want you. They're the ones who will teach you who you really are, Your Highness," she added.

I felt the current rolling between Shake and Shimmy again. It was almost like the feeling of the magic when it shot through my blood. All at once, Shimmy shifted gears.

"Poor Callie," she said suddenly. "You've had a bad time, haven't you? And so much to wrap your head around. You deserve a treat. Both of you." She tossed a smile toward Jack. "I tell you what. Why don't the pair of you go to the pictures?" She got her purse from where it sat on the back of the piano and pulled out two green cardboard stubs.

"Shimmy . . . ," said Shake. "That is not a good idea."

"Oh, hush. It's a fine idea."

"You'll be sendin' 'em straight to . . ."

"The movies." Shimmy cut him off firmly and laid the tickets down on the table.

Jack and I glanced at each other. Did we have our own current that Shimmy and Shake could feel?

"I don't . . . ," I started.

"Go on, go on, take them." She pushed the tickets toward me, and I remembered how I'd pushed that bread pudding toward Letitia Hopper, just before I tried to lay her out with Mama's silver tray. "Enjoy yourselves for a change. It'll be good for you. We can talk more later."

To my surprise, Jack picked up those tickets and slipped them into his coat pocket. "Thank you kindly, Miss Shimmy," he said. "We were just talking about how much fun it would be to get to the picture show, weren't we, Callie?"

Sometimes you don't need a kick in the ankle to get the hint. "That's right. We were talking about that."

"Well then!" Shimmy spread her hands and beamed.

Shake frowned hard, shook his head, and lit a fresh cigarette. The smell of all that smoke made my stomach churn.

Shimmy grabbed Shake's new cigarette from his fingers and took a long drag. "Have fun, Callie LeRoux," she said, exhaling smoke with her words. "And we'll see you around."

"Yeah, yeah, sure."

And that was that. With Shimmy and Shake grinning like Christmas morning and the Fourth of July, Jack and I walked out the door into the twilight that had fallen across Constantinople. The door swung shut behind us. Jack grabbed my hand and hustled us both off the porch. He didn't stop until we were a good twenty yards down the street.

"What do you think?" Jack asked, jerking his chin back in the direction we'd come.

There were a thousand answers to that, but none of them were any good. "I think she wanted us to go to the movies awful bad, but Shake didn't. Why do you suppose that was?"

Jack shoved his hands in his pockets. "That was a con game if ever I saw one."

"What do you mean?"

"You want to get a mark, I mean a person, to do something they shouldn't. So you and your partner, you stage an argument. Make out like one of you is telling the mark something they shouldn't know. Your partner says, 'No, no, don't tell him that!' which makes the mark think he's on to something, that maybe he's outsmarted you. Next thing you know, that mark's doing exactly what you want."

"Like in the story when Brer Rabbit says to Brer Fox, 'Don't throw me in that briar patch,' when that's exactly what he wants to have happen." I did not like the sound of it. I did not like the smile on Shake's face or the light in his glittery eyes.

Jack glowered hard back toward Shimmy's. The dark was lowering slowly, covering the clapboard houses and all the world around them. "Besides, they were lying to your face about what they want with you."

"What?"

"They didn't say a word about the prophecy. It was all about Princess Callie and how your family wants you back so bad. Nothing about gates or worlds or choices."

He was right, of course, and I could have kicked myself for forgetting. I'd been all caught up in the idea that I had kin who might actually want to see me. Part of me started wondering if it was Letitia Hopper who'd been lying, but I shook that off. She'd been too far gone with her own hunger to fool anybody. I knew what that felt like now.

"So what do we do?"

"We don't go into that briar patch," said Jack firmly.

"What else are we gonna do?" Shimmy wanted us—wanted *me*—to see something, that much was certain, and I was already wondering what that something might be. Shimmy had played it smart. She'd told me just enough of the truth to get me thinking about what else I could find out from her. It was a con game, all right. Just like Jack said.

"We get to the rail yard and hop the first train west. When we find your parents, they'll be able to tell us what's really going on."

He was right. Of course he was right. We couldn't do what Shimmy and Shake wanted because we couldn't trust them. Probably that whole princess thing was a kind of fairy story, just to try to get me to come along quietly. Probably I didn't even have grandparents.

Jack set his face toward the rail yard, pulled his hat down low against the spreading dark, and started walking. The only thing I could think to do was follow, never mind that I felt like I was leaving bits of myself in the dust with every step.

13

What Is a Vigilante Man?

I used to like trains. I'd watch them go by out my window and wave to the people. I'd even envied the hobos. At least they were on their way somewhere, while I was stuck in the dust. The train songs were my favorite, whether Mama sang them to me or we listened on the radio: "Rock Island Line," "This Train," "Chattanooga Choo Choo," even "Little Black Train." And of course "The Midnight Special."

But I'll tell you what, now that I was in the middle of all those trains, I didn't want anything more than to find my way out again. Nothing makes sense in a rail yard at night, and there's no way to see where you're going or what's coming toward you. Huge sheds rose up to our right like giants' caves, with steam engines bigger than any storybook troll squatting inside. The lines of train cars—Pullman cars, refrigerators, tankers, open-top coal cars, flatbeds—rose up on every side, cutting off any easy way forward or out. We had to squeeze between or under those silent, empty cars to get anywhere. But even then, the only place we were getting was deeper into the dark, broken maze. A wind stinking of oil, diesel, metal, and sawdust wormed its way between the cars, following us. Things clanked and creaked, but I couldn't tell where any of the sounds came from or what they belonged to. Anything could be hiding here, and we'd never know until it was right behind us.

Jack held my hand so we'd keep together, and I didn't mind at all. I startled and tripped on the rails and the ties as I tried to cross. I wished a thousand times we'd just gone to the movies. Whatever waited inside the Bijoux could not have been scarier than all these shadows. Jack acted like he knew where he was going, but nobody could in all this dark, with all these giant cars and all these sounds coming from nowhere. Part of me knew this was just fear shunting my brains around, but it surely made a good job of it.

Finally, Jack pointed to a bunch of dark bundles beside a stack of railroad ties. I thought they were coal sacks until I saw one unfold itself and arch back to stretch its shoulders. Those bundles were all people, huddled close in the dark.

I wanted to hang back, but Jack squeezed my hand and marched us forward. As we got closer, I could see there were dozens of people, maybe as many as a hundred. All of them hobos, bums, Dust Bowl refugees hunkered down together because as bad as it was here, being here alone would have been worse.

Jack picked out one man from all the others, a wiry

fella in overalls and a loose undershirt, his thin hair brushed back. He wasn't huddled on the ground. This man leaned against the stack of ties, staring hard at the dark, his big, crooked nose making him look like a hawk. Jack walked us both into a patch of floodlight and went straight up to him.

"How do?" Jack asked politely. The man nodded.

"Been here long?"

The man shrugged. "Few days."

"All right we set down too?"

That man's eyes were sharp and clear as he looked us over. I would have bet money he could see in the dark. Not because he was a magic man or anything; just because he'd been watching so hard and so long.

He shrugged again. "It's a free country."

"Thank you kindly," said Jack.

I'd seen plenty of hobos. They came to the Imperial looking for work almost every time a train pulled into the station. But I'd never been in a whole camp of them like this. All these people were dried out and wrinkled by sun and wind, and then starved down so far that their bones rode right under their skin. Even the babies looked old. The families clustered together. Women sat with skinny children around their knees and in their arms, their men standing watch while they dozed. The boys traveling on their own hunkered down a little ways away. Some of those boys with their hats pulled low and their hands shoved in their jacket pockets might have been girls, but their faces were just as hard and exhausted as any of the others.

All of them waiting to hop a train. All of them trying to get someplace, anyplace where there might be work and a chance at keeping body and soul together just a little bit longer. They watched us settle down between them with hollow, hungry eyes. I remembered the barbeque, and guilt squirmed around inside me, making itself all comfortable.

"So, what now?" I said to Jack. "We wait for the Midnight Special?"

He chuckled. "I wouldn't have thought you'd know that song."

I shrugged. "Mama sings it all the time. One of her favorites. I never heard it on the radio or anything. I always thought . . . maybe it was something Papa taught her."

Jack shrugged. "Could be, I guess. I heard it on the road. A fella told me the prisoners in this big jail over in Texas, they said if the light from the midnight train touched you as it went past the jail, you'd be freed."

I let that sink in awhile. The idea of Mama spending her life trying to keep the Imperial from falling down and the whole time singing a song about getting out of jail was not one that sat well with what was already in my head.

"Better get some sleep, Callie." Jack stretched himself out right on the ground, using his cap as a pillow. "Nothing going to be leavin' before mornin'."

I shook my head. "I don't like this." Something bothered me about all those people squatting in the dark, and I needed to dig it out before I could rest.

Jack opened one eye and peered up at me. "What's the problem?"

I had it now, and I didn't want it. "Bull Morgan. The man from the lunch counter. He said he didn't allow hobos on his trains, or in his town."

I wanted a different answer than the uncertainty on Jack's face. "Bull Morgan?" he repeated. "As in railroad bull?"

I knew that one. A bull was a private detective hired by the railroad company to keep bums and thieves out of the yard. "He had a badge," I said. *And a club. And a gun . . .*

Jack thought about this. Then he got to his feet and walked slow and easy back over to the man with the hawk nose.

"There been any trouble with the bulls?" Jack asked him.

The man shrugged. "Naw. Some of us lent a hand with the digging out after the duster. Stationmaster said it was okay if we set here for a while; he'd warn Morgan off."

"That guy was not goin' to give anybody a pass." I remembered those cold gray eyes and I shivered. "And he said he didn't allow hobos in his yard."

The man's face went hard, just like Jack's had when we got into Constantinople. I wondered which of those women and kids were his. He strolled over to a couple of the other men who were leaning against the stack of ties and said something soft to them. They nodded, straightened their

hats, and closed in behind him. I knew what they were doing, and I was glad. They might have the stationmaster's
word, but they were going to check things out for themselves.

Jack drew himself up to his full height and started after
the men. I went to follow, but he put up his hand.

"No, Callie. You stay here. You'll just get lost."

I wanted to argue with him, but I already knew he was
right, so I nodded and let him go. The men walked off,
melting into the shadows, and in a minute it was like they'd
never been there at all.

I went back to our spot and sat down cross-legged. A
baby started crying, high and thin and persistent in the
darkness. A woman's voice rose up soft: *"Hush, little baby,
don't say a word . . ."*

But Papa wasn't going to buy that baby anything at all,
never mind a diamond ring. Hope and despair wound like
the dusty wind through that song. I thought again about the
barbeque dinner I'd made, and about all the heavy worry
that held the people around me. Worry had worn itself deep
into their minds and souls, but it was still finding new chan-
nels to dig. I wanted something to do, like Jack. I didn't
want to just sit and wait.

*"And if that diamond ring turns brass, Papa's gonna buy
you a looking glass . . ."*

I'd wished up a whole dinner at Shimmy's. Why
couldn't I do it again? I knew how this time. I could hold
the power together and shape the wish. It didn't even have

to be a barbeque; it could be something smaller . . . a kettle of stew or something.

"And if that looking glass gets broke, Papa's gonna buy you a billy goat . . ."

I picked myself up and moved deeper into the shadows. Lamb stew. One big kettle. Enough for one meal. Just to let people get through the night, just to ease the worry a little. I cupped my hands, like I was catching water coming from a pump, but instead I caught the feeling of that lullaby, the worry and the tired, desperate wish to make it all better. It was a strong feeling, and it sank right into me, to the place where I could spin it into a wish.

A wish for food. Everybody here wished that wish. I could feel the aching, gnawing hunger bound together with the worry. Hunger as plentiful as dust. I took that hunger, I took that song, and I wished for food. For lamb stew, with rich broth and new potatoes. A big kettle full of it. I could smell it, hot, meaty, savory. A whole kettle of stew to feed the people. I held my hands out. It was almost here. Almost.

But something was holding on to it. Something heavy pushed that wish back while I tried to pull it forward. I leaned into it and wished harder. But the whatever-it-was pushed harder yet.

She's here. That's her. I know it is!

Quiet!

My eyes snapped open, and the wish flew into a thousand pieces. Everything Shimmy had tried to tell me about how I'd feel the wishes around me, how they'd make me itchy, came rushing back. She'd been right. I was surrounded by worried wishes, and they had made me so itchy, I'd forgotten I still had people out looking for me. The Hoppers had been the beginning, not the end.

I needed to find Jack and warn him. Trailing the fading scent of hot stew, I lit out into the shadows.

14

Get Away

It probably took more than two minutes to get me completely turned around, but not much. Shadows, rail lines, and looming train cars knotted up my sense of direction. Then the fear carried it so far off, I couldn't have told you which way was up if you'd pointed at the sky. The moon hung overhead, bloated and bloody red from the dust, with a white ring round it. A dog barked somewhere behind the train cars.

I had to calm down and get my bearings. I made myself stop and turn in a slow circle, looking at the telegraph poles, the darkened signal lights, the sheds, anything that I might be able to use as a landmark.

As I turned past the nearest shack, movement caught my eye. A thin man's shape ducked farther into the shadows. I hurried toward it. Maybe it was Jack, or the hawk-nosed man. It didn't matter as long as they knew where they were going. . . .

Hands yanked me backward. I started to scream, but a hat was stuffed into my mouth.

"Shhhhhh!" ordered Jack.

"What's going on?" I demanded against his cap, which, I've got to say, tasted awful. Jack pointed into the shed.

It wasn't just one man moving in there. It was a whole crowd of them. I shook myself free from Jack and his hat and crept up to the shed door, crouching low. Jack was right at my shoulder.

Bull Morgan stood in front of maybe two dozen men. Every last one of them carried some kind of weapon. Some had clubs made of shovel ends or ax handles. Many had shotguns.

This wasn't just a crowd. Bull Morgan had put together a vigilance committee.

One man, the one I'd seen moving, slipped up to the front right next to Morgan and took the ax handle a neighbor passed him.

"Are we in place?" growled Bull Morgan.

"Just about, Mr. Morgan." I heard the snappy salute in the smaller man's voice.

"And the bums?"

"Some of them's slipped out. Charlie'll round 'em up."

Morgan grunted. "As long as they don't get back to warn the others."

"Hadn't we better move out now?" asked somebody from the middle of the crowd. "Them bums might be gettin' antsy."

Morgan calmly pulled a toothpick out of his pocket

and stuck it in his mouth. "They'll stay put. After all, Mr. Stationmaster Reynolds told 'em they could stay. He'd just look the other way while they broke the law. Ain't that right, Mr. Reynolds?" Morgan grinned toward the shadows deeper in the shed. I squinted through the shifting thicket of pant legs and work boots and saw a huddle of other men. These men wore dark coats and peaked caps, and all of them had rags stuffed in their mouths and their hands tied together in front of them. I'd've bet any money one of them was the stationmaster.

Bull Morgan had told me he didn't allow hobos on his trains. And he'd taken over the rail yard to keep his promise. These weren't lawmen. They were going to go into that crowd of kids and families and . . . and . . .

They were going to do whatever they felt like with those ax handles and those shotguns, and there wasn't anybody within hollering distance to stop them. Except us.

"So we're just gonna stand here all night, then?" grumbled a man.

"Shut yer gob, Grady." Morgan chewed lazily on his toothpick and pulled out his club as a reminder that he was armed too. "I told you, we go when I say."

Some other man snickered. "In a hurry to get home, Grady? I hear that wife of yours isn't the patient type."

"Come over here and say that, you . . ."

Morgan smacked his club into his big, hard palm. "Save it for the bums, you two!"

Jack and I didn't have to say anything to each other. We were both thinking the same thing. We had to warn the others. The fastest way would be to make some noise. It would also be the surest way to get caught.

Jack eased backward, and I went with him. There was a pyramid-shaped pile of oil drums against the side of the shed. He pointed to it, and we ran, as quiet as thought, around to the far side of the stack. Jack put his shoulder to one, and I saw his plan. I put my hands up beside him.

From inside the shed, we heard Morgan say, "Time . . ."

Jack shoved. I shoved. Those empty barrels came down like thunder in high summer.

Inside the shed, the men sent up a holler. Dogs bayed and barked in answer. Jack and I whooped like wild Indians and took off running. I glanced back to see the vigilante men pouring out of the shed in time to collide with those rolling barrels. The men fell, yelling words their mothers never taught them, and the barrels bounced and banged all around them.

A shotgun blast tore through the dark. Startled, I tripped over a rail and Jack yanked me to my feet. Holding on to each other, we ran. Actually, he ran. I got dragged along.

Screams filled the yard, echoing off the sides of the train cars. Men, women, and kids shrieked, cursed, and cried. Another shot exploded, followed fast by an unsteady pounding—a sick, hollow kind of sound, like wood smacking against wood, except I knew it wasn't. We hadn't been fast enough. Morgan's vigilantes had been ready, and that pounding was the ax handles and the clubs saying a bloody hello to people's skulls.

"Don't let them get away!" called Bull Morgan from

somewhere in the dark. "It's time these bums got what was coming to 'em!"

People streamed between the cars, a great, huge river of noise and panic. A shotgun flashed. The pounding wouldn't stop. I could feel the pain. All of it. I couldn't see. I couldn't think. There was nothing but the pain and the fear and Jack wishing he could do something to stop it.

A woman passed us, a little kid clinging to her skirt, a baby held sideways under her arm. There was something wrong with her other arm; it was dangling funny. I saw the gleam of the shotgun barrel rising up behind her. I saw the vigilante take aim.

"NO!"

My magic snatched up Jack's wish and threw it hard at the man. The vigilante hollered and fell backward, and the shot went straight up to the bloody moon. The woman and her kids vanished between the boxcars.

"Come on, Callie!" Jack tugged at me. "Let's go!"

"Why?" I hollered. "I can take 'em all on! I got the magic!" All these wishes, all this feeling, it was power for me. I could use it, turn it against Bull Morgan's vigilantes. I knew I could.

"Because they'll see us standing here, you dope! And I ain't bulletproof!"

That hit me. I wheeled around to follow him and collided with his back. Because he'd run straight into Bull Morgan.

"Gotcha!" Morgan's meaty hands clamped down on our shoulders.

I gritted my teeth. "Let us go!"

"Well, well!" Morgan shook me away from Jack. "If it ain't the little girlie bum. I thought I warned you off, girlie."

"I said, let us go!"

"You ain't goin' anywhere except onto the chain gang," Morgan crowed. "I'm sick of you whiny bums helpin' yourselves to what ain't yours. No respect . . ."

I didn't even think. I just reached out to that powerful feeling pouring around me to take it for a wish.

It was like I'd stepped into a furnace. There was nothing but pain. Pain like stars, like flames filling the whole world. I was surrounded by the roar and burn of a thousand thoughts, a thousand feelings.

. . . *hurt, hurt, hate, no, no, gotta run, help me, please help me, where are they, where is he, where is she, hate you, hate you . . .*

I couldn't move. The hate and the pain of the riot rushed into me, cutting me off from my body.

. . . *gonnakillyouallhateyouhateyouturnaroundandfightyouhelpmehateyouhelpmehateyouhelpme . . .*

My body fell, and I couldn't do anything about it. I stared up at Morgan's swollen face as the railroad bull bent over me. There was a flash of movement and a yell, and Jack kicked Bull Morgan in the kneecap. Morgan leapt back, but Jack kicked his other knee and Morgan toppled over. I felt his pain too, and his wish for the one who caused it to be dead, dead, dead.

"Callie!" Jack had hold of my wrists and tried to pull me to my feet. "Callie! Come on, get up!"

He wished I'd get up. My scattered thoughts grabbed hold of that wish, knotted around it like his hands were knotted around my wrists.

And I could stand. I could see. I was all right. Except I was all right in time for Bull Morgan to rear up behind me.

"Run!" shouted Jack. He bolted backward, and I bolted forward. Morgan was reaching for his club, but I got there first and yanked it right out of his holster. Morgan stumbled, and with all the fear and strength I had in me, I slammed that club against the side of his head. There was a sharp crack, and Morgan sprawled into the dirt. I was staring again, because there was blood spattered on his temple, and on my hands.

Jack shoved me sideways, knocking me down, and dragged me under the nearest boxcar, pushing at me until we scrambled out the other side and took off running. All the while I felt how Bull Morgan wasn't moving, wasn't even breathing, and his blood mixed with the dirt on my hands.

"He's dead." I panted. "Oh, my God, he's dead. I killed him!"

"Stop it!" Jack jerked hard on my hand. "Just run!"

I closed my mouth and ran.

There should have been plenty of places to hide in that dark yard. But at every turn there was somebody in front of us, somebody with a gun or an ax handle or in the thick of a fight. It went on forever, the flashes of light, the cracks and the screaming. I was crying and Jack was cussing, taking us this way and that. We climbed over the couplings between the trains; we dodged around sheds and coal piles. My lungs burned and my legs got heavier with each step, and the whole time my head was babbling, *No way out, no way out, no way out. . . .*

"There!" boomed Morgan's voice. "There they are!"

I looked. I couldn't help it. Bull Morgan reared up in the floodlights like a monster, with a crowd of shadows at his side. He pointed at us with his club.

"Get 'em!" he bellowed. "Bring 'em here!"

Men surged forward, guns and ax handles ready.

Jack swore and we ran. Ahead, I spotted the livestock pens.

"Jack!" I pointed. He saw, and he dove forward.

We were small, and we were running for our lives. We slid between the slats; we climbed over gates the blow dirt had drifted shut. We even ran on the top rail of the criss-crossing fences, a game every farm kid has played. The men swore and stumbled and got stuck and swore some more. But they kept coming.

Bullets sound like hornets when they pass too close to your head. After a while, the world closes down. You can't hear much, you can't see much, just the way ahead, the next slat, the next open gate. All you know is running; the only place that's real is away.

Finally, we hit the edge of the stockyard. Jack swerved

toward the lights of Constantinople. I hesitated, but when a truck engine rumbled up from behind us, I tore after him. If we headed out to the prairie, they could drive us like rabbits. Back among Constantinople's houses, we'd have a place to hide, and maybe the vigilantes wouldn't be so ready to fire off their guns in the middle of town.

Not that I was thinking that straight then. I just followed Jack as close as I could. Jack dodged into the streets, ducking around buildings, trying to get walls between us and the headlights and shouts.

"Gotta get inside somewhere." He panted. "Gotta . . ."

"Movies!" I shouted, pointing at the lit-up Bijoux.

Jack swallowed hard. This time, I took the lead, and after a split second, he followed.

There was a small, plain door in the back of the theater. I grabbed the knob and yanked it open, and all but fell inside.

Jack slammed the door, fumbled for the latch, and shot the bolt home. As it snapped shut, I felt the world twisting around us.

15

Looking for a Woman That's Hard to Find

"Jack?" I whispered. He was near me. I could feel him, but I couldn't see much.

"Yeah?"

"We're somewhere else."

"What do you mean?"

I hesitated, trying to dig up words to explain. Now I could make out shelves stacked with boxes. We were in a storeroom, except, of course, it wasn't just a storeroom. "I got this feeling when I walked into Shimmy's juke joint, like the whole world had turned around. I just felt it again."

"Okay." Jack swallowed. "Okay."

We both stood there, trying to catch our breath and not doing a very good job of it. We were both thinking about the riot, and the vigilantes in the streets, and Bull

Morgan in front of all of them. Jack had his hand on the door, but slowly, he lifted it back. I understood. We couldn't leave by that route. We didn't know what was in here, but we for sure knew what was out there.

There was another door ahead of us, partly open. Through it, we could see the red carpet and gold trim of the Bijoux's lobby.

"I guess we see the show," said Jack. Side by side we walked toward the light.

I'd actually been in the Bijoux before. Mama used to take me to the pictures when we could afford it. The last time was to see *Tarzan the Ape Man* with Johnny Weissmuller and Maureen O'Sullivan. I played Jane-Being-Kidnapped for weeks afterward, until I tried swinging on the drapes in the Moonlight Room and Mama put a stop to it.

The theater looked exactly like I remembered, with the red carpet and drapes, velvet ropes, and shiny gold paint on the curlicue trimmings that reflected the light from the chandeliers. I started to think maybe I'd been wrong about what I'd felt. There was nothing strange about this place. It was just a movie theater. The popcorn smelled warm and buttery, and the candy counter was laid out with a crazy quilt of Jujubes, Baby Ruths, Milk Duds, Zagnut bars, and licorice whips. None of which we had money for. That was okay; I was still full of barbeque. I did wonder if I could gin up some money, though. If the Hoppers could do it, why couldn't I?

We handed the tickets Shimmy had given us to an usherette with frizzy gold hair, short pants, and a jacket like an organ-grinder's monkey's. She popped her gum and led us to our seats in the half-empty theater, shooing us in place with the beam of her flashlight. We sat where she told us and stared at the closed scarlet curtains up front. The theater was air-cooled, and at first it felt like Heaven. Now, though, I was shivering. Jack gave me his coat, and I huddled into it. I was tired. The longer I sat there, the less I liked the quiet. I felt for sure something was sneaking up on us.

"Don't worry," whispered Jack. "If Morgan and his bunch come in, just duck down in the seats."

I nodded and bit my lip. Something squeaked, and I jumped. But it was just the curtains up front pulling away to reveal the rippling silver screen. Above and behind us, the projector whirred. A beam of flickering white light shot out over our heads, and the picture show started.

The newsreel came first. President Roosevelt waved to crowds and talked about the New Deal. The courage of the American businessman was on the rise. Then it was over to New York City. The United Nations was complaining about Germany's rearmament policy. Adolf Hitler didn't seem to care; in fact, he was making military service mandatory. Lefty Gomez opened the season for the Yankees.

After that, there was a Betty Boop cartoon. Despite everything, Jack and I both started laughing at the silly dancing and the crazy machines Betty's grandpa invented to help out with their party. It felt good to just laugh, even for a minute.

The screen went black, and to my surprise I almost felt okay. If Morgan had been on to us, he would've been here by now, wouldn't he? And as for this being someplace else, some fairy place . . . I must have been wrong about that. Just my worried mind borrowing trouble. I mean, how in the world could fairies get their hands on a Betty Boop cartoon?

Then the projector started whirring again, and the white light flickered. Fresh music blared out of the speakers, and a new title card appeared on the screen:

THE PARADE OF GLAMOUR

"*This* is Los Angeles!" declared the announcer as the camera panned across an expanse of straight streets and squared-off buildings. "A city of commerce . . . recreation . . . and of course . . . glamour!"

There was the HOLLYWOODLAND sign. Next shot was of a beach with clean sand and rolling ocean waves. Women in bathing suits and floppy hats stretched out under striped umbrellas. Then there was another shot of a straight white street with a big Rolls-Royce car driving past a row of palm trees.

"And *MovieTime News* has been granted an exclusive look at what the nation's official glamour capital will be wearing this summer!"

The scene blurred and cleared. Now we were shown a

stage with a long platform stretching out in front. Spangled translucent curtains screened off the back, but behind them you could see the silhouettes of women carefully posed in overstuffed chairs.

Two little girls wearing big hair bows and dresses with pleated skirts came forward, unrolling a length of carpet to make a runway. Jack made a strange noise, like a squeak. I thought he was starting to laugh and elbowed him in the ribs to keep him quiet. But he wasn't laughing. If anything, he looked like he was going to be sick.

I stared at the screen, trying to see what was so terrible. The music swelled as the little girls walked back to draw the sparkling gauze curtains open.

"We'll start with Maggie," said the narrator. "Maggie's modeling a daring little evening number, perfect for cocktails by the sea. . . ."

The woman strolled forward. She wore a silvery, shimmery dress that went down to her ankles and draped loose around her neck. Diamonds sparkled at her throat and on her hands. She sauntered easily down the runway and turned to show how the back of that silver gown pretty much wasn't there. My fingers dug hard into the arms of my seat. Maggie, the smiling woman wearing that daring little evening number, was Mama.

Mama looked relaxed and comfortable. More than that. She looked young. She smiled a dazzling smile that I'd never seen on her before. She looked so happy as she walked back slowly to join those other beautiful women.

The announcer kept talking. Other women walked down the stretch of red carpet the little girls had laid down. I didn't hear anything. I just stared at Mama. She lounged in her seat on the stage and rested her chin in her hand as she watched the other models parade for the camera.

"What's she doing there?"

"I don't know," said Jack softly.

That shook me out of my confusion. "How do you know my mama?"

"Your mama? Where?"

I pointed at "Maggie."

"Your mother's in Hollywood?"

The shushing started up all around us. I shook. A woman in a flowery skirt and sleeveless top was parading down the runway now. At the back of the stage, Mama held out a cigarette in a long holder for another woman to light. She looked perfectly at peace as she leaned back and blew a languid cloud of smoke toward the ceiling.

"I gotta get out of here." I was on my feet and heading up the aisle without even bothering to see if Jack followed me. I was all the way into the lobby before I realized my cheeks were soaked with tears.

I made it as far as the glass-and-bronze front doors. I put my hands on them, but I didn't have the strength to push. I just stood there, shaking and crying, until Jack came up all quiet next to me.

"It can't be true," he whispered. "What was on that screen. It can't be."

He'd seen something too. Something or somebody. I knew I should ask about it, but I couldn't get any words out at all right then. I just made crybaby noises and wiped at my face.

"They're liars, Callie," Jack said. "You said it yourself."

"They told some of the truth," I whispered.

"Why would they tell the truth about this?" His face went from pasty white to angry red. "This is just another trick. They want you to go with them, that's all."

"Yeah, yeah, that's it." That had to be it. I couldn't trust them. I couldn't trust any of them.

"Come on," said Jack. "Let's get out of here."

"What's your hurry, honey?" said a brassy voice from behind the curtain. "You ain't even seen the main feature yet."

We both jumped. It was the usherette, the blond woman with her flashlight. She stepped out from behind the curtain at the back of the candy counter, popping her gum and grinning at us with her wide red mouth. There was something different about her this time, a sharp, sly look to her face that hadn't been there before.

She sauntered around the lit-up counter with its Jujubes and Zagnuts, swinging her light from the loop around her wrist. She had white gloves on her hands and sheer stockings on her perfect legs. She looked like she'd just stepped out of a Busby Berkeley feature, like any minute she'd start dancing and a screen would lift to reveal a dozen other blond girls, dressed just like her.

"We've got plenty more to show you." The usherette grinned straight at Jack and popped her gum. "Both of you."

"Who's we?" I whispered.

"Silly! Who do you think we are?"

I knew. But I didn't have the words. I could just about remember the ones Shimmy used. "You're the Shining Ones."

The gum cracked like a gunshot. "We're the ones who got your mama, sweetie."

16

Come and Drag Me Away

"You . . . you . . . ," I stammered at the blond woman.

"Oh, yeah." The usherette leaned her bottom against the counter and crossed one perfect ankle over the other. "Now, maybe where she's at ain't quite as pretty as what you saw up on the screen, but she is with us now. Not that we really want her." She examined her perfect fingernails, which were the exact same shade of scarlet as her mouth. I got the creepy feeling it wasn't lipstick or polish making them match up like that. "She's pretty used up now. Not much fun for anybody anymore. But you knew that, didn't you, sweetie?"

Hearing somebody speak your most low-down thought may be the worst thing that can happen. Anger bunched its fists up tight inside me, ready to strike. "What do you want?"

"You, silly."

"Why?"

She shrugged, rippling the perfectly fitted shoulders of her red-and-gold jacket. "Not my business. But if you want your mama to go free before anything permanent-like happens to her, you'll come with me, nice and easy."

Jack moved up close to me. I wanted to grab his hand, but I didn't want the usherette to see how scared I was. "We're leaving, Callie," he said, his voice iron-hard.

"You sure about that?" The usherette leveled her gaze at him, like she was bringing up her flashlight beam. "You really sure, Jacob?"

"Don't call me that. Nobody calls me that."

She jerked her pointy chin toward the theater and grinned wide, showing the pink wad of gum clenched in teeth that were too big for her red mouth. She was Hopper kin, all right.

Whatever she meant, Jack understood. The last of the color left his cheeks. "You're just a bunch of liars."

"Now that's where you're wrong, Jacob. You've got something we want, and we've got something you want. We're ready to do a deal. All you've got to do is turn around and walk away." She waved her flashlight toward the front doors. "And she'll be right out there waiting for you."

"She?" The penny dropped. I said, "That was Hannah up there, wasn't it, Jack? Your sister?"

"No, it wasn't." He meant to snap those words, I could tell, but his voice was shaking too bad. "Hannah's dead!"

The usherette shrugged. "You think that matters to the

Seelie King? He's connected, ain't he? He puts a word in the right ear, and bingo! She's right back with you, all smiles to see her brother, Jacob."

Jack stood there as if he'd been struck dead himself. Just his lips moved, shaping one word but making no sound. I didn't have to hear it. I could feel the word thrumming through the air.

Hannah.

"Walk away, Jacob Hollander," said the usherette. "All you gotta do is walk away."

For one terrible moment, Jack hesitated. His eyes darted from me to the door, with the dark, empty street on the other side of that thin piece of glass. My heart rose up slowly, pushing its way into my throat while I watched my only friend in the whole, wide, terrible world make up his mind.

"I ain't leavin' without Callie." Jack spoke the words like he knew he was closing a coffin lid, and I hated myself for having doubted him.

The usherette sighed and shook her frizzy blond head. "I tried to be nice about this, but have it your way. . . ." She twisted around. "You can come out now, Mr. Morgan."

The curtain lifted again. Jack's arm wrapped around my shoulders as we both backed up.

Bull Morgan seemed to have swelled since the railroad yard. He towered over us, his face puffed up and pale. His fleshy jaw worked back and forth on his toothpick, and the usherette kept time with him by cracking her gum.

"There you is," Bull Morgan whispered hoarsely between chews on his toothpick. "The no-good pickaninny bummin' brat and her little Jew-boy friend. Got you both this time." He shifted the pick to the other side of his mouth with his big, tobacco-stained tongue. "Good job, Trixie."

"Sure thing, Mr. Morgan," said the usherette, Trixie. "Always glad to help an officer of the law."

"He ain't breathing," croaked Jack. "Have mercy, he ain't breathing."

Jack was right. Bull Morgan walked toward us. Handcuffs dangled from his thick fingers. He chewed his toothpick and grinned, but he wasn't breathing, not even a little bit. It's such a tiny thing, you wouldn't think you'd notice it looking at another person, but trust me, when it ain't there, you notice right away.

Bull Morgan was dead.

You think that matters to the Seelie King? Trixie had said. *He puts a word in the right ear, and bingo!*

Then I felt something else, something sharp and bright pressing against that extra sense I'd found. Headlights glared on the other side of the glass doors, and I heard a car's engine. I swung around, taking Jack with me. A big silver Packard screeched up to the Bijoux, bumping right over the curb. Shimmy leapt out, ran to the theater doors, and rattled the handles.

Trixie looked at her and hissed. Bull Morgan lifted his heavy head.

Jack and I dove sideways, in opposite directions. I ran

for the doors. Jack ran toward the theater. "Where you think you're goin', Jew boy?" laughed Morgan, stumping heavily after him.

He must have thought Jack was heading back into the movie, but Jack ducked sideways, grabbed up one of the poles with the velvet ribbon, and charged, aiming straight for Morgan's big stomach. Morgan clamped his hands around the pole and tore it away like it was nothing.

Trixie, in the meantime, sauntered up to me. I rattled the door handle. I banged on the glass. On the other side, Shimmy did the same.

"You don't have to worry none about her, Callie," said Trixie. "She can't get in here. Our gates don't open for *her* kind."

I spun around fast. Trixie was bringing her flashlight up to shine on me. I decided not to wait for that.

I kicked her. I missed her knee, but I got her shin and she screeched. For good measure, I grabbed a fistful of that frizzy gold hair and yanked with all my might, spinning her around and slamming her into Bull Morgan, who had Jack by the arm.

I didn't wait to see how they all untangled themselves. I whirled around again and laid both my hands on the handle of the outside door. Shimmy hammered on the other side of the glass so hard the door shook. I dug down deep into the place where my new sense waited, and I remembered the twisting key-in-the-lock feeling. I felt it in my heart and my stomach. I wished for it with all my might.

Click. Click. Click. The world key turned, the door opened, and Shimmy toppled inside.

For a moment, I was certain I saw a spasm of fear on Shimmy's face before she grabbed my wrist.

"Come on!" she shouted.

"No! Jack!" I twisted out of her grasp, yanking her halfway inside.

Shimmy gave a wordless shout of frustration and pulled herself up straight on the threshold, jamming her heel into the door to keep it open. Jack wriggled in Bull Morgan's grip as the dead man lifted him off his feet, squeezing hard around his middle.

"We don't 'low *your* kind in here," Trixie sneered to Shimmy. "Girls! Show this one out!"

The curtain behind the candy counter lifted again, and this time the chorus line appeared: a dozen Trixies, all dressed alike, all with the same hair and the same scarlet mouth and bright red nails, marched in time from behind the candy counter. Mr. Berkeley would have been on his knees to see those girls, all exactly the same, all swinging their perfect legs in perfect time.

All lifting up their flashlight beams to shine straight at me and Shimmy.

That light hit us, and it felt like hot honey pouring over my skin. It melted me down like I was made of wax, and I began to crumble.

Shimmy drew herself up in the light, spread her arms, and started to sing.

There were no words, just loud, clear, rich notes of pure sound, rippling up and down the scale. Shimmy's voice cut through the light, cut through the fear, and I grabbed hold of it like a lifeline. I even knew the tune, "St. James Infirmary Blues." She'd been singing it when I first saw her in the juke joint.

Let him go, let him go, God bless him . . .

The Trixie chorus line staggered in perfect synchronization, first left, then right. Then they all fell back, their flashlight beams scattering every which way. I charged them, barreling through, not letting any of them stop me. Trailing Shimmy's song and all its power behind me, I ran straight up to Bull Morgan, who was squeezing Jack so hard his eyes were bugged out and his mouth was open to gasp and gag. My stomach lurched up and down, but I grabbed hold of Bull Morgan's ice-cold arm. I buckled my knees and let my weight drag on him, grabbed tight hold of Shimmy's music, and *wished.*

Let him go, let him go!

It was like trying to punch through a marshmallow wall; you went in deep and got stuck. For a minute, I couldn't breathe. Jack choked hard, and I got hold of his fear with Shimmy's music and we all started pulling back. Morgan's grip loosened. Jack dropped to the floor. I grabbed Jack by the arm, and we ran straight for the Trixies. They swung round in a circle, ringing us in, bringing their lights up. Morgan growled. Jack snatched up one of the Trixies' hands and shined her own light into her eyes. She gave a

SARAH ZETTEL

weird groan and slumped to the ground again, taking the rest with her.

We leapt over the sagging heap of usherettes. Shimmy backed up and shoved the door open, and we ran through. I felt the world twist again, and we were back in Kansas, with the dusty night wind blowing around us and a big, old silver Packard with its engine running right in front.

"Get in!" hollered Shimmy.

I dove into the backseat with Jack piling in behind and partly on top of me. We didn't even have the door shut before Shimmy threw the car into reverse and stomped the accelerator so we tore backward with squealing tires. With another clash of gears, we shot forward. Vigilantes and civilians flashed in and out of the car's headlights as Shimmy clutched the wheel with both hands and drove hell-for-leather down Constantinople's main street.

"What was you thinking going to that rail yard?" she shouted. Jack had managed to get the door shut, which was good because we both spilled against it when the car tipped up onto two wheels as Shimmy cornered tight around the hardware store. We untangled ourselves in time to see the highway swinging into place under the headlights. With another hard bounce, we hit the pavement and raced forward into the dark.

Jack and I sat up, trying to catch our breath. It was not comfortable knowing that Shimmy had saved our lives. Worse, it was setting in that we were stuck with her in a speeding car.

170

"Where're we going?" Jack asked.

"Away," Shimmy snapped.

I tried to rally some nerve, but found precious little left to work with. "Look, thank you for getting us out of there, but . . ."

"You think you want me to stop?" Something small and dark flew toward me. I caught it automatically. It was a compact, the kind that usually held rouge or face powder. "You have a look in there, and then you tell me how much you want to get out of this car, missy."

My fingers fumbled with the compact's catch and finally got it open. There was a mirror under the lid, and I looked into my own hollow eyes, but only for a second. While I watched, the mirror turned solid silver, just like a movie screen. And just like a screen, it showed a moving picture. Except this picture was in color, and clearer than anything I'd ever seen in any theater.

There was Bull Morgan, sprawled on his face in the shadowy rail yard. A thin, dark trickle of blood ran down his temple. My stomach clenched, and Jack, who had leaned close to look, cussed softly.

Some vigilantes came around the corner of a boxcar and saw Morgan lying there. They rushed forward and rolled him over. They listened to his chest; they slapped his face and shouted. One of them ran away, probably to get help.

Morgan didn't move.

Slowly, though, the light around the vigilantes and the

railroad bull began to brighten. The men didn't react. They just kept shouting and slapping Morgan. The light was almost as bright as day now, and it coalesced into a ring of candle flames, each as tall as a human being and as white as snow. The candle flames changed, flickering and becoming . . . people.

They were beautiful beyond words, beautiful beyond understanding. So beautiful, I wanted to tear out my heart and hand it over, because after seeing them, I surely wouldn't have any more use for it.

They spread wings of pure light over Morgan's body. He groaned, long and low.

Please. I heard the word, but I don't know if Morgan actually spoke. *I don't want to die. Please, I ain't ready.*

"Then live, Samuel Morgan," said one of the shining, beautiful people. "Live, thou good and faithful servant."

"Thy labors are not yet finished," said another.

"Rise up, Samuel Morgan," commanded another.

"Rise up. Rise up," they said together, their voices blending in a sonorous chord, like the deepest note on a church organ. I knew that voice—part of it, anyhow. I'd heard it on the wind and in the dark. I'd heard it somewhere else too, but I had too much going on in my head to remember where.

The men couldn't see the light or hear the voices. But Bull Morgan could, and his eyes opened wide.

"My God," he whispered. "My God."

"Rise and walk!" the Shining Ones commanded.

And Morgan did rise. Not like a normal man trying to stand, but as if someone had shoved a board under him and was now levering him upward. The vigilantes fell back, cursing and swearing. Morgan ignored them. He took two steps forward and went down on both knees before the Shining Ones. In that white light, I could see his upturned face was ashen and his lips were ringed with blue. His eyes were the worst, though. His eyes were turned up, and they didn't blink. It didn't matter if his body was moving. His eyes were dead.

"The girl, Bull Morgan," said the Shining Ones. "The mixed-blood girl. You know her kind are an abomination."

"Yes, I do know it," whispered Morgan reverently.

"You will bring her to us. Nothing shall deter you. We grant you clear sight and unfailing strength. No rest, no food will you need for your righteous quest. You will find the abomination, and you will bring her to us so that we may clear away the stain of her from this earth."

A terrible peace stole over Morgan's face, as if everything he held most dear had just been proven true. "It will be as you say."

"Go then with all our blessing."

Their brilliance faded, blending back into the stark white of the yard floodlights. Morgan climbed to his feet and turned slowly around to face the vigilantes clustered behind him.

"What're you mooks standing around here for?" His voice was soft and rough, like he couldn't get enough breath to raise it to a shout. Maybe he couldn't. "We got work to do."

The mirror went dark.

"It's not true," said Jack. "Nothing they show is true."

"It is true." The compact slipped from my numb fingers and clattered to the floor. I just let it go. I couldn't explain how I knew it was the truth we'd seen, but I did. It was a feeling deeper than any in the bone. "That was them, wasn't it?" I asked Shimmy. "The ones like Trixie. Those were the Seelie."

"Got to be," said Shimmy, keeping her eyes on the road.

"What do they want with me?"

"They think if you're dead and your mama's out of the way, your papa'll come round and marry their girl, and then they'll get to take over our share of the territory."

While I tried to find some kind of sense past this new roadblock in my head, Jack, as usual, got right down to the practical.

"Where're you taking her?" I noticed that he said "her," not "us."

"The city gates," said Shimmy. "I just hope we can get there fast enough."

"Where are these gates?" asked Jack.

"At the moment, Kansas City."

Kansas City. That was east of Slow Run. A long way east. Shimmy was taking me and Jack in the exact opposite of the direction we needed to go to rescue my parents.

Panic squeezed my stomach, and all at once I couldn't

catch my breath. We were going the wrong way. I couldn't let her do this. I was already too far away from Mama, and I'd been gone too long. But what was I going to do? I had no way to make Shimmy stop the car, and even if she did and Jack and I could get away from her, what would we do then? It was the middle of the night and the middle of nowhere. We'd show up on the dunes as plain as paint, and Bull Morgan would find us and take us to his new bosses, dead or alive.

Tears swam in front of my eyes, and I fought to swallow them down. Jack saw, and he covered my hand with his. But because of what had happened in the theater and what we'd seen in the little magic mirror, the two of us sat in the big backseat of that Packard and let Shimmy drive us the wrong way into the dark.

17

Rattled Down That Road

Something nudged my leg. I swatted it away, but it came right back. Nudge, nudge.

With the fight and the fear all done, and Shimmy not showing signs of taking us off anywhere more terrible than the dust fields east of Constantinople, I'd fallen into a doze and was looking for a way deeper into sleep. But that little nudge kept on, and reluctantly, I opened my eyes.

The sun was up, and we were still driving. The fields passing by had been ridged and plowed in an effort to stop the blow dirt, in case maybe this year a crop could be saved. Jack leaned against the other door and stared out the window on his side, but his hand was nudging his battered black notebook at me. It was open, and the page read:

She watching us?

I glanced at Shimmy. She had both hands on the wheel and hummed random bits of tune as she took us down that highway straight toward the orange sunrise. It wasn't just a song; she was working some kind of wish with it. I couldn't tell what kind, but I could feel how that constant wishing took up most of her attention.

My stomach squirmed, trying to get comfortable around this new way of knowing. But the feeling was too lumpy to allow that, and my stomach finally gave it up as a bad job.

Jack's pencil stub lay in the fold of his notebook. I picked it up and, moving as carefully as I could, wrote

Don't think so

on the page and pushed the book back to him. He flicked his eyes briefly down to read.

We went back and forth like that for the next few miles, both pretending to stare out the side windows, letting Shimmy drive us farther away from where we wanted to be, and all the while writing our notes.

What do we do now?

What can we? Morgan's never going to stop looking for us.

Was it true? In the mirror?

You saw Morgan in the theater. What's it matter if the mirror showed true?

It matters.

My face wanted to screw up tight when I read that.

Because they can bring back dead folks?
Because the mirror can show us stuff. You can work it.
BAD IDEA. Every time I do magic, they find me.

Jack read this, made a face, and stared out the window for a while.

A mule cart took shape in the dusty distance, coming toward us. Shimmy's hum changed pitch, and the wordless tune slowed down. As we passed the cart, I saw a black man in dungarees slouched in the driver's seat, with about a ton of baled cotton piled high behind him. We drove by slow and easy, but he didn't look up. I would have bet all the money I didn't have that he didn't even see us.

Shimmy's hum picked up tempo and turned all happy again. I pulled Jack's notebook back toward me.

You think they've got your sister, don't you?

Jack read it, and his face went funny and tight.

Do you?
I don't know.

For a second, I thought he was going to tear the book in two, he looked so angry.

We have to find out. If they've got Hannah somehow like they got your folks, we have to get her away.

I thought about this. Hannah was dead; how could anybody be holding her prisoner? But then, Bull Morgan was dead and they had him up and walking around. But then, the Seelie were liars. But then, Letitia Hopper was one of them and she'd told me some true things.

It was just too many thoughts, spinning too fast. I tried to sort out the one that was really important. Jack wanted me to find out whether the Seelie had Hannah like they said they did.

HOW?

Jack thought about this.

Get her talking.

He drew an arrow to point between Shimmy's shoulders.

She already likes you. Find out what you can.
Then what?

He glanced at Shimmy to make extra sure she was still watching the road, then wrote four words slowly and carefully.

We steal this car.

I nodded once. Jack erased the last line, closed the book, and stashed it in his coat. The movement caught Shimmy's eye and she glanced back at us. Jack yawned and wiggled like he was trying to scratch an itch between his shoulder blades.

"Miss Shimmy, are we gonna stop soon? I gotta"—he glanced at me like he didn't want to offend my delicate sensibilities—"stretch my legs."

"Yeah, me too," I said. "And I'm hungry."

Shimmy sighed, short and sharp. "All right, all right. Next roadside stand, we stop. But no funny business. I ain't got enough juice to be chasin' the pair of you all over hell and creation, you hear me?"

"Yes, ma'am," we chorused.

Shimmy snorted at our docile agreement and kept driving.

We'd reached a county where the spikes of sunburned cotton stems still stuck up above the dunes. The broken bolls trailed sad streamers of white fluff that combed the blow dirt out of the wind. The road sign said BURDEN. The cluster of gray houses and one lonely gray church were behind us almost before we saw them coming. But on the far side of Burden, Kansas, there was a low white building all on its own. Gas pumps and picnic tables stood watch in front of it, and a peeling sign read FLORA'S.

Shimmy eased the car to a stop on the patch of dusty dried grass beside the fry shack.

"Here, young man, you go and make yourself useful." Shimmy pulled a beaded purse out of her handbag and laid two fifty-cent pieces on Jack's palm. "You go in and buy us some food, and be sure you bring me all the change."

"Yes, ma'am." Jack pushed his cap back on his head and put his wide-eyed young boy look on. He walked into the shack, jingling the coins in his pocket the whole way. I could see him through the window as he stepped up to the counter. Somebody had worked hard to keep that glass clean. The fry cook, a skinny man in a white shirt, glowered at Jack, his face as hard and ugly as grease at the bottom of a jar. Jack pushed those coins across the counter, and the fry cook nodded. But then he looked through that sparkling-clean window at me and Shimmy, and his face tightened up into ugly again.

Shimmy didn't seem to notice. She just took a white hankie out of her handbag, dusted down a spot on the picnic table, and sat. The fry cook nodded, turned back to his flat top, and began cracking eggs from a big carton onto the grill.

"Well, I suppose there's some use having that boy around after all." Shimmy got out her compact and looked herself up and down in the mirror. But I wasn't really watching. Shame curdled through me from the cold suspicion on the fry cook's face. I'd been out in the sun for days now, without a hat or gloves. I looked down at my hands, and to my shock, I barely recognized them, they were so brown. Mama would've had a fit. I touched my tangled hair, which had come loose from its braids days ago. If I went in there, would that man let me sit beside Jack on one of his stools? Or would he throw me right out again?

I didn't want to think about that. I had enough problems. Starting with how to get Shimmy talking. Jack wanted me to find out about Hannah, but I had a whole heap of my own questions I wanted to tuck into.

"Shimmy?"

"Mmm-hmm?" She dabbed at the corner of her mouth with one fingertip.

"Why didn't you say anything about the prophecy?"

"Prophecy?" She snapped the compact shut and stowed it in her handbag. "What prophecy?"

"See her now, daughter of three worlds," I recited, trying not to see Letitia Hopper's bug eyes while I did. *"See her now, three roads to choose. Where she goes, where she stays, where she stands, there shall the gates be closed."*

"Oh, *that!*" Shimmy laughed, but for the first time her laugh sounded thin, like she was stretching it too far. "That's been around for donkey's years. Some fool'll trot it out every time a half-fairy girl gets herself born, and pretty soon everybody's in a tizzy." She held her hand up to her mouth like she was whispering sideways to some other body leaning in close. "'Is it her? Is *she* the one? Oh, my stars, I think it's *got* to be her.'" Shimmy laughed again and waved all those invisible folks away. "They even said it about me when I was still an itty-skinny thing. It's why Their Majesties didn't want anybody marrying outside the fold. Gets folk all worked up." She frowned at the shack. Jack was sitting on a stool at the counter now, swinging his legs. "What is takin' that boy so long?"

But I wasn't ready to let it go so easily. I couldn't forget the turning-key feeling, the way I'd opened the time window to show the railroad work camp, and how I'd felt it again when I opened the doors between the theater and the normal world. "Can all of . . . us open gates?"

"Oh, sure, sure," Shimmy said breezily. "Ain't nothin' to it."

Then why couldn't you get into the Bijoux? But I knew. She couldn't open that door. That was a door between the regular world and whatever kind of world the Seelie lived in, and Shimmy didn't have the right kind of magic to get through.

I was going to ask more questions, but Jack was shouldering open the shack's screen door. He carried white paper bags filled with fried egg sandwiches and fat slices of apple pie. Jack and I shared a bottle of milk between us, and he'd gotten Shimmy a coffee, which she thanked him all pretty for and drank down like she'd never tasted anything so good.

Jack watched Shimmy closely as he took another swallow of milk, wiped the bottle rim with his sleeve, and passed it to me. "You know, Miss Shimmy, you must be tired by now. Why don't you ride shotgun a ways? I can drive."

"Nice try, *Mr.* Jack. But I'd rather keep things as they are. Now"—she picked up her purse—"I'm going to make use of the outhouse. Don't you let Mr. Jack here get any ideas, Callie. I've made sure no one can move that car but me."

She left me and Jack sitting there with a mess of paper wrappers and the remains of our breakfast.

"You think that's true?" Jack picked at the pie crumbs and kept an eye on the direction Shimmy'd gone.

"Can't say." I frowned at the car. From where we sat, it was just a car. "But it could be."

"Might make the rest of this trickier." Jack measured up the Packard with his eyes. I got the idea he was seeing through the hood to the motor and the wires, figuring how long it would take him to start the engine without the key.

"Might." Then I screwed up my nerve to ask something that had been bothering me since Constantinople. "Jack, are you really a Jew?"

"Yeah. So?"

"Nothing," I said. "But if you're a Jacob Hollander, shouldn't we be callin' you Jake?"

"Sometimes it's not so good for people to find out what you really are." Jack crumpled the sandwich wrappers together and stuffed them into one of the sacks. "Like, for instance, are you really a Negro?" he asked without looking at me.

I'd known that was coming. But my answer didn't have such a straight road to travel. "I think my papa had brown skin, but he was a fairy too, so I don't rightly know what I am."

Jack was quiet for a minute. "Well, from what I seen so far, being a Callie LeRoux is plenty good enough. Maybe you should just stick to that."

I found myself liking Jack a whole lot right then, no matter what name he chose. I'd never really looked at a boy before. The ones I knew in Slow Run all seemed small and mean, nothing you'd ever want to stop and pay attention to. But as frustrating as he could be, I truly did want to pay attention to Jack. Maybe it was because he was older and had been places and seen all kinds of things I never had. And, of course, with those other boys, if I looked at them too close, they might look back at me and see something I couldn't afford to show.

But Jack already knew.

"I'm sorry," I said.

"What for?"

"You had a plan. You were going to Los Angeles, get a newspaper job. . . ." The corner of my apron had three threads hanging off it. I pulled at the longest one. "And then I got you all caught up in . . . this. I'm just sorry, that's all."

"It's okay, Callie. Just think of the story I'm going to have when we get there!" Jack grinned, and his whole face lit up. "You know, it'd make a great Sunday serial, maybe for a magazine."

"Sure would." I made myself smile back. I was faking, but I started to feel a little better all the same.

Jack stuffed the trash into a can beside the table and settled the lid down tight. "So, what are *you* gonna do?"

"Do?"

"Yeah, after this is over?"

My brain went blank, like a blackboard when the eraser swipes across it. I'd never thought about doing anything. My life had been the Imperial and taking care of Mama. I kind of knew other kids had plans about what they were gonna do and where they were gonna go when they grew up. There'd just never seemed to be any world outside Slow Run for me.

But I was out of Slow Run now, and there *was* a world. In fact, there was more than one world. But I still couldn't see past what was happening right this minute. I wasn't used to looking ahead. Not like Jack. Maybe that was why he had that ready grin. I could see through the dust, but he could see through time, and he didn't even need magic to do it.

Before I could answer, Shimmy came marching around the corner of the shack, her face set in hard lines like she wanted to level some kind of curse on the outhouse.

It would have deserved it.

18

Gone and Left Me

By the time Shimmy parked the car in the dusty yard for Thompson's Motor Lodge, night had come back round for another visit.

"Now, we don't know what kind of place this is," said Shimmy as we all climbed out. The air had gone still and settled heavy over a line of little white cabins and dead live oak trees, one per cabin. Crickets chirped in the dark, each letting the other bugs know they hadn't starved out yet. "You two just let me do the talking."

To my surprise, Shimmy unlocked the Packard's trunk and pulled out two big suitcases. Jack moved to take one, but Shimmy brushed him off and made us both walk ahead of her to the little office, humming as she did. She smartly rang the bell on the desk. While we waited, Shimmy tugged on her white gloves and smoothed her blue-flower dress.

A squared-off white man with gray stubble on his hard

jaw and no hair left on his speckled head came up to the desk.

"What can I do for you folks?" His eyes slid straight over Shimmy, to Jack and me. My throat tightened up until I caught a glimpse of us in the window glass. In the reflection, we were all clean and well kept. Jack's clothes were mended and dust-free; even his shoes and stockings were whole. My hair hung in neat braids down the back of a tidy yellow dress. More important, though, my skin was nearly as white as Jack's. Shimmy's, on the other hand, had darkened up by several shades.

"These kids with you?" the motel man asked Shimmy slowly. It was a stupid question since we obviously were, except that wasn't what he was really asking. He was really asking if *she* was with *us*.

"Yes, suh," drawled Shimmy. Like the shade of her skin, her voice had changed, becoming deeper and slower, with the edge and shine all dulled. "Takin' 'em out to Kansas City to stay with they gran'ma. Mrs. Holland's laid up something awful after the last baby, and Mr. Holland out on the road so much . . . well, I'll be seein' 'em safe to ol' Mrs. Holland an' gettin' back just as soon as I can." She blinked rapidly and smiled way too big.

Jack fell right in with the act, slipping into the role of man of the party like he'd been there all his life. "We'd like two cabins for the night, if you please."

But the motel man was taking his sweet time deciding whether the story he heard matched what he saw in front of him. I tried to stand tall and trust in Shimmy's magic, but the disguise she'd thrown over us felt paper-thin. I hadn't liked Slow Run a whole lot, and Slow Run hadn't liked me. But I was a piece that fit in the puzzle of that town. This man didn't know us. I was nothing to him. All he had to go on was what he saw, like the fry cook back at Flora's. Like everybody we'd meet from now on.

"You can have six and seven," the man said finally, turning the registration book toward Jack and handing him a fountain pen. "Seven dollars, cash, in advance. No pets. No cooking in the cabins. No noise after ten o'clock. Shower house is round back. Soap and towels, ten cents extra."

Jack put his hand in his pocket but shifted his eyes toward Shimmy, who gave out her short, sharp sigh.

"I tol' you you shouldn'ta bought all them magazines, Mr. Jack." She handed Jack a ten-dollar bill from her purse, and Jack put it on the counter for the man, who gave him the change and two brass keys, along with a pile of towels and two cakes of soap from under the counter.

"If you kids want breakfast, it's in the dining room, eight sharp," he said as Jack gathered up the towels and Shimmy picked up the cases. What he meant was we could eat in the dining room but Shimmy couldn't. I couldn't have either, of course, if he'd gotten a proper look at me.

"Thank you, suh," said Shimmy with a big smile. "I'm sure it'll be right good too. Come along, chillun."

I tried not to scurry out of there.

Cabin six was one little dingy room. The cabins had

been electrified, but that maybe wasn't such a good idea, because when Shimmy snapped the light on we were able to get a good look at the place. The gingham curtains needed a wash, bad. The sheets on the two narrow, sagging beds would have given Mama a lemon-juice face for a month. I reached out to pull down the shade over my bed and to look at cabin seven. There was Jack, doing the same. He waved and gave me a thumbs-up.

There was a mirror over the dresser. It showed that my skin was back to its own color in here. So was Shimmy's. Shimmy pulled off her hat and set it on the dresser. Her hair was pulled into a tidy bun, except for the line of curls that lay flat against her forehead. She ran her hand carefully over her hair. I knew that gesture. I'd done it plenty. She was making sure it was still straight enough.

"How do you do that?" I asked, sitting on the edge of the bed.

"Do what?" She snapped the case open and shook out a fresh dress, this one with green flowers. She hung it from the clothes bar.

"How'd you do the magic?" *How'd you make me pass for white to that man?* "Is it safe? Every time I've tried . . . they find me."

"That's because you use too much. Not your fault, you ain't had no training. But you have to use as little power as possible when you're making wishes come true. It's like pepper in the soup—you want just enough to do the job, and no more." Shimmy lifted another dress out of the suitcase. This one was bright green with white cuffs and collar and looked too small for her. In fact, it looked about my size.

"But . . . they're still looking for me . . . us . . . aren't they?"

"See for yourself, why don't you?" She nodded toward her handbag.

It felt a little strange digging into Shimmy's bag. The silver compact was round, with an engraving of leaves and flowers on the top. This time, when I pressed the catch, awareness of a change rippled over my fingers. It wasn't exactly the turning-key feeling, but it was something close. For a minute, I saw my own eyes and sunburned cheeks in the clear mirror beneath the lid. This time the glass turned black, like the fade-out between movie scenes. When the next scene brightened up, I saw Bull Morgan. He had both hands planted on the counter of a general store. Damp stains spread under his coat sleeves and around his shirt collar, and sweat—or something—dripped down his puffy face. He leaned in close to a skinny little man with a bushy beard and one eye drooped almost shut.

"She'll be travelin' with a darkie woman and a Jew boy," Morgan said in his soft, husky voice. "They got themselves a big silver Packard. Probably stolen."

The little man tried to back away, but he bumped up against his own shelves. He coughed, and coughed again. I thought how Morgan must be smelling pretty bad by now. "I ain't seen nobody through here like that," the little man wheezed. "But maybe you wanna check over ta Burden. They been sayin' the road's clear thatta way."

Morgan nodded at the man, hooked his badge back on his belt, and stumped out to the truck. Two men with shotguns and slouch hats were waiting. Both looked awful fidgety.

"Sam . . . ," began the one wearing the brown canvas jacket and the scraggly beard.

"What?" Bull Morgan climbed heavily into the driver's seat.

"Me and Eddie was thinkin' . . ."

"Well, you can cut that out and get in the truck." Morgan jerked his thumb at the open back.

"We're hungry, Sam," said the second man. He was flagpole skinny, and kept his blue jeans tied at the waist with a piece of old clothesline. "We gotta slow down."

"If you'd even just let us go in there and get something to eat . . ." Brown Jacket pointed to the store.

"Shut yer yaps, both of ya, and get in the truck!"

The man with the rope belt pushed his hat back on his head. "It's just a couple of kids, Sam. They ain't even in our town anymore!"

Morgan heaved himself out of the truck. The mirror didn't show me his face really clear and I was glad. What I could see was his puffed-up hands curled into fists. Despite the fact that they were both carrying guns, the other two men backed up. "I said shut yer . . ." But Morgan stopped. Not paused, stopped dead. He cocked his head to one side, looking carefully. No, listening carefully. Except no one was talking.

"All right," said Morgan, but he wasn't talking to the two in front of him, just like he wasn't listening to anything they could hear. Slowly he shifted his eyes back toward the other vigilantes. "You go on and ask the guy where there's a good diner."

"Okay, then." The vigilante settled his hat back into place and started for the store. Sam Morgan shoved the other guy away from the truck and jumped in faster than somebody so big should have been able to move. He'd barely slammed the door when the truck shot forward in a cloud of dust, with the two vigilantes running behind, waving their arms and shouting.

Then I saw my own reflection again.

Shimmy came over to my side and looked down at me with sympathy shining in her eyes. She took her compact out of my hand and checked the mirror.

I wished it wasn't her here. I wished it was Jack. I needed to talk to somebody I could trust. I couldn't trust Shimmy, but I couldn't not trust her either. Jack was my friend, but it was Shimmy who knew what was really going on.

"Shimmy?" My voice sounded awfully small, even to me.

"Mmm-hmm?" She stowed the compact back in her handbag and snapped the catch shut.

"When you said we were kin . . . you meant you're . . . you're half . . ."

"I'm a daughter of the Midnight People, but my daddy was a mortal man." She returned to her unpacking, pulling pajamas and underthings out of the suitcase and laying them in the dresser drawers. "Now, I'm none so high up and powerful as you, of course, but I do have me a foot in both worlds."

"And the . . . the . . . Midnight People . . . they wanted you there?"

She turned and looked right at me. Her eyes were big and brown, and as human as mine. "More than anybody ever did here." She nodded in the direction of the office. "You know what we are to that sort. You know the names they'll call us because we're a strange color in a strange town."

I folded my arms and tucked my hands into the pits.

Shimmy's eyes narrowed. "She tried to hide you, didn't she? Your own mama tried to hide you." I nodded, ashamed, and she shook her head. "It's all right, Callie. We both know what's what. But you have to understand this. The Midnight People don't care *that*"—she snapped her fingers hard— "for your skin color or whether you've got good hair or good eyes. Why *wouldn't* I go live with folk like that?"

"But you're not there now. You're here."

"I was on watch. Now that my shift's over, I'll go back."

"What's it like where they live?"

"It's everything you want it to be." Shimmy plunked herself on the other bed and clasped her hands together, her face suddenly all distant and dreamy. "It's beautiful as Heaven and sweet as Christmas morning. Everything's easy and free. No hunger, no hard times, never. Just music and dancing. Pretty boys too, though maybe you're a bit young for that."

"But . . . but . . . what do people *do* all day?"

"Whatever they like to do best."

I had to admit it sounded peachy keen. Tired, filthy, and frightened like I was, the idea of someplace where I could do whatever I wanted, or not do anything at all, seemed pretty wonderful. Then I remembered the Trixies, and Bull Morgan rearing up in the dark.

"That ain't what it's been like so far."

She laughed. "Oh, you ain't been on the other side yet. You've only been inside the tunnels from the twilight hills. Once we get to Kansas City, we'll go through one of the main gates, right into the other lands."

"You think it would be like . . . like you said for me?"

She laid a hand on my head, smoothing my wild hair down. "For you, sugar, it'll be even better. You're the princess, don't forget."

That was a peachy keen idea too, although I was having a hard time picturing myself done up in a long dress with a crown and all. Still, it might be fun to try.

But I wouldn't be trying. I wasn't going to be anybody's princess. I was going to California with Jack, to find Mama and Papa.

I looked at my brown hands again and tried not to see my skin.

The shower house was dark, but there was a kerosene lantern by the door and the water was hot. The towels were a lot cleaner than the sheets, and wherever Shimmy got the clothes from, she'd remembered to get a soft pink bathrobe and a white-and-green-sprigged nightgown in my size.

I lay down under the sheet and tried not to squirm. Shimmy put the light out, and before too long I heard faint snores. I stared into the dark, waiting and thinking.

Tap, tap, tap.

I sat up and peeked under the shade. Jack, fully dressed, was on the other side of the window, tapping on the pane with the tip of one finger.

I tiptoed across the floor, freezing when the boards creaked. Shimmy kept right on snoring. I eased the door open and stepped out onto the cabin's tiny stoop.

Shimmy had clearly packed Jack's suitcase like she'd packed hers . . . ours. He had on a pair of long pants now, a clean shirt, and new work boots. Even though he'd kept his newsboy cap, he looked older. It was funny how clothes could do that.

Jack looked hard at my nightgown, like he couldn't believe I changed out of my traveling clothes. I don't know what he thought I was going to do, go to bed fully dressed with Shimmy right there?

"Let's go," he whispered.

"Jack . . . maybe we shouldn't." I didn't ask him to look at my skin or my hair. I couldn't find a way to explain that I couldn't travel like this. I didn't know how to put on an act like Shimmy did to get past the hard, suspicious eyes. I'd never learned. Instead, I told him about what I'd seen in Shimmy's mirror.

Jack swallowed hard and glanced toward the Packard, hunkered down low in the dark.

"Not much we can do about Morgan," he said. "We'll just have to be careful. I tell you what: we can take the car into the next town and sell it there. Use the money to buy a couple of train tickets west and . . ."

"And what? When we get there, what'll we do?"

"We'll find this house of St. Simon that Baya told you about."

"But *how*?"

"I don't know. But we will. With your magic . . ."

"My magic I can't use," I reminded him.

"So what? You're saying we should go with Shimmy to Kansas City? What're we gonna do there?"

"Find my family." It was the first time I'd said it out loud. It felt warm and right. I had family, and they were waiting for me.

But Jack didn't see things that way. "You can't mean it."

"Why not?" I asked, the anger creeping out from where I'd shoved it back before. Why'd he want us to do this the hard way? "They can help us."

"If they could help your papa, don't you think they would have by now? He's their son! And they didn't exactly come running to help your mama while you were growing up, did they?"

Which was true, but I didn't want to think about it too hard. "Well, maybe if we tell them what Baya said, they'll know what to do, or where to look. They can . . ."

"When did you start trusting Shimmy?" he snapped.

I shrugged, and Jack shook his head. "She just wants you to come along quiet. I'll bet the Unseelie, the Midnight People, whatever they call themselves, have got some kind of bounty out on you."

"A bounty? They're my *grandparents.*"

"You don't know that! You've only got Shimmy's word for it!"

I was angry. I was frightened. I didn't want him to be right. "What do you know? You just want to go to California because you think the Seelies've got your little sister out there."

"So what?"

"So, they're even bigger liars than Shimmy! They're just trying to lure us over into their territory so they can grab us!"

"Keep your voice down, dopey! You'll wake the whole place up!"

"Don't call me dopey!"

"All right. All right! Just . . . just pipe down, will you?" Jack sat on the little board porch with his hands dangling between his knees. When he finally looked up at me, I saw moonlight shining in his tired blue eyes. "What do you want to do, Callie?"

I grabbed the edges of the fluffy pink robe Shimmy had given me and pulled them tight around my throat. I didn't look at Jack. I wouldn't be able to go through with things if I looked at him too much right now.

"I want to go to Kansas City," I said. "Just for a little

while. Just to ask for help. If they won't help, we'll turn right around and head out on our own." The whole time I talked, I ignored the part of my brain telling me there was no way on God's green earth it would be that easy.

Jack sat there quiet for a long time, looking out at the dark, listening to the crickets. "Okay," he sighed at last. "If that's what you want."

"Thank you."

He smiled all lopsided at me as he got to his feet. "Sure. Go ahead and get some sleep."

I turned around and headed into the cabin, but stopped on the threshold and looked back over my shoulder. Jack, tall and slim, stood right on the edge of the patch of light from the pole by the office. "I'd never have gotten this far without you," I said.

Jack tipped his cap to me. My heart squirmed around to find a new position under my ribs. I closed the door fast before I could say something really stupid.

In the morning, Jack and the car were gone.

19

Whirlwinds in the Desert

"I am gonna skin that boy alive!" Shimmy's anger tumbled over me like wind in a dust storm.

"It's not that bad," I whispered. But it was. My knees were shaking so much I had to sit down on the edge of my bed. Jack was gone. I wanted to run back outside hollering for him, like he might just be hiding in one of the other cabins, or on his way to the showers. But I knew he wasn't there. He'd lit out and left me, and taken the car with him. I'd thought he was my friend. I'd thought . . . I'd thought all kinds of things, and now they were all gone too.

"The motel owner's got a truck. I saw it," I said, trying to sound like it was the missing car that was important, not the fact that Jack took it. Not that Jack left me. Us. "We can ask him to give us a lift to town. . . ."

"And tell him what?" Shimmy demanded. "We spun him a story about you two being in my mammy-ass charge.

How's that gonna fit with that boy running off and stealing the car? Do you know how much glamour it'll take to get him to believe something else? We'll have the whole Shining Court on us like flies on sugar!"

I swallowed and clenched my shaking hands over my shaking knees. "I don't understand. You weren't worried yesterday. . . ."

"*Yesterday* we were in a car. Haven't you noticed by now? Iron and steel raise Cain with magic. I just had to concentrate on keeping us going in the right direction, and all that bright metal kept us safe and hid. Just one more car in the dust. Now they're gonna have a clear line of sight. . . ." Shimmy's anger wavered, and for a minute, I saw her fear. I wanted the anger back right away.

"What about Shake?" I asked desperately. "Couldn't you call him, or send him a telegram or something? He'd help, wouldn't he . . . ?"

She just looked at me like she couldn't believe I'd say something so dumb. "Shake's not anywhere a phone call's gonna find him. He's . . . he's gone on ahead." Shimmy slumped down on the bed and smoothed her hair back. "Go get your breakfast. I gotta think."

I nodded and left her there, closing the door softly behind me.

The dining hall was a single-story building, painted white to match the cabins. It had one long table down the middle, covered by a faded red-and-white-checked cloth. A pair of traveling men sat at the near end, and an old couple at the far. There was no mirror. I couldn't see what I looked like to them. I sat right in the middle and tried to make myself as small as possible.

A stout woman with stringy gray hair straggling down around her ears brought out big bowls of Cream of Wheat and a platter of ham slices. There was a jug of molasses and another of milk. I tried to eat, but I could only choke down a few spoonfuls of the hot cereal. Shimmy's anger still crawled across my skin, and that wasn't as bad as the big hole inside me from where Jack had pulled up stakes.

Maybe he isn't really gone. I used the fork to pick my ham slice into little pink bits. *Maybe he just ran into town to check out where we were headed, or hock his suitcase to buy me and him those railroad tickets. Maybe he's on his way back right now. I'll walk out of here and he'll be driving up, and he'll get out of the car and I'll feel bad for having not trusted him again. . . .*

Of course, when I walked out, the parking spot under the dead live oaks was empty of everything but tire tracks. But as I stood there trying to stop my chin from trembling, I heard the rumble of a car motor coming up behind me.

Jack!

Shimmy's big silver Packard turned into the motor court, and sure enough, there was Jack behind the wheel. He braked and I ran up to the passenger side to yank the door open.

"Where in the world . . . ?"

My question died an early death, because Bull Morgan

was sitting up in the backseat. His revolver was out of its holster and aimed right at the base of Jack's neck. His swollen thumb held the hammer cocked back.

"Call that gal you made off with." Morgan's toothpick bobbled with each word. A smell rose up when he spoke, like old meat left out for the dogs. His cheeks sagged. The skin on his fat hands sagged. Runnels of damp trickled down his face like he was sweating hard, and his lips still had that blue tint, like he was freezing cold. "Get her out here now, or I'll shoot this one dead."

Jack didn't look around. He sat there, breathing hard from the fear, staring straight ahead. His hands gripped the steering wheel, and he tried to lean forward, away from Morgan's gun.

The worst part was there was nothing I could do except what I was told.

"Shimmy!" I shouted. "Shimmy! Come out here!"

Look out the window first, I prayed. *Please, look out first to see what's happening.* But no such luck. The cabin door squeaked open right away.

"What on earth are you hollerin' about . . . ?" I didn't need to look behind me to know she'd stopped dead in her tracks.

"Get in, both of ya," Morgan growled. "Right up front next to your boy here, where I can keep an eye on all of ya."

I looked to Shimmy. Her eyes burned bright with anger, but she dropped no hint that I should do anything but follow Morgan's orders. So I slid into the car beside Jack, and Shimmy climbed in beside me. She sat up poker-straight, both her hands clasped around her white beaded bag. I hadn't seen it in her hand when she came out of the cabin. Hope slid in under the fear. Shimmy still had her magic and, unlike me, she knew how to use it.

"Drive," Morgan snapped.

Jack shifted the car into reverse and swung it around, carrying us all back toward the highway. I thought that when the motel man found our empty cabins, he'd congratulate himself for making guests pay in advance. I wondered if he'd find the suitcases, or if they'd turn into something else without Shimmy there, like how the Hoppers' fifty-dollar bill had become a dried leaf.

Morgan ordered Jack to head west. Jack did as he was told. He glanced at me, and his mouth moved. I thought he was saying *Sorry.*

"What happened?" I whispered.

Jack made a strangled noise, and Bull Morgan chuckled. "Oh, you go on and tell her, boy." He prodded the revolver's barrel into Jack's shoulder, but before Jack had a chance to draw a breath, Morgan just kept on talking. "The local sheriff's a good man. A righteous man. When I explained to him we had a car thief on the road, he helped me set up the roadblock, easy as that. This one thought he could run it through, but he plowed into the drift instead."

While Morgan talked, Shimmy started to hum, low and quiet, a tiny trickle of sound. Morgan swung his arm over to press the revolver barrel right against her scalp. "You keep quiet, gal, or I'll blow your brains out all over this nice up-holstery. You understand me?"

"Oh, yes, sir." Shimmy's words cut like broken glass. "Yes, I surely do understand that."

I knotted my fists over my thighs. There had to be something I could do. We couldn't be just sitting here, letting Morgan take us to . . . to . . . *them.* I thought about the Trixies and the Hoppers. I didn't want to know what else waited out there.

Maybe I could get Jack and Shimmy out. If we split up, whoever chased us would come after me. Probably. Maybe then I could work up a plan.

"What do you want with them?" I said out loud. "I'm the one folks are after."

"That is true." Morgan chomped a few extra times on his toothpick. "But you might not behave so nice if you ain't got your mammy here to make you mind. Or your little boyfriend." He brought the gun back around so it rested under Jack's right ear. Jack winced, and the car wobbled.

"Careful there, Jew boy," Morgan snarled. "You keep it on the road, or my hand might just slip."

Jack's jaw clenched, and I felt the anger flash through him. He wanted to do something, wanted *me* to do something. He was wishing for it, wishing hard. But I glanced at Shimmy, and she shook her head.

"That's better." Morgan grinned. Blood speckled his blue lips.

"Where are we going?" I asked.

"Oh, there's plans for you, girlie. You're gonna be took care of good and proper, you are."

My heart turned upside down and tried to burrow itself behind my stomach, which was already working up a good sick from the fear and the stink.

"Why are you doing this?" Jack asked suddenly. "Why not just shoot us?"

I knew what he was trying to do. He was trying to get Morgan talking so maybe he'd let slip something we could use. But still, that was not the kind of thing you wanted to hear from your only friend, especially after he'd run out on you and gotten himself kidnapped by a dead man.

"Now, there's a thought," sneered Morgan, and the revolver swung toward me. "What do you say, girlie? Should I just shoot you?"

A gun is a terrible thing. It's a dark hole pointed at you, and that hole swallows up everything else in the world, your friends, your nerve, until there's nothing but you and what's waiting in that little round space of dark.

"I asked you a question, girlie," wheezed Morgan. "Should I shoot you?"

"No, sir," I whispered.

"No, sir." Morgan grinned. His teeth were black with blood and dirt. "Didn't think so, somehow. You just keep your fine ideas to yourself, boy, and keep drivin'."

Jack kept driving.

"Pull over here," Morgan ordered.

We'd been on the road about an hour. Morgan had

made Jack turn off the main highway a while back, sending us bumping slowly over dirt roads between dunes and what was left of old farm shacks. Where he ordered Jack to stop was the edge of what had been a cornfield. Rows of broken brown stalks still rattled in the wind, their bases all tangled up with the remains of grass stems and tumbleweeds. No one had cut down last year's plants, let alone tried to plow the ground to hold the blow dirt, or attempted to sow a crop for this year. To the north I could just see a hogback ridge curving above those chattering, whispering cornstalks. An old gray house stood sentinel on the ridgetop, the light glittering on its broken windows. Just another abandoned farm in the middle of the Dust Bowl, and we were in the middle of it with a dead railroad bull.

Morgan marched us straight into that tall, dead corn until I lost sight of the ridge and the house and the road. The only thing that told me we were still headed south was the sun over our shoulders. I thought maybe now I could cut and run. I told myself that Morgan wouldn't really shoot Jack or Shimmy. I was the one he wanted. He'd follow me, and I was smaller and faster than him. The other two could run away on their own.

Except he might just shoot them before he came looking for me. Or he might shoot me in the back while I was running. I saw the black hole of the barrel pointing at my face again, and a wave of weakness ran down my spine.

We broke through into a little clearing in the corn, and Morgan ordered us to stop. There was no sound except the rattle of the dead and broken stalks. I tried to remember how to pray. Jack flexed his hands, like he was gauging whether he could knock Morgan down before the bull got a shot off.

Shimmy, though, Shimmy had her nose up in the air, like she was trying to catch a whiff of something on the wind.

"What's out there?" she murmured. "What is that?"

Morgan just grinned and held the gun steady in his saggy gray hand.

I twisted my head around, trying to figure out what Shimmy was talking about. To the north, where that ridge had curved up, I saw smoke rising. No, not smoke. I squinted. It was dust. But not like a dust storm. It was a long, puffy gray cloud lifting up from the ground, like something was moving closer. Something big.

With the dust cloud, a jangling, clanging noise came drifting down over the corn's endless chatter, the sound of dozens of pieces of metal being slammed together.

The corn in front of us rustled and bent. A rabbit raced by so fast it was nothing but a streak of brown and white. It was quickly followed by another, and a third. All of them tore through the corn in the mad dash that means the critter is afraid for its life.

The banging got louder. The corn shifted and swayed, and more rabbits—six, eight, a dozen—sped past us. One bounded right over my shoe tops, like it didn't even notice a human was standing there. It was just trying to get away from whatever was coming up, making all that noise.

Then I knew. "It's a rabbit drive."

Shimmy's eyes went wide. "Have mercy."

"What?" croaked Jack. "What's a rabbit drive?"

Morgan grinned his rotting grin and gestured with the revolver barrel, telling me to go ahead.

"Since the dust came, there's no grass for the rabbits to eat, so they eat the crops, when there are crops," I told Jack. My voice had gone hoarse, and I couldn't even find the breath to clear my throat. "So in some places folks round up all the rabbits and kill 'em. They get in a long line and they walk in the same direction, making a big noise with pots and pans, and that scares the rabbits and they run . . . but there's a big pen set up in front of them and the drovers herd 'em in and the people waiting . . . they shoot 'em or club 'em to death. . . ." My voice faltered. The banging was getting louder. That'd be the drovers, banging on their pans as they marched through the old, dead corn. The rabbits would run from the noise and the line of people. The people would keep moving forward, herding the rabbits toward the pen. Others would be waiting behind that pen with shotguns and clubs. The first rabbits would run into the pen and be trapped. But the other rabbits would keep running in until they all piled up, clawing each other to try to get over the edge of that big pen, and they'd just be clubbed back down. . . .

"They shoot some on the way in, if they's too slow." Morgan straightened his arm to level the revolver at us.

Shimmy grabbed my wrist, backing away and pulling me with her.

SARAH ZETTEL

"No," whispered Jack. "The people won't hurt us. Not if they're just after the rabbits. . . ."

"There's magic happening here," snapped Shimmy. "You think we're gonna look like people to whoever's coming?"

"If I was you, I'd run." Morgan cocked the revolver's hammer back another notch.

We ran.

20

Shot

We slammed through the cornstalks and stumbled over tangles of dead weeds. A living river of jackrabbits ran in high flood around us. Brown, black, and white, they squealed in fear. We couldn't see the drovers, but we felt them at our backs. They raised the dust and their banging filled the air, louder even than the chuckling of the corn.

They were getting closer.

I tried to cut sideways, but I tripped over the solid mass of fleeing rabbits and fell sprawling into the dirt. Rabbits squealed and leapt over me. Their claws scraped along my back, and got tangled in my hair. I screamed and screamed, trying to beat them off and keep my head covered at the same time. Jack hauled me to my feet. Shimmy grabbed my hand and dragged me forward.

A gunshot exploded above the banging. And another. I heard Morgan laughing, back there in the corn. He'd joined the drovers. I knew it. He was marching with them, his revolver held high.

"They wishin' dead." Shimmy panted. "Can't get hold of anything. . . . All they wishin' is dead. . . ."

I knew what she meant. I could only catch glimpses of the people moving through the corn in a big curving line, but their anger rolled over me like the noise. With every beat, every footstep, the drovers wanted the rabbits dead. They wanted us dead. That single wish was in the banging pots and the rustle of the corn. *Die, die, die.* Every inch, they drove us closer to the open pen and their kith and kin, waiting with clubs and guns.

That couldn't be all there was, I thought desperately. There had to be something else. But I didn't dare open my magic sense to try to find it. I'd tried in the rail yard and was paralyzed by the anger and fear that I found. If I froze up now, I would die. Those people back there wouldn't see me. All they'd see was another varmint destroying what little they had left.

A rabbit flashed in front of me, too close. I tripped and plowed face-first into dirt and dead weeds. Dust drove into my eyes and under my nails. I pushed myself up, hacking and coughing like the dust pneumonia had come back.

"Get up!" screamed Shimmy, hauling on my wrist. "Get up!"

I staggered to my feet, trying to blink the dust away as I ran forward. *Die, die, die.* The wish pummeled me. I coughed, and knuckled the blow dirt out of my eyes, and kept running. Sweat streamed down my face and turned the dust on my cheeks to mud, and all at once my mind clamped tight around a new thought.

There was another wish, a wish that every person in Kansas wanted to come true, even these people driving us to die. They wanted it more than the death of the varmints they'd set out to slaughter, more than revenge against a world gone so wrong for so many years.

They wanted rain. They wished for rain each time they stepped out into their dead fields. They wished for it now, under the banging of the pots and the pans.

"Shimmy!" I shouted. I put on a fresh burst of speed and held out my hand to her. "Help me!"

She grabbed hold of my hand, and I felt her magic rise up. I squeezed my eyes shut and let her drag me along, blind. It didn't matter if our enemies could find me from the wishing magic. They were already here. Bull Morgan had brought their magic with him to blind the folks behind us. I squeezed Shimmy's hand, and with all my might, I wished for rain.

I remembered the cool smell of rain filling the wind as I ran to the top of the hogback ridge near the Imperial, and how the black and gray clouds built up into mountains overhead. I remembered the hard smack of the first drop against my skin, and the way the goose bumps spread out from the touch of cold water on a burning-hot day. Then there'd be another drop, and another. Soon there'd be too many to count, pattering on the ground, making a sound like paws.

I'd wished for rain every day since the dust came, just like all the folks behind us did. It was my wish and their wish, all together, as strong and as real as the wish for food among the hobos in the rail yard.

The wind blew hard and suddenly cold. Behind us, the clamor faltered. The light turned dirty-canvas yellow and then smoky gray. I risked a glance up. Clouds churned in the hard blue sky. But these weren't brown dust clouds. These were thunderheads, great piles of them, filling the sky.

Something cold hit the top of my head. Then my arm, and my cheek, and my brow.

Rain.

Fat, ice-cold raindrops hit the ground and raised puffs of dust. They smacked against the dead cornstalks, making the stems buckle and sway. I could see the people between the drooping cornstalks now. The whole line of folks in dusty clothes, with hats on their heads and dented pots in their calloused hands, stood with their faces turned toward the sky.

"My God!" someone cried. "My God!"

They stared openmouthed at the sky. The individual drops now turned into a solid sheet of water, rippling in the wind, pouring down over the dead earth and the desperate people. The rain fell faster and thicker with every heartbeat. It poured out of the clouds, out of my wishing, and out of me too, until I swayed as much as any of the cornstalks.

"No!" bellowed Morgan. "Get after 'em, you fools!"

But no one was listening to him. The rabbits vanished into the corn, splashing through the new puddles as they made their escape, and no one cared. The people laughed and held their arms out to the sky, mouths open wide to let the rain pour right in. They hooted and hollered and banged on the pots, the ones they weren't holding up to catch the water. They danced among the cornstalks, swinging each other around and shouting hallelujahs.

With the rain, I felt something else dissolve. The spell on their eyes. My rain washed that magic clean away.

I wasn't the only one who felt it. Bull Morgan roared. He swelled like he was a bag filling up with the rain, and he teetered toward us, the revolver stretched out in front.

"You're dead, you darkie brat!" he howled. "Abomination! Gonna kill you dead!"

"Run!" hollered Jack.

I tried, but my legs had turned to rubber and I just sagged. Jack caught my arm and kept me upright. Shimmy grabbed my other arm, and between the two of them they dragged me deeper into the cornfield. Shimmy pushed me forward into Jack's arms so he could pull me with him while she shoved us both from behind.

There was a shot, and another. How many bullets had that been? How many did Morgan have left? My head spun. My stomach heaved. I was jouncing and jolting, deadweight in Jack's arms. The clouds I'd called up hid the sun. I had no sense of direction. Jack swung around to the right, like he knew where he was going. Maybe he did. He always had before. Behind us, Morgan shouted and plunged through the corn and the pouring rain.

A hollow opened up in front of us. Jack threw himself flat on his face in the mud and pulled me down beside him. Shimmy dropped to her knees and then to her belly beside us. There was something wrong with her dress. It had a dark stain across the shoulder, something shining and wet that mixed with the rain and the mud. Shimmy put her hand on my back and held me down like she thought I might get up and start dancing. I couldn't move. Each raindrop that hit me felt like it weighed five pounds. I was being pummeled flat into the ground by my own rain.

"Give it over now, Callie," Shimmy said. Then she coughed. "Give it to me."

"I don't understand."

"The—the wish." She coughed again.

Panic was blooming inside Jack. I could feel it like the rain battering my skin. Something was wrong, very wrong. I knotted together the last of my strength and made myself look at Shimmy, and at that dark, spreading stain. It wasn't just a stain; it was a tear, straight through her shoulder.

She was shot.

"I got it now." Shimmy's voice trembled. "You let go."

"But you're . . . you're bleeding. . . ."

She coughed. "It's not so bad."

I made my eyes roll up to look at Jack. He shook his head. Shimmy was lying.

"I can't let you . . ."

"Yes, you can!" Shimmy snapped. "You wish you felt better, don't you, sugar? You wish you could run. Give it to me now."

Shimmy huddled on the slope of the hollow. I didn't know what to do. Bull Morgan was thrashing around up there with his gun, looking for us. It was a matter of seconds before he tripped over us in that little hollow, and I didn't know how many bullets he had left, but I figured it was enough. The rain was punishing me down to my bones. I had no strength for another wish.

"You got to get away," croaked Shimmy. "Take the car, get to Kansas City. You got to promise me you will."

"Okay." I swallowed hard. "I promise."

Shimmy smiled, and I saw the glimmer of golden light in her brown eyes. "Don't look like that. You just be sure you tell our king and queen that Shimmy never let you down." She wrapped her hand around mine. It was as cold as the rain, as cold as death. I felt her reach inside me, felt the spark of mischief and determination, and her wish. I felt Shimmy wish I could give her the rainstorm, and I passed it over to her. Simple as breathing.

It was like a whole sack of stones rolled off my back. I could stand. I could back away.

Shimmy rose up from the mud. She was tall and solid, more real than the storm overhead or the mud underfoot.

"Bull Morgan!" she shouted. "Bull Morgan! Come here!"

Jack pulled me deeper into the corn and the rain.

We heard Morgan shout. We heard Shimmy laugh.

We broke through the edge of the corn, and there was the Packard, parked crooked on the side of the road. Jack had known where he was going after all.

A shot split the air like thunder, and another.

I dove into the passenger side of the Packard while Jack cranked the engine to life. I dug into Shimmy's handbag for her compact. The tires spun and squelched in the mud as Jack forced the car forward, rocking and bumping across the dirt road's ruts. I flipped the compact open.

Show me, I demanded of the mirror. *Show me!*

The mirror went black again, then gray and shimmery with rain. Then the rain cleared away.

Bull Morgan was squinting, turning drunkenly in place, waving his revolver. Looking for us. For me. Shimmy lay in the mud at his feet, and she wasn't moving.

"Where are they?" he shouted like she could still answer him. "Where?"

The wind blew until the cornstalks bent almost double. Then, slowly, the light began to change. It grew clean, bright, and hard. The rain slowed, then stopped. The white light turned Morgan's sagging skin the color of chalk, like he'd walked off the screen from some old silent film.

"You have failed us, Samuel Morgan." The voice came from nowhere and everywhere. There were no beautiful beings this time, just this voice that belonged to Judgment Day.

"No . . ."

"We gave you our trust and our favor, and you have failed!"

"No! No! I can still find her. I know where she's gone!"

"Your time is over, Samuel Morgan."

The light faded. Bull Morgan cried out and staggered forward, but he collapsed to his knees. He sagged slowly, deflating like a tire with a slow leak. I watched, my heart in my mouth, as Morgan slumped forward until his hands pressed into the dirt.

"No. No. Don't leave me! I can find them. I will find them."

But the magic was gone. The light was only the bloody twilight over the ruined prairie. The long stripes of the cornstalk shadows fell across him like bars. Morgan's elbows buckled until his forehead touched his hands.

"They ain't gonna escape. They ain't. I ain't givin' up. Bull Morgan don't. Give. UP."

Ever seen a movie that's been run through the projector in reverse? The cars and the people all head backward, and anything that has broken apart flies into one piece again. That was what this was like. Morgan's head lifted, and his neck drew back into his collar. His hands lifted themselves up, and first one knee straightened, then the other, and he stood.

But the strength that had puffed him up before was gone, along with the light in his eyes. His colorless skin sagged against his bones, like all the juice had been sucked out of him. It even puckered unevenly around his flat, dry eyeballs as he stared into the twilight. One hand, the skin loose and rumpled around the finger bones, felt for his club, then his gun, then his badge.

Morgan turned from where Shimmy lay and blundered through the rain-drenched corn.

My hand went cold and curled into a fist, snapping the compact closed.

"What is it?" shouted Jack. "What did you see?"

"Drive," I told him as the tears ran down my face to mix with the last of the rain that had saved our lives. Ours, but not Shimmy's. "Just drive."

21

Ain't Gonna Be
Treated This a-Way

The next town we came to was Madison. We sold Shimmy's Packard for seventy-five dollars to the one auto dealer, and bought two tickets for the bus to Kansas City. I kept Shimmy's handbag with her compact and her wallet. There was a paper in there that told me everything I needed to know about what to do once we got into the city.

There wasn't any discussion about where we were going. I said what was going to happen and Jack agreed, and he set about dickering with the auto man, who already knew we'd take whatever he cared to offer. Jack wasn't even looking in my direction any more than necessary, and that was just fine with me. If he hadn't run out on me, Shimmy wouldn't be dead. I clenched her white bag in my hand and looked out the bus window. Things were going to be different from here on out. Something had changed inside me when I'd made that wish come true, and again when I'd passed it over to Shimmy. That was all right too.

Kansas City was another world.

It was still flat, and the sky overhead was still colored by the dust. But unlike Slow Run, or Constantinople, or sad little Burden, Kansas City teemed with life. People filled the paved streets, crowding the sidewalks between stone and timber buildings. Some of those buildings were as much as ten stories tall. Cars, trucks, and wagons jostled each other in the streets. It smelled of exhaust and excitement. I wanted to plunge straight into the crowds and find out where they were going and where they were coming from. I wanted to wrap my arms around the city and hold it so close it would become part of me. Even the hard parts—the cops in blue coats and hats, with their clubs and guns on their hips, who seemed to stand on every corner; the men lounging against the walls, unshaven, cigarettes dangling; the apple sellers, with ragged families tucked in the shadows; the long line of people in front of the mission waiting for bread and soup.

Even in my excitement, there were parts I could have done without. Along with the signs for hotels and shops and cinemas and food, I saw the signs on the doors that said WHITES ONLY and NO COLORED. They hadn't needed signs like that in Slow Run. Sheriff Davis kept anybody with brown skin from staying in town overnight. Mama kept the black hobos she put up behind closed curtains in the Imperial's rooms. If Sheriff Davis came to inquire about who she had there, she distracted him with her cooking. But Kansas City was too big for simple tricks like that, and there were too many colored folks walking the streets. They had to be told straight-out where they weren't welcome.

But I wasn't going to let that matter to me. Not this time.

Jack wanted us to find some cheap boardinghouse where we could hole up, but I wasn't having it. From the bus station we hailed a taxi. I climbed into the backseat and looked right into the eyes of the skinny white driver.

He wished we were rich folks. He needed to make the rental on his cab for the day, and he wanted a good fare, maybe somebody going to the Savoy or the Muehlebach Hotel. So I took that wish and made it come true. Just a little, just enough so he saw exactly what he wanted: a pair of rich white folks in his cab.

"Take us to the Savoy," I said.

"Yes, miss." He tipped his hat to me and pulled the taxi into traffic.

Jack opened his mouth, but I looked at him too, daring him to say a single word. He didn't.

Finally, we pulled up in front of the biggest, grandest building I'd seen yet. I counted bills out of Shimmy's purse. Of course there was enough. I should have known. There was all we needed, plus enough for a big tip.

A doorman with deep black skin, wearing a red coat with gold buttons and white gloves, opened the car door. He tipped his shining top hat to us as I marched through the front door and up to the registration desk.

The manager wore a pin-striped suit and a tight frown. He looked down at us with watery gray eyes. His name badge read WENTWORTH, and he wished that was his real name, instead of Weinstein.

"May I help you?" Mr. "Wentworth" asked in the sort of voice that meant the only help he was going to give was the kind that would get us out of his shiny marble and gold lobby as quickly as possible. Like the cabdriver, he wished we were rich folks, maybe movie stars on our way to Hollywood.

"My name's Callie LeRoux," I said to him. "I've just signed a three-picture deal with MGM Studios. I'm going to be the next Shirley Temple, but the train to California is delayed by a dust storm and I need a place to stay until the track is cleared."

My magic shivered between me and Mr. Wentworth, and those watery eyes flew wide open. He shot out from behind the mahogany registration desk, rubbing his hands and all but bowing to me.

"Miss LeRoux, please allow me to welcome you to the Savoy. We are delighted to have you here. I'm so dreadfully sorry to hear about the delay of your train. Of course the Savoy will be more than happy to accommodate you."

He took us up in the elevator to the top floor. He opened the doors of a suite so big, the entire staff quarters of the Imperial could have fit in there and still would've had space to rattle around. It had a sitting room with a dining nook, three bedrooms, a private bath with a claw-foot tub, and a balcony facing the distant green river.

I pulled a knot of bills out of Shimmy's purse and laid them on the table for the manager to pocket. I wondered about that money, whether it was real or like the Hoppers'. Not that it mattered. Mr. Wentworth wished it was real, and that was enough. The manager bowed and smiled and rubbed his long, clean hands as he backed out the door.

As soon as he was gone, Jack turned to me. "Callie . . ."

"I don't want to talk about it," I told him. I didn't care what "it" was. I was done talking and worrying. And I wasn't going to show up in front of a king and queen looking like a Dust Bowl refugee. That wasn't how Shimmy would have done it. For her sake and mine, I was going to do things up right, and Jack could see how it felt to trail along and not know which way *he* was going for a change.

I bought us a huge luncheon in the Savoy's dining room—Waldorf salad made table-side, steak, and lobster in butter sauce with heaps of french fries. We had banana splits piled with whipped cream for dessert. I told Mr. Wentworth I needed to do some shopping, and he phoned over to

Kleine's department store so the floor manager was waiting at the door with a small army of store clerks when we arrived. We were ushered up to the third floor and seated on plush chairs in a special alcove. Women in starched white aprons brought us lemonade and cookies. Boys in green jackets who looked about Jack's age brought us one outfit after another for our approval. I bought us both enough fancy clothes for a week and paid with more cash from Shimmy's purse.

Through it all, Jack looked like a hound dog whose owner had died. I told myself I didn't care, and I almost believed it.

Back at the hotel, the bellhops carried the boxes filled with new clothes into our suite. I tipped them all, then used the private phone to order room service. Steak and french fries and more ice cream. It was going to be a long night, and I wanted a good dinner.

"Callie . . . ," said Jack behind me. "What are you doing?"

"I told you I didn't want to talk about it."

"I'm sorry," he said. "I've been trying to tell you. I'm sorry about Shimmy and about running out on you."

"You left." I shrugged. "You got caught, and Shimmy saved us both. What else is there to talk about?"

"It's my fault Hannah's dead."

That turned me around. Jack stood in the middle of all that fancy furniture, his shoes sinking into the thick carpet. He hunched his shoulders up and stuffed his hands in his pockets, like he was trying to make himself even skinnier than he was, maybe so skinny he'd disappear.

"My family didn't just run liquor during Prohibition; they made it. It was cheaper that way, and the syndicate bosses didn't really care if you made a little on the side, as long as the good stuff from across the border got to the right warehouses.

"When I wasn't out helping with the deliveries, it was my job to stay home and watch Hannah, and the stills. Moonshine stills . . . you gotta watch them close. If the steam pressure gets too high, you'll ruin the brew, and the still can explode." He licked his lips and took a deep, shuddery breath.

"I was supposed to keep Hannah out of the basement. I was supposed to keep an eye on the stills. But she was being a pain. She wanted me to play dolls, and I wanted to read, and I hated the cellar. There were rats and . . . I thought I'd locked the door. I always did, and it had always been all right before. But Hannah got down there and I guess she was playing with the knobs, or maybe there was a pressure buildup. . . .

"The explosion shook the whole house, and by the time I got through the cellar door, the fire was burning, and she was . . . she was . . ." He didn't finish. He didn't have to. "That was when Dad started laying down the beatings, and Mom started drinking harder, and the government said they were gonna repeal Prohibition, and the bosses were saying they had other work for my brothers and me and . . . I couldn't stand it. I ran out and hopped a freighter. I thought maybe I could just get away from everything. But you can't get away from a thing that's your own fault."

There were all kinds of things I should have said right then. Because way down inside I knew that what had happened wasn't Jack's fault. None of it. Not just with Morgan and Shimmy, but also with Hannah. Not really. I mean, what were his folks even thinking, leaving a kid alone with stills and a little sister? Mama might have kept me holed up in the Imperial, but she looked after me and did her best to keep me safe however she could. Jack's parents were running 'shine and making their kids drive the car. It was plain crazy.

But saying any of that would have meant I still cared about Jack, and I didn't want to care. Not after the rabbit drive and Shimmy. Not after he'd up and left me.

"What's that got to do with anything?"

"Hannah followed me. I see her every night in my dreams. And when I met you and found out about the Seelie and saw that movie, I thought . . . maybe they do have her. Maybe that's why I can't get rid of the nightmares. I had to try to find out, don't you see? That's why I left. I told myself you had Shimmy, you'd do all right. Hannah only had me. I had to get to her. But Morgan caught me instead."

I couldn't figure out where the anger was coming from, but it had a tight hold on me. It didn't matter he'd been scared. It didn't matter he thought the little sister he loved was being held prisoner. What mattered was he'd left me all on my own with a woman he didn't trust. He'd barely even tried to get me to go with him, and if he had made it out to California, well, he wouldn't have come back, would he? The only person who'd never run out on me, who'd stood up to everything that came after me, was Shimmy, and because of Jack Holland, Shimmy was dead and she hadn't even gotten to take Bull Morgan down with her.

Maybe if I'd thought about all that slow and straight, it wouldn't have made much sense, but I was way past thinking straight.

"It doesn't matter." The words came out even and hard. Three words to let him know that if he left, he was on his own. I wouldn't be coming after him any more than he had come back for me. "You do what you gotta. I don't care anymore."

"What're you going to do?" he asked.

"I'm going to eat dinner, and then I'm going to find my grandparents."

"How do you even know where to look?"

I pulled out the paper I'd found in Shimmy's purse and laid it on the table.

Jack stared at it. "Oh, now that just can't be right."

Because the flyer read:

KANSAS CITY DANCE MARATHON!
WHO WILL BE THE LAST ONES STANDING?
FABULOUS PRIZES
THRILLS, SUSPENSE, AIR-COOLING

MUSIC BY KANSAS CITY'S OWN
BILL "COUNT" BASIE AND HIS BAND
Starting April 14, 8 o'clock
AT
FAIRYLAND
KANSAS CITY'S PREMIER AMUSEMENT PARK!

"It's right," I said. "And that's where I'm going."

22

Bound for Glory

Jack tried to tell me that we—meaning I—needed to be careful. That we shouldn't just go rushing off through the streets. After all, he said, Bull Morgan was still out there.

As if I'd forgotten that for one minute. The truth was, I hoped Bull Morgan would find us. I really did. I hoped he'd come right up to me like I was still that frightened little girl he'd chased through the dust. I'd show him what was what. I told myself that the only reason I didn't go out looking for him was that it was more important I find my grandparents. I was telling myself all kinds of things right then. Telling myself things was like the wishing magic. The more I did it, the easier it got.

We ate our steak dinner. Well, I ate mine. Jack picked at his. You'd think he would've been grateful I let him stick around after he'd run out on me and Shimmy like that. I wasn't sure why I did, really. Maybe I just wanted him to see how wrong he'd actually been.

It took a while to get ready for going out. The fancy new clothes were pretty complicated to get into. There was the slip, petticoats, and frilly drawers to sort out. The green velvet dress I'd chosen had prickly starched lace cuffs and a collar that had to be attached separately, and there were about a million silver buttons up the back. Then came the white stockings and the patent-leather Mary Janes.

My hair wasn't cooperating either. The Savoy's pretty gold-and-white vanity table was outfitted with brushes and combs and a big jar of pomade, in case some fine lady forgot hers. After a whole lot of wrestling, I managed to get my hair into one long braid and coil it up on my head like Mama did when we went to church at Christmastime. My hands shook as I worked the strands of the braid. I hadn't really thought about Mama in days. I wondered where she was now, and what the Seelie were doing to her. I wondered if they were even keeping her and Papa in the same place.

I told myself this was best, even if it took a little longer. Even with my new hold over my magic, there wasn't a whole lot I could do on my own, was there? If I couldn't even keep Shimmy alive, how was I going to pull my parents away from the same things that could bring Bull Morgan back from the dead?

I fixed my braid with a mess of pins, then added a headband that sparkled with green glass gems. I had white gloves with pearl buttons, and a silver locket with a matching bracelet.

I smiled at the girl in the mirror and she smiled back.

But I didn't know who she was. She was pretty, I guess. But I couldn't connect that girl in her brand-spanking-new clothes with the small, mean person I felt living inside my skin.

I snatched up Shimmy's handbag and ran away from my reflection.

Jack was already out in the sitting room. He wore what the man at the store had called evening dress: black jacket, black trousers, stiff white shirt, and white bow tie. He'd slicked his brown hair down hard. He didn't look any more comfortable than I felt, but he for sure looked fine in those new clothes. Any other time I would have told him so. Well, I think I would have. The truth was, he looked too grown-up for me, and despite the fact that I was still mad as sin at him, my insides were starting to squirm around all over again just seeing him.

For his part, Jack was looking at me funny. I wanted to know whether he saw the pretty girl from the mirror or the tiny, mean one. But there was no way to ask. So we just picked up our new coats and walked out to the elevator, and then across the lobby and out to the street, where the doorman hailed us a taxi.

If Kansas City during the day was a marvel, at night it was pure magic. Electric lights shone from every window and turned the shadows into decorations, like curtains on a stage. Cars filled the street, honking and ducking between each other in a raucous dance, carrying people in fancy clothes who laughed and drank out of flasks and smiled at the world. I all but pressed my face up against the window. It was light and color wrapped in velvet black. It was like the biggest jewel box in the world.

But the best part was the music. There was music everywhere. It poured out of the doorways and second-story windows into the smoky city air. Hot jazz and cool blues clashed with the clamor of the car horns. Through drawn shades, I could see the silhouettes of men at upright pianos. People leaned out of open windows and sang along to whatever tune was closest. They stood on the corners, laughing and singing as they swayed back and forth. A boy and girl jitterbugged on the street corner with a bunch of kids playing harmonica and ukulele. Men in sharp suits and broad-brimmed hats danced close and slow with women in spangled dresses with orchids in their hair. I rolled the taxi window down and breathed deep, like I could inhale that music and store it up in my bones, where my magic lived.

At last, our taxi pulled onto a straight street with a broad white wall on the side. Steps led up to a wide-open gate. A neon sign shone orange and red over the archway:

FAIRYLAND

"They got to be havin' us on," said Jack as we climbed out. "They're havin' us on, aren't they?"

"No." I paid the taxi driver and started up the steps.

"How do you know?"

"I know."

I paid our admission at the ticket booth, and we pushed through the turnstile. The bars clattered as they went round, and I felt the turning key inside and outside, but not all the way, not yet. This was a sort of in-between space, like Shimmy had talked about, a passage from the regular world to whatever world the fairies lived in, like the theater and the juke joint. The real gate to the real Fairyland was farther on inside.

I'd never been in an amusement park, and it was plenty like another world for me right then. There was the Ferris wheel lit up red, white, and blue and turning slowly against the black sky. The roar and screams from the roller coaster washed over us to mix with the colored lights and tinny music from the carousel. The air smelled like popcorn and cotton candy and fireworks. This late there were no little kids, just teenagers and adults in their evening clothes, laughing with each other over candy apples, Cokes, bottles of beer, and glasses of gin.

Jack was trying to put on his hard hobo look, but it wasn't working. The excited kid kept shining through. We both rubbernecked like the tourists we were as we walked down the boards of the midway. Jack stared so hard that some of the colored light bled into his eyes.

"Hurry! Hurry! Hurry!" called a barker from one of the wooden game booths. "Three chances to win the prize of the night! All ya gotta do is put the ball in the basket. You there, sir, whaddaya say? Win a gold ring for the little lady. . . ."

The barker wore a striped coat and a straw boater, and his skin was emerald green. I stared, and he grinned, but then that grin faded and he took his hat off.

"Oh, I do beg your pardon, Highness! I didn't recognize you. Please, with my compliments!" And he handed me that golden ring.

I slipped the ring on my gloved hand and inclined my head toward him. It seemed like the right thing to do. The barker held his straw hat over his heart and bowed back.

After that, I started seeing all kinds of things. A goblin squatted on the bell for the test-of-strength game, swatting the weight back down whenever a man hit the lever so that no one made the bell ring. The pretty lady in the bathing suit sitting on the platform above the dunk tank was a mermaid. A spotty-faced cook at the lunch counter dished up steaks and fries to a pair of wolves in straw boaters and white linen suits. A couple dressed for dancing was having an argument out front of the Tilt-A-Whirl and a whole crowd of knee-high imps in ball gowns gathered around them and cheered.

This was the in-between place. Fairies and humans both walked here. Except while the fairies could see the humans, the humans couldn't see the fairies.

But I could. For a moment, I felt this couldn't be right, but that feeling was gone in a heartbeat, and it all just seemed funny to me. It was funny and beautiful and just like it should be.

Under all the other voices and commotion, I heard

more music swinging. It was a big band playing hot and strong, just like on the radio. I wrapped my arm around Jack's, and he looked startled for a second, but then he grinned and let me steer him toward the music.

A white pavilion with three peaked glass roofs sprawled ahead of us, glittering in the neon and incandescent bulbs. The music flowed through its arched windows. On the boardwalk out front stood a big sandwich board sign:

FAIRYLAND DANCE MARATHON!

I knew about dance marathons, although I'd never actually seen one. They were contests for prize money, sometimes as much as ten thousand dollars. The idea was that folks would dance and keep on dancing. If they stopped, or fell down and didn't get back up, they'd lose. People danced for days and days, even a whole month without stopping. They had to eat while they danced and try to sleep in each other's arms while still moving around the floor. I guess they must have done something about letting folks use the lavatory, but I didn't know how that worked, and I probably didn't want to.

When I was about nine, a bunch of men organized one in Slow Run. Mama wouldn't let me go see, no matter how much I begged, not even when I said it was just to hear the music, because they had a swell band. All the other kids at school got to go. They said it was a great show. Evan Carter won some money betting who would be the first people to drop. I opened my windows at night, watching the folks coming and going from the lit-up Grange Hall, and listened to the music swinging in the summer air.

But then, after twenty days of dancing, somebody died from exhaustion right on the dance floor, and the guys who ran the show took off with all the entrance fees. The city council outlawed marathons after that.

So I wasn't crazy about the idea of heading toward a dance marathon, but this was where Shimmy had been headed, so I was going too.

The pavilion steps were covered in red carpet. A red velvet rope stretched in front of the open double doors. Behind that rope waited a man with skin and eyes like pure moonless midnight who wore white tie and tails and perfect white gloves. He carried an ebony cane with a silver tip and a handle made of a clear faceted jewel. Anywhere else, I would have thought it was glass. Here, though, I knew it was a real diamond.

"Welcome, Your Highness!" The man bowed deeply to me with his hand over his heart. "Their Imperial Majesties have instructed me to bring you to the receiving hall as soon as you arrive. If you will be so good as to follow me?"

Jack looked at me in a new way, with wonder and respect in his blue eyes. That felt just fine. I drew myself up, put my nose in the air, and waited for the man to unhook the velvet rope and usher us both inside.

The man led us down a hallway, carpeted in red just like the stairs. I think we walked a long way, but I couldn't be sure. The soaring feeling inside me made walking so easy it was hard to gauge the distance. I tried to notice details, but there weren't many. The walls were painted white, and the carpet was pure, bright red over the polished floorboards. There seemed to be a whole lot of framed paintings on the walls, or maybe they were windows. I wasn't sure, and I found I didn't particularly care.

Finally, the corridor opened onto a magnificent hall. The dance was in full swing. A crowd of couples, all dressed in bright gowns and tuxedos, circled the floor to the music of a big band that filled the main stage to overflowing. Men in neat gray jackets sat behind their music stands. They played clarinets and trombones and cornets. There was a double bass and a steel guitar. But up in front of them all was the shining baby grand piano. The man at the piano had a round face, medium-brown skin, a mustache, and a receding hairline, and he smiled and waved his right hand in the air, marking time for the others as the music soared up sweet and clear.

At the far side of the hall stood a smaller, higher stage carpeted in black. At the top were two thrones carved of black wood or maybe black marble. In them sat a man and a woman.

My grandparents.

I knew who they were the second I saw them. But I was stunned by the notion that such swell people could be my flesh and blood. The woman was built full and strong. Her dress was black lace and jet beads, and the train spread out down the steps. Diamonds circled her neck and wrists, and more diamonds sparkled in the tiara that crowned her white hair. Half a dozen women in sparkling ball gowns lined the stage beside her, ladies-in-waiting.

The man was dressed in white tie like all the rest, but his gloves were dove gray and a black cloak lined with gray silk fell from his shoulders. His salt-and-pepper beard was trimmed close to his chin, and he wore a tall golden crown studded with diamonds and emeralds. He had an attendant too, a tall, slim man dressed like him, with gray gloves and a long cape. But that man had a gray sash across his chest, with a golden star shining right in the middle.

The man who'd led us in thumped his cane twice on the floor.

"Her Royal Highness, the princess Calliope LeRoux!"

The dancers stilled and turned and saw. They drew back, making an aisle from me to my grandparents.

"At last." The woman on the throne held her hands out. "Oh, Calliope, at last!"

I walked forward. Maybe the turning-key feeling was in me, or maybe it was just the dizziness of my blood hammering in my ears, but the walls seemed to shift and lean back. All the dancing people bowed as I passed, but they never stopped swaying in time to the music that swelled until it filled the whole world.

I reached the foot of the Midnight Throne. The woman, the queen, my grandmother, stood slowly. I trembled as she looked down on me; there was so much strength in her. A

Kansas twister could have come through the room right then, and she simply would have stared at it until it unwound from shame. She came down the steps to me. I didn't dare move. Her hand slid under my chin, lifting it until I had to look her straight in the eyes. Those eyes were silver, gold, and midnight black. They were like the city at night—dark, light, beauty, sorrow, and danger all mixed up together. They were familiar too. I'd seen them before, but I couldn't remember where.

"Yes," whispered the queen. "I see her father in her." She turned her eyes away from me, and I realized I'd been holding my breath.

From up on his throne, the king of the Midnight People smiled down at me. "Welcome, child," said my grandfather. "Welcome home."

23

Gotta Dance a Little Longer

The people in front of me were royalty. I took hold of my skirt and bent my knees, doing my best to imitate the curtsies I had seen in the movies. Behind me the dancers applauded politely, and I flushed. *Welcome home.* The words echoed in my head and my heart. *Welcome home.*

"Now, granddaughter." The queen, my grandmother, turned toward Jack. "Make this young man known to us."

"This is Jack Holland, ma'am." I grabbed Jack's hand and pulled him forward. He looked next to panicking, but I had no idea why. My anger was all gone. Nothing that had happened outside the gates seemed to matter now that I had been welcomed home. "He's the reason I was able to make it this far. He saved my life a bunch of times."

"Did he?" boomed Grandfather from his throne. "Then we are deeply in your debt, Jack Holland." He inclined his head regally.

"Yes, indeed." Grandmother grasped Jack's hand and

smiled down straight into his eyes. Immediately, a change came over Jack. The panic bled away, and he stood up straighter. He bowed low over my grandmother's hand, and even clicked his heels like a foreign count in a dime novel. It should have looked dopey, but it didn't. It looked . . . debonair. The swaying dancers applauded again. Grandmother's smile went a little tight, and her eyes slid sideways to Grandfather. He nodded.

"We had help from Shimmy too," I told them, and for a moment my rising happiness faltered. "She never let us down."

"Shimmy?" repeated my grandmother.

"She means Shiraz," said the thin man beside the throne. He trotted down the steps, coming close enough that I could see him clearly. Shock knocked my jaw loose.

"Shake!"

Shake bowed. Now I knew why my grandmother's silver and gold eyes looked so familiar. I'd seen eyes like hers when Shake first looked at me, a thousand miles and a thousand years ago.

"Hello, Calliope. Welcome home." Shake smiled his big white smile. "Perhaps I should introduce myself properly. I am Lorcan deMinuit, and I am your father's brother."

"You . . . you're my uncle?"

Shake—Lorcan deMinuit—bowed again.

Anger tried to elbow its way past shock. "Why didn't you say so?"

"I apologize for that. But it is dangerous for our kind to go wearing our names openly in the world beyond. They can be turned against us, which is something you have yet to learn." He said those last words as pleasant and polite as Sunday morning, but there was something in them that didn't sit quite right.

"She . . . Shimmy told me you went on ahead. . . ."

"I did, to make sure all was prepared for your arrival. Where is Shiraz . . . Shimmy?" Lorcan craned his neck to see between the dancers, as if Shimmy might have gotten lost on the way from the door.

Now I had proper hold of my anger, and it was fresh and piping hot. Why hadn't he stayed with her, with us? We could have used his help. Maybe Shimmy would still be alive if we'd had some full-bore fairy magic when Bull Morgan set us in front of that rabbit drive.

"She's dead," I told him.

The music faltered, and the whole crowd gasped. Grandmother's smile faded. Up on the throne, Grandfather said, "Tell us what happened."

So I told them about how Shimmy had come to save us from the Trixies and Bull Morgan in the Bijoux, and about the long car ride and the motel, and about the rabbit drive. While I talked, I felt the anger rising in the room. It made the kind of heaviness in the air you feel when the weather's changing. I glossed over Jack's running out on us as best I could. This might have been my home and family, but there was danger here. I could feel it all across my skin, and despite everything, I didn't want it aimed at Jack.

When I finished my story, Grandfather bowed his

head. "Shiraz was truly one of the Midnight People. She shall be rewarded for the service she has rendered in bringing you home."

I almost opened my mouth to ask how she could be rewarded for anything when she was dead. Then I remembered I was in a magic country now. *Dead* didn't mean the same thing to these people . . . to my family. Hope rose up in my heart. Maybe Shimmy wasn't gone after all.

"Now, I know you have a thousand questions." Grandmother squeezed my arm. "And they will all be answered, I promise. But tomorrow. Tonight we dance. When tomorrow comes, we will talk about your future."

"Play on!" Grandfather raised his hand to the musicians. "We will dance! For Princess Calliope is returned to us!"

A cheer rang around the room, and a single high note rose above the band. It sounded almost like a siren, but the music swept that warning note away and the dancers swarmed to the center of the floor, swirling around, swinging to the hot new tune.

"Come on with me, Jack," said my uncle, Lorcan. "Let me introduce you to some people. We'll let Callie talk with her grandmother for a bit."

Jack hesitated, but Lorcan had a hand on his back and was already steering him toward a group of young women and men, who I was pretty sure were all fairies. Some of those girls were awfully pretty too. Something made me uncomfortable about letting Jack go away like that, but I was having a hard time concentrating. The music swept over me too, sinking into my skin, making me feel all light and easy. Was it possible to get music-logged like you could get waterlogged from lying in the bathtub too long?

"Aren't they magnificent?" Grandmother said, her gold-and-midnight eyes sparkling as she looked toward the bandstand. "Mr. Basie is but lately come to our court. I expect he will be invited back again soon."

"But . . . why did you bring them here?" Because it wasn't just the musicians who were humans. Most of the dancers were too. There were some fairy couples scattered among them, but mostly it was humans out there. I could see the difference now. It showed up in Jack as he stood talking and laughing with the pretty girls on the edge of the dance floor. There was something missing from him, and them, or maybe there was something extra with him. I couldn't make up my mind. But he felt different, and so did the dancers, and so did the band. "And why so many?"

"Bring them?" Grandmother laughed. "We do not bring them. They come to us, my dear." She beamed proudly across the dance floor. "The makers, the beautiful, the ones cast out because their light was too brilliant for the world beyond. The ones who wish true and deep with their whole hearts for more than they have. They come here, and we love them."

"We do?"

"Oh, my dear, of course we do, and they need our love. They are so lonely, so unsure, so hungry for the success of the daylight world. They come here and bring that hope and those wishes to us, and we accept all they have to give."

All. That one word was heavier than the others. It made the music falter. Except it couldn't have, could it? I rubbed my temple. I couldn't sort out my feelings. All the music and happiness were like the wind around my ears. They pushed and pulled at me. But there was something else too. Something tugged at my mind, trying to tell me that I shouldn't relax too much, but I couldn't hear it plainly.

"Is something wrong, dear?" asked Grandmother.

"I, um . . . I was wondering . . . about the music. On the way here, I was listening to the music out on the street and it made me feel kinda funny."

"Oh, my dear." She laughed, but nicely. "Yes. Music is strong drink for our kind. It's so full of feeling and unmet wishes that when you're not used to it, it can go straight to your head. But you're home now, dear. You'll take no harm from the entertainment we have for you. In fact, I think you'll find it quite . . . liberating."

Uncle Lorcan was coming back across the room alone. He bowed to me. "My dear niece, may I have this dance?"

"I can't dance." That wasn't strictly true. I'd danced with Mama in the parlor just for fun. She'd taught me a little swing and how to jitterbug, and every kid at school had to learn how to waltz. But I'd never actually danced in front of, well, people.

"I'm sure you dance beautifully. It's in your blood,

after all." My uncle held out his hand, and Grandmother smiled and gave me a little push toward him.

I was blushing all over, but I let him lead me out onto the floor. The music had changed, slowing down from the swing time to a slow, country sound. One, two, three, one, two, three. Uncle Lorcan put his hands under mine and began to waltz. It was polite, formal, and easy, a simple rhythm that my feet seemed to know better than my head. All the while, Lorcan hummed under his breath, and I remembered Shimmy's humming, and remembered how I'd first met this man.

"Why did you try to get me to think you were my papa?" I asked him.

He smiled, small and kind of sad. "It was something in the nature of a test, I'm afraid. I didn't know what kind of person you were, and I had to find out. I am pleased to say you passed with flying colors."

"Oh."

"You don't have to make that face. You don't realize how important you are, Callie LeRoux—or I should say Callie deMinuit. Without an heir, the Midnight Throne has been in deep danger."

"But you were here. You said Papa abdicated. So wouldn't that make you next in line?"

"If this were a human court, yes. The problem is, you were born before your father completed the ceremony of abdication. He did not know that, of course. But by our laws that makes you the legitimate heir, and me, well, I am second in line."

"But Grandfather's the king, isn't he? He can just change the law."

"You're still thinking like a human, Callie. Human laws have no real hold on their people. It is different for our kind. Our laws—the laws of light and shadow—are born into us. If they are broken, our whole world, our very existence, is broken. You are the heir to the Midnight Throne, Calliope, and will be as long as you draw breath."

I felt like I should say something, although I wasn't sure what. "I'm sorry," I tried. "I didn't want to be . . ."

Uncle Lorcan shrugged. "We can none of us help being born, my dear niece. That is one thing our kind shares with the likes of your young man." Uncle Lorcan nodded toward Jack, who was watching me while one of the fairy girls leaned in and whispered something in his ear.

I felt my face flush all over again. "He's not my young man."

"Well, you would be the one to know." Something I couldn't read glittered in my uncle's eyes. "But you need to take care, Callie. Not everyone wants you here."

Fear touched the back of my neck, a cold, heavy feeling like the press of Morgan's gun.

Uncle Lorcan nodded once. He knew I'd gotten the message. His serious whisper vanished, and he was all smiles again. "Now, you've talked enough with your dull uncle. Let me take you back to Her Majesty."

The music had changed again. No one else stopped dancing, but Uncle Lorcan led me through the swaying, spinning couples. The human dancers seemed to turn pale as we passed, and their faces . . . they were all smiling, but their smiles seemed strained. There was something shifting and rippling between me and them, like a gauzy curtain had fallen over them. That was familiar too, but before I could place it, I was back beside Grandmother.

"Well, my dear, how do you like your celebration?" She spread her hands out to take in the entire hall.

"I love it, but . . ."

"And is not Mr. Basie's music so wonderful?"

"It is, but . . ."

"I think your friend would like a dance, my dear."

My tongue froze against the top of my mouth. Jack was coming across the floor, leaving the fairy girls behind. I'd never danced with a boy. I mean, not really. Not one I liked. There was waltz class at school, but that was a lot different. This was Jack standing in front of me in his fine evening clothes, making me feel funny again. He looked so much older dressed like that, with the wonderful music rising up behind him. He could have been Fred Astaire smiling for Ginger Rogers.

Jack bowed to me, just like he had to my grandmother. "May I have this dance?"

I giggled and made a curtsy. It seemed the thing to do. Then Jack took my gloved hand in his and led me onto the dance floor.

"I probably oughta let you know, I can't actually dance," he confessed.

"It'll be okay," I said. Because now that I was in the

middle of the dance and the music, I knew I could dance however I pleased. What's more, I could help Jack do the same, as easy as breathing. Easy as wishing.

I took Jack's hands, arranging them so one held mine and the other rested against the small of my back. The current of the music and the magic ran through me into him, and just like that, Jack could dance too.

And he was really good. He could swing and sashay and tango and lindy and jitterbug. He swung me around and lifted me up high. I laughed and came down and whirled around with him. I was swimming in the music like a dolphin in the ocean. It had gotten into my blood and my feet. I could have flown to the moon or danced along a high wire. I could do anything. This place was perfect, with its colored lights, its deep shadows, and its music, and I was perfect in it. For the first time in my entire life, I was comfortable in my own skin. This was right where we needed to be. I knew it for sure.

Jack was perfect too. He steered me beautifully during the slow numbers, and when Mr. Basie's band picked up the pace again, we stomped down and kicked back into a swing step.

"Callie . . . ," Jack whispered like someone coming up for air.

"I know!" I cried as the next song began. "Isn't it wonderful?"

There was just a heartbeat before his great big grin spread across his face. "Sure is!"

Jack gripped my hands tightly, and we plunged in deep among the taller, slower dancers. We spun around each other, kicking and jumping high. The music washed through me. I was made of music.

But then a new noise rippled beneath the music. It was a kind of distant roaring, like the wind rushing around the eaves. Out of the corner of my eye, I thought I saw someone fall down.

I blinked and turned my head, trying to see better. All at once, I wasn't in the middle of the glittering crowd anymore. I was in a dim and dusty pavilion. Daylight filtered through tiny strips of window high above. Around me, people in faded dresses and overalls staggered around the dance floor to the strident, off-key music of a tired band. Next to the door hung a sign:

FAIRYLAND DANCE MARATHON!
27 DAYS AND COUNTING!
WHO WILL BE THE NEXT TO FALL?

But Jack, following the music, turned us again, and I caught sight of my grandparents on their thrones. I was in their dance hall again, and I knew that other place was just my imagination. The dance marathon was a whole world away. This was my party. I could dance forever; I was that strong and that free. I grinned at Jack.

But Jack didn't look quite right anymore. He was kind of pale, and his coffee-and-cream freckles stood out sharp against his skin. He was sweating, and he had to close his mouth around his breathing to smile at me and swing me around again.

KANSAS CITY DANCE MARATHON. The words from the flyer I'd pulled out of Shimmy's handbag flickered in front of my eyes again. Why was I thinking about that? This wasn't a dance marathon. This was a celebration, the celebration of my homecoming.

Jack stumbled. I tightened my grip on his hands. His cold hands.

"Jack?"

His jaw sagged open again. "Callie . . . ," he croaked. "Callie, I think something's wrong with me. . . ."

But what could be wrong, with the music and the lights and my grandparents smiling down at us? It was perfect and magical. Like time was standing still.

Like time was standing still. My head surfaced briefly above the current of the music. How long had we been dancing, anyhow? An hour, maybe? I had no idea. There were no clocks in the hall, and I hadn't worn a watch. There were big bay windows that looked over the midway, but as I turned again, I saw all the heavy curtains were closed. I couldn't see anything through them but some faint, flickering light. The peaked ceiling sparkled like glass, but it was just a kind of shimmery solid silver that didn't seem to be letting anything in, either dark or light.

Jack stumbled again.

"Jack . . ."

"Gotta . . . gotta keep moving . . . ," he gasped.

"No. Let's go sit down, okay? I'll get you something to drink."

"Can't. Can't. Gotta keep moving. They say I gotta keep moving."

"Who, Jack? Who says?"

He stared at me. His eyes were clouded over, milky. "Don't know," he wheezed. "Just . . . gotta keep dancing."

I whipped my head around, turning us, trying to catch my grandparents' attention. But they just waved from high on their thrones.

The current of the music pulled hard at me. My grip on my worry started to loosen, and I wanted to let it go. This was where I belonged, inside this life and vitality. I needed to drink it all into myself. I'd be even stronger than I was now. I'd be able to dance forever, and that was all I wanted, wasn't it? Sure, I wanted to talk about who I was and what had happened to my papa. But there was time enough for that later. Grandmother had promised we'd talk when tomorrow got here.

Which was a funny way to say "later." Like when Shimmy said Jack would take no harm walking into her house, when we weren't in her house.

We weren't in her house now either. We were in a magic country where even Death could be pushed around. Could they push around Time too? Thought and memory shoved hard against the music, trying to get up to where they could be seen.

I'd torn time right open back on the prairie, back when it was Jack who believed I was half fairy and I tried to tell him that was all baloney. What if my fairy grandparents could stop time in its tracks?

The music slowed down, becoming sultry. A woman in a sparkling red gown had stepped in front of Mr. Basie's piano. I blinked, and looked, and blinked again.

"SHIMMY!"

Shimmy waved and smiled at me like nothing had ever been wrong. Then she took hold of the microphone and raised her voice to sing.

"Woke up this morning . . ."

Shimmy had a fine voice, full of feeling. She sang—she wept, really—about a man who'd done her wrong, and about how she should never let him go, never, ever let him go.

Jack slumped into my arms, but that didn't seem important. What was important was that Shimmy was alive and well, and right where she wanted to be, home among the fairies, singing for their delight. Grandfather had promised she'd be rewarded, and she was.

I felt I should listen to that song about holding on to your man. I should hold on to mine forever and never let him go.

"Gotta keep moving," Jack said. He was right, of course. I couldn't leave the music or the dance. I didn't belong out there. I never had. I belonged right here, just like Shimmy did. I waved at her, and she winked at me.

But Jack's head lolled against my shoulder, and a bolt of fear shot through to my heart. It touched the spot where I could still muster a sense of right, and that feeling spread up my spine to my drowning head. It occurred to me that this much magic might not actually be good for a normal person. As much as I belonged here with my family, it wasn't Jack's world. I thought maybe I should get him out into the fresh air, away from some of the swirling power.

"Okay, Jack. We'll keep moving." I stretched my neck to see past the dancers until I got a bead on the double doors we'd come through. Jack was supposed to be leading because he was the boy, but he could barely support his own weight now, so I had to take over. I struggled with the rhythm but slowly steered us toward the edge of the dance floor. If I could just get him back outside to the midway, it would be all right. I was sure of it.

"Callie, my dear, where *are* you going?"

I turned us both around, and there was my grandmother.

She didn't look so happy anymore.

24

Gonna Bring This Proud House Down

My hands went cold, and I groped quick after a lie. "I . . . uh . . . I was gonna go ride the Ferris wheel. I've never had the chance before, and neither has Jack."

"Oh, poor thing, he's tired, isn't he?" Grandmother cupped Jack's cheek with her hand. "Well, we're just about to have dinner. You'll both feel so much better after a good meal."

"Oh, yeah, sure." I forced a smile.

"I know it's all very confusing, Calliope," said my grandmother. "But you just finish your dance. When tomorrow gets here, you'll understand. For now . . . well, we're celebrating, aren't we?"

Of course we were. That was exactly what we were doing. How could I forget?

Except those thoughts weren't coming up from inside me. I could feel it now. Those thoughts were from outside, like the music. They pushed their way past my own thoughts and memories. Grandmother was trying to put ideas in my head, and I had the very scary feeling she hadn't even tried her hardest yet.

"Yes, we're celebrating. Of course." I said it because I knew it was what she wanted. It was the direction the current of music and magic moved, and it would be so much easier to just go along with it. If I tried to cut across it, I'd stumble and fall, just like I had during the rabbit drive, when Shimmy died.

But that wasn't important, said those outside ideas to me. That was all long ago and far away. What was important was that Jack and I would finish the dance, and then there'd be a banquet, bigger and grander than anything either of us had seen yet.

Jack would eat too, because he was so hungry. I could feel that as well. This time, he wouldn't be able to hold out. Even though he was the one who told me that if a regular person ate or drank in Fairyland, they'd be trapped.

"Come on, Jack." I shook the hand I held. "We haven't finished our dance."

"Gotta keep moving," murmured Jack.

Grandmother smiled as hard and bright as the diamonds in her crown, and stepped back so I could steer Jack deeper among the dancers.

The band was swinging again, fast and hot. All around

us on the dance floor, people hopped and swung, fast and frantic and happy. Desperately, crazily happy, their eyes as wild as their movements. I dragged Jack over to the bandstand, and as we swayed back and forth, I looked hard at the musicians. They were desperate too. But they weren't happy. They were scared, almost scared to death.

How much time had passed for the regular people? Jack was turning gray. He was going to be sick. I saw waiters laying out platters of food on long tables. Jack's head turned that way, and he groaned like he was starving. And he might have been.

Shimmy wasn't up at the microphone anymore. I turned us around, searching for her. I finally spotted her standing in one of the alcoves with Uncle Lorcan. He cupped a hand around her cheek. She was laughing with him, all loving. All forgiven.

I felt I was being watched. Sure enough, Grandmother was by the door and Grandfather was on his throne, both with their glittering eyes trained right on us. I moved away from the bandstand again. This time, I tried to keep to the edges of the dance. I had to do something and I had to do it soon, or neither one of us was getting out of here. Not that I wanted to. I mean, I had just come home. But Jack couldn't stay.

I bit my lip and tried to think. *These are regular people dancing around us. There must be wishes here.* I reached with my extra sense gently, like I was trying to move through the dark without being heard. But there was not one single wish in that whole hall to catch hold of. All the wishes here were fulfilled. Taken. Grandmother and Grandfather, this place, it had made all their wishes come true, or at least it made them think they had. For them those wishes were so true they noticed nothing else. Not even that they were dancing themselves to death.

I all but dragged Jack to the edge of the dance floor, as far from the music as I could get. It filled my mind like fog, like dust. I couldn't see past it. It made me one of them, the Unseelie. I only cared that the music went on, never mind what it did to the people. But I didn't want to be like that. I strained, searching for a wish, a need, anything I could get my senses into and wrap my wishing power around.

"You'll never get out that way."

It was Uncle Lorcan. All smiles and charm, he had slipped up beside us, and now he stood there, looking out over the crowd, tapping his toe in time to the music.

"Oh, I'm not trying to get out—"

"Of course not." He cut me off, laughing softly. "And he's not your young man dying in your arms. Their Majesties are stronger than you can ever imagine, Callie. You'll never get out of here using magic."

"Help me," I whispered.

Lorcan glanced around, with a huge smile but hard eyes. "There is no help from your father's people. They have you exactly where they want you. You must accept, or you may just burn."

With that, my uncle strolled away.

Jack sagged further. "I need water," he whispered. "Please, Callie. I can't . . ."

I was crying, and even as the sorrow trickled out of me, I felt the music coming in. No one wanted me sad. They wanted me happy. Jack was happy, just a little thirsty. If I relaxed, if I just listened like he did, I'd be happy and it would be all right. I looked to the stage, to Mr. Basie and his band. Mr. Basie was grinning and marking time with the cigarette he pinched in the fingers of his right hand, while his left kept a steady beat on the piano.

There is no help from your father's people.

But it wasn't only my father's people here.

You must accept, or you may just burn.

Mr. Basie put his cigarette back between his lips and returned his full attention to the keyboard. I thought about my uncle when he was still Shake, back in Shimmy's juke joint. I looked at the sheet music on the piano, looked at the curtains, looked at all the cigarettes in all the ashtrays around the musicians and smelled all that tobacco smoke. I remembered how I called down the rain over the rabbit drive and felt it wash away the fairy spell in the folks chasing after us.

If water could wash away magic, what could fire do?

Jack groaned, and his forehead thumped against my shoulder. A plan formed in my head. A crazy, dangerous plan. But I had to try. If we were going to get out of this place, I had to break those doors open with something stronger than the happy magic.

I steered Jack back to the bandstand. I waved and beamed at my grandparents and felt their satisfaction swell over me. You know how you feel when you want to make someone happy? And how it is when you know they're truly proud of you? This was that feeling in tens and twenties.

Holding tight to Jack's hand, I climbed up the bandstand steps to Mr. Basie's piano.

"Well now." Mr. Basie smiled, but his voice was hoarse from smoke and thirst. "What can I do for you?"

"I just wanted to say how much I've been enjoying your music," I said. Then I whispered, "How long have you been here, Mr. Basie?"

Count Basie blinked, then coughed. "You ain't like them," he whispered back. "You gotta get outta here."

"We're all gettin' outta here," I told him. I couldn't leave these other people any more than I could leave Jack. It wouldn't be right.

Mr. Basie was looking toward the throne. "I took this gig and I thought, I thought I'd be gettin' me some good luck with it." He shook his head. "Ain't been like that so much."

"Can you play 'Midnight Special'?" I asked.

"That ain't a dance tune. They"—he nodded toward my relatives—"might not like it."

"Then you turn it into a dance tune. Make it swing. You can do it. Please, Mr. Basie."

The piano player looked at me a long time. He had seen the fairy in me; now I had to pray he saw the human.

"Okay." He nodded. "Freddie!" He jerked his chin to the guitar player. They conferred for a moment, shuffling around sheets of music. The rest of the band kept on playing. The trumpet and the saxophone wailed to each other, carrying on the dance.

Grandmother glanced at me. I smiled big and broad at her and swayed a little, moving my fingers like I was snapping them. Jack swayed where he stood, but he stared at the buffet tables heaped with food like he couldn't see anything else.

Freddie was back with the band, giving them their instructions. Somewhere a long ways away, a siren sounded.

"And now, ladies and gentlemen," said Mr. Basie with a smile that was as bright as any Shake had ever used against me, "me and the boys would like to do our version of 'The Midnight Special.' And as an extra treat, we have Fairyland's very own Callie LeRoux to sing for us. Miss Callie?"

Applause rose up all around me. I had to let go of Jack's hand. He dropped into a chair beside the piano. My grandparents' approval poured over me as I stepped up to the microphone. I was adding to the current of music and magic. They were happy about that. They wanted me to sweep all these people away and be swept away myself.

The microphone was big and square and shining black and silver in the fairy lights. I thought about Mama's humming as she moved around the Imperial, singing a song about wishing for freedom. I thought about the hobo families in the train yard. I thought about Jack's hand in mine as we ran from Bull Morgan, and how Jack always seemed to know which way to go.

I opened my mouth, and I sang.

"Let the Midnight Special shine a light on me . . ."

The current of magic around me doubled. I wasn't just in it now, I was truly a part of it. I could feel the people dance. I could feel their love and their happiness to have all their wishes fulfilled, and how that good feeling meant more than anything in the world. More than life itself.

"Ain't nothin' on the table, ain't nothin' in the pan . . ."

Mr. Basie played. It was the tune I knew, but it leapt and danced all on its own, the meaning of the words hidden down deep behind the syncopation. The music had power, but not from the fairy magic. Mr. Basie was right; this wasn't their song. This wasn't a happy dance tune. This was a song of the dust and the trains and everybody trapped on the work gangs, wishing they would lose their chains. This was the song my mama sang to me, wishing for my papa to come home.

"Yonder come Miss Lucy. How in the world do you know?"

I swayed and I turned, dancing there all on my own. On the floor, someone faltered, and someone fell. I turned again, not fighting the current, letting it carry me around. Like the words, the power of this song was hidden deep down, but I could feel it. It was an entirely different spark from the fairy power. It burned, burned as bright as the matches and the cigarettes the musicians brought in with them.

"She come to see the governor. She gonna free her man . . ."

I grabbed the cigarette burning in the tray, and I stabbed that nasty thing hard against Mr. Basie's sheet music. The sharp smell of smoke hit me a second before the yellow flame jumped up.

Mr. Basie jumped up too.

"Fire!" he yelled. "Fire!"

I snatched the paper. Heat bit my fingertips. But I didn't wave the flame out; I ran for the curtains rippling behind the bandstand and dropped the burning paper on the floor. The heavy velveteen caught, and the flames started licking their way up the dark fabric.

The musicians took up Mr. Basie's shout. "Fire! Fire!" They grabbed their instruments and ran for the doors.

Slowly, the dancers staggered to a halt. They blinked. I felt the moment every one of them smelled the smoke, and the moment they saw the flames chewing on the curtains.

They screamed. They screamed and broke and ran, following the musicians racing for the big open doors.

"Stop!" shouted a bass voice. It was Grandfather, on his feet in front of his throne. "Stop!"

But fire is stronger than magic, and it was spreading. It was licking across the curtains. One of the trumpet players tripped over his chair, and a bunch of chairs and papers and drinks spilled across the bandstand. The liquid hit the burning curtains, and blue alcohol flames leapt up from the floor. The pavilion was burning, and the crowd was shoving its way out the doors, past the point where any glamour, any wishing magic could call them back.

"Time to go, Jack." I grabbed his hand. He blinked too, and looked at me, really looked at me. He was still sick and gray and weak, but he was back. He stumbled to his feet behind me.

The doorway was clogged with struggling people. There was no getting out that way. But there were windows. I jerked open the curtains and saw the bright lights of the midway. Jack and I knew what to do with windows.

Jack yanked off his tuxedo jacket and I pressed my hand right up against his, lacing our fingers. He got the idea and wrapped the jacket around both our arms, tying us together.

"On three!" I reached for my magic. Jack reached for the last of his strength. "One, two, three!"

"STOP!" The force of wish and will tumbled over us, but it was too late. Together, we punched out that sparkling glass. The world key turned, and turned again. I grabbed Jack's shoulders, pulled us forward, and we fell.

And we kept on falling.

25

The Little Black Train's a-Comin'

We fell through a blaze of color. We tumbled and pinged and slammed back and forth. Jack screamed. I screamed. I wanted to pull out my powers and stop the storm. But if I did, we'd stop flying. We'd be stuck in whatever world this was. Their world.

I let us fall.

We hit the boardwalk hard. I screamed some more, and Jack cussed and groaned. I couldn't see straight. The crazy colors we fell through had blinded me. But then I smelled the smoke and cotton candy. I heard the other screams, and something in my brain beyond all the magic jerked itself upright and took me with it. The world cleared, and we were in the amusement park again.

The white pavilion was burning down. People streamed

out of the building, adding their screams to the roar of the fire. There were sirens and bells clanging, and everybody who wasn't running away from the fire was running toward it to watch the show and cheer it on. A fire engine thundered up the boardwalk, and men in heavy coats and red helmets swarmed out and started shouting orders.

"We made it," gasped Jack. He was doubled over, his hand pressed against his belly. "We made it."

But I looked up and saw the green-skinned carnival barker who'd given me my ring. The goblin from the test-of-strength tower sat on the counter at his right hand, and they both had their beady fairy eyes trained on me.

"Not yet, we haven't," I said, more to myself than to Jack. We were back in the tunnel, the passage between. I grabbed Jack's arm. "Come on, we got to get to the outside gate."

But Jack staggered forward two steps and sank to his knees.

"I can't . . . ," he gasped. "I can't. . . ."

He had to. I looked around us and spied an abandoned cart advertising soda pop, five cents a bottle. I reached into its cooler, grabbed a bottle of root beer, and used the opener. I felt no magic or glamour around it, and I ran back to Jack.

He turned the bottle up and drank that root beer like he meant to down it in a single gulp. The screams had lessened, but the smoke was filling the air around us and firelight flickered on the boards. White sparks flew overhead, and the artificial lights all winked. There was just the fire now.

"Come on, come on, come on," I murmured, hoping Jack wouldn't hear me over all the other noise.

But that was a mistake. Because that was me making a wish.

Thhhheeeerrrre shhhheeee issss. . . . It was the voice again, the soft, beautiful, deep voice that had followed me from that first awful day when I'd wished so hard to get out of Slow Run.

No. Oh, no, no, no, not here! "Get up, Jack! They're coming!"

Jack surged to his feet. He followed me as I ran through the heat and the flickering firelight. The stupid Mary Janes pinched my toes, and the slick leather soles skidded against the boards, making me stumble.

"Calliope!" a woman's voice called. "Calliope, where are you going, child? Come home!"

Hearing the sound of my name was like slamming up against a brick wall. I couldn't go forward. It hurt. My feet turned, skidding and sloppy under me.

"Come home!" called Grandmother. "Calliope deMinuit! Come home!"

"Callie, no!" Jack grabbed for my hand.

But Jack wasn't strong enough. I was slogging forward, as helpless against the pull of my own name as he had been against the pull of the dance music.

The touch of Jack's hand slipped away. He was gone,

run off. Again. He'd left me alone to stumble through the stinking smoke and hot ash toward the fire. The little imps in evening dress circled around my knees, cheering. I looked up and saw my grandparents silhouetted against the flames, their arms out in welcome. A deep hole filled with the swirling colors of madness opened behind them.

WHAM!

I was sprawled on my belly. Jack rolled off me before I knew what had hit me, and he stuffed something in my hands. I stared.

It was a frying pan. A big black cast-iron frying pan. Over his shoulder I saw the lunch counter with its stove top, and the human fry cook hollering and leaping over the counter.

"Calliope deMinuit!" called Grandmother again.

But this time, the drag was gone. Jack looked down at me and grinned.

"Let's go!" he said.

I was on my feet and we ran, fast and crazy, away from the fry cook and my grandparents and everything. We were going toward the gate. I didn't need my magic to tell me. Jack always knew the right way to go.

The shot exploded past my ear without warning.

I screamed, Jack screamed, and we both faltered and skidded sideways around the Tilt-A-Whirl.

Bull Morgan walked out of the smoke. And he wasn't alone. A slim male silhouette walked beside him.

Where issss shhhheeee? The voice rode the wind and swirled together with the smoke.

"There!" said Bull Morgan, who despite everything was a human being and couldn't be fooled by iron or steel. He pointed at us with his revolver.

"Thou good and faithful servant!" laughed the man at his side. No. Not a man. I knew the voice now. I'd heard it calling to Bull Morgan, raising him up and driving him back down into the dust. But I'd also heard it singing "St. James Infirmary Blues" in a deserted honky-tonk, and trying to talk me into believing lies about who my father was.

It hadn't been the Seelie who had sent Morgan after us. It had been my uncle, my father's younger brother, the one who would have been the heir to the Midnight Throne if it wasn't for me being born. The one who told me straight-out that I was the heir, as long as I drew breath.

"You're slow, Callie deMinuit." Uncle Lorcan smiled his big white smile down at me. "But then, so was your papa." He turned calmly to Bull Morgan. "Shoot them. We'll toss them into the fire afterward."

"You planned this. You wanted me to start the fire so you could kill me and make it look like an accident."

He bowed. "Their Majesties would be most upset if I spilled family blood, even bastard blood. But a tragic accident, precipitated by your unwise passion for this little mortal boy . . . ah, well. Shoot them," he said again to Morgan.

"You left Shimmy to die," I croaked. "You never told her she was helping to get me killed."

"Poor Shimmy." He shook his head, but his smile never once wavered. "She was so anxious to curry the favor of the court. As if any half-and-half who wasn't the prophecy girl could ever find welcome here. Yes, I used her, and she was glad to be used."

"She never let me down."

"Never, pathetic creature."

"She's behind you!"

He jerked around. I whacked him hard with my frying pan in the small of the back. Jack tackled Bull Morgan, and they rolled over and over on the boardwalk. The ground shook underneath us. The boardwalk was made of wood, and it was still burning. There was a shot. The frying pan in my hands shuddered, and something smacked against my head so hard I staggered. Something went squelch. Now I couldn't see straight. Salt stung my eyes, and all the strength left my hands, so I had to drop the frying pan.

"Callie!" Jack grabbed my hand and dragged me after him. "You gotta wish us outta here, Callie!"

But I couldn't see. There was something dark getting into my eyes. My ears rang louder than the fire alarms. My head was burning, and I wondered if I'd caught fire.

"Stop!" bawled Morgan. "Stop in the name of the law!"

"'The Midnight Special,' Callie!" cried Jack. "Sing it!"

I wanted to get away. I wanted to get Jack away. I felt my name being called, and I had no iron to get in the way of that summons. I opened my mouth, but I could only whisper:

"Let the Midnight Special shine a light on me . . ."

My head was spinning. I couldn't hold my thoughts together. All the other train songs rattled around in my frightened skull: "Rock Island Line," "This Train," "Little Black Train." All the words all mixed up in the wishes and commands and fire.

"If you wanna ride it, gotta ride it like you find it . . . this train she's bound for glory . . . don't carry no gamblers . . . let the Midnight Special shine a light, shine a light, shine an ever-lovin' light . . . this train she's bound for glory . . . gotta ride it, gotta ride it like you find it . . . this train . . ."

And I didn't care. I didn't care which train, which gate or door we could find. I had to get out of there. I had to get Jack out of there. I had to. There was no one else, not with the smoke and the fire and my treacherous family all behind us.

This train, this train, this train . . .

"I got yer mammy!" said Morgan.

I skidded to a stop and turned my head. Too slow, too late. Morgan didn't have hold of Shimmy, but my hesitation was just enough, and his big, soft, cold hands clamped around my waist, lifting me high. Jack hollered and swore, and Morgan kicked him aside. He started to squeeze hard, squeeze all the air out of me.

"Die! Die, you stupid pickaninny brat! Gonna kill you dead like you killed me!"

"No!" cried Jack. I couldn't breathe, couldn't scream, couldn't see.

Mama! My heart wailed to the black sky. *Help me! Mama!*

This train, whispered the wind that blew down from that sky. *This train . . .*

A new note cut across the roar of fire and fear. Louder than any alarm bell, longer than any note from any horn. New light fell across us, blinding white and strong enough to cut through any smoke. Morgan hollered, and his killing grip around my middle let loose. I dropped to the boards, and Jack was on his knees next to me, pulling me up and wrapping his arms around me.

A clanging and a chugging filled the world, followed by the squeal of brakes and the hiss of steam. I tried to look up, but the new light was so strong, I could only squint.

There on the edge of the boardwalk stood a railroad engine. It was shining black iron, bigger than anything else in the whole world. Clouds of steam wreathed around it, and the brass ringing of its bell drowned out all the other noises.

I stared. Jack stared. Morgan hollered and fell back. The gun in his hand went off, and the bullet pinged off the side of that big black engine and did no harm whatsoever.

The engine pulled a string of passenger cars, just as black, with the shades pulled down so no light came from the windows. The door on the first car swung open smoothly, and a man in a white porter's jacket and a shiny billed cap walked down the stairs. He was treetop-tall and had skin as black as the Midnight Throne. He saw me and Jack huddled on the ground gawping up at him, and folded his arms. But it wasn't us he was frowning at.

"I been waitin' on you, Samuel Morgan." His big black hand clamped around Morgan's shoulder and lifted him up off the ground. "You just about done throwed off my whole schedule."

26

Kind Friends,
This May Be the End

Dangling from the porter's grip, Morgan raised his gun and pointed it at the man's broad face. The porter just looked disgusted and wrenched the revolver out of the railroad bull's gray fingers, tossing it away into the steam clouds.

"Last call!" cried a voice from deep inside the train. "All aboard!

The giant of a porter looked down at me and Jack. "You two coming?"

Weakness washed over me, mixing with the pain in my head and the feel of the flames at my back. But Jack pulled me to my feet and shoved me in front of him up the steps of that black Pullman car, climbing in behind.

You know how people talk about the weight of the world slipping off their shoulders? That was what I felt as

276

soon as I reached the top of those stairs. All at once, I wasn't tired anymore. I felt fine. Nothing hurt, and I could see perfectly well. I could stand. I could walk. I wasn't even hungry.

The porter came up the steps behind us, carrying Bull Morgan at arm's length as easy as he'd carry a rotten apple by its stem.

"Okay, Mr. Jones!" he called toward the engine. "We got 'em."

There was a narrow pass-through behind me. I could see the sooty confines of the engine, and the engineer in his dusty overalls. The firebox was open, and the burly fireman shoveled in a load of coal from the big pile next to him. The engineer mounted the cab. The whistle sounded, and the train pulled smoothly forward.

"These two are my prisoners!"

Bull Morgan straightened himself up. He wasn't swollen, damp, and gray anymore. He was the living man as I'd first seen him in Constantinople. As if to prove it, he yanked his club out of its holster and waved it at the porter. "You got no right, you . . ."

But the porter just clamped two huge fingers around the club and pulled it out of the bull's hand. He closed his fist around it. There was a loud, short crunch, and sawdust trickled down to the carpet.

"I am the porter in charge of this train, Samuel Morgan. You will sit yourself down and mind your p's and q's until you get where you're going."

He put his hand on Morgan's shoulder again and

pushed him into the nearest seat. He snapped his fingers, and Bull Morgan's head dropped back. His mouth opened, and for a second I thought he was dead, until I heard the long, rumbling snore.

Apparently satisfied, the porter turned to smile all the long way down to me and Jack, and touched the brim of his hat. "Pleased to have you on board, Jacob, Calliope."

"We can't ride this train," Jack whispered. "We don't have tickets."

The porter chuckled. "Oh, everybody on my train's prepaid, don't you worry. You just be comfortable. We'll be at the station shortly." He pulled a gold turnip watch out of his pocket and checked it. "Yes, indeed. Right on time." He tucked the watch away and touched the brim of his hat again. "You need anything, you just pull the cord and ask for Daddy Joe, porter in charge. Now, if you and Calliope will excuse me, there's some folks in the back I've got to see to." He walked briskly down the aisle. The train rattled and bumped over the tracks, but Daddy Joe didn't so much as sway as he strode toward the rear of the car.

I turned to Jack, my mouth open, and I swallowed my words.

If I'd gotten better, Jack had gotten worse. He was sick and gray again as he stared around the dim car at all the passengers.

"*Shema yisroel, adonoi eloheinu, adonoi echod,*" he croaked. "*Boruch shem k'vod malchuso l'olam vo'ed.*"

"Jack!" I shook his shoulder. "Jack, what is it?"

"Don't you see, Callie?"

I looked around. I saw a Pullman Palace Car stuffed full of people, all kinds and all ages of people. There were women with babies in their arms, and all sizes of kids, both with their parents and on their own. There were old people tricked out in their Sunday best, sitting up straight and calm. Some were smiling like they were on the way to a vacation they'd been saving for forever; others looked sad; some looked even more scared than Bull Morgan had when he saw Daddy Joe the porter reach down for him.

"What do you see?" I asked Jack.

"They're dead, Callie. That one . . . that one's been shot, and that one's got her head on her lap, like she needs a hatbox. That one's got the scarlet fever, and that one . . ." He shuddered and closed his eyes. "What do you see?"

"They all look fine to me. They look . . . they look like they're on a train trip. Nothing special, except . . ." Then I realized what was special, what I'd missed before. "Except black and white and brown, they're all sitting together. Nobody's split them up."

Then I looked at them harder. "Can you see their eyes?" I asked Jack.

"Yeah."

"I can't. They've got no eyes." They didn't. Where their eyes should have been in all those calm, slightly curious faces were nothing but black holes.

"Which of us do you think is seeing true?" asked Jack.

"I think we both are." I paused, and slowly touched

the place on my head where I'd been hit by . . . something. My skin and skull didn't feel smooth like they should. They felt ragged and loose. "Jack . . . Jack, what do you see looking at me?"

He swallowed, and he struggled. "You're . . . you're shot, Callie. Your head."

Which was really all I needed to know about that. "Okay."

"Does it hurt?" he asked softly.

"No. I don't feel anything at all." I didn't even feel afraid. It was like I was cut off from all that. Jack, clearly, wasn't having any such luck.

"Maybe we should sit down," I suggested.

"Yeah."

We found a couple of seats right at the front, where Jack could stare at the wall and not have to see the other passengers. I took the window seat. The shade was down, but I hooked one finger around the edge and pulled it back, just far enough to see.

White clouds billowed all around us. Not steam clouds. Clouds. Overhead stretched the sparkling white river of the Milky Way. Down below, the earth spread out like a carpet, all green and brown in the sunrise.

I let the shade drop into place and fell back against the plush seat.

"What did you see?" asked Jack, but I just shook my head. He did not want to know.

"Can you wish us outta here, Callie?"

I swallowed, and I stretched out my senses, but there

was no feeling. No, that wasn't right. There was plenty of feeling, but it was beyond me. It was like trying to wrap my hand around the wind. These people were past my touching, past anybody's touching. Or maybe it was because I couldn't feel my own self anymore. Maybe if I could have still gotten to my pain or my fear, I would have found my magic, but that was all gone.

I shook my head again. No wish was going to get us off this train. I reached for Jack's hand. It was cold. But then, so was mine.

I don't know how long that ride took. Maybe it took no time at all. But it didn't feel like the timelessness of Fairyland. There was nothing frenetic about this, nothing hidden under any veil. The train held a calm like earth and stone.

At last, Daddy Joe the porter came up the aisle. "Union Station!" he called. "Union Station, last stop! All out at Union Station! All connecting trains at Union Station!"

The rocking and rattling slowed. The brakes shrieked and the steam whooshed out. Light streamed in around the shades. People got to their feet. No one reached for any luggage. They just moved into the aisles and climbed down the stairs.

I looked at Jack. Jack looked at me. "I guess we gotta," he whispered. I nodded.

We joined the queue of passengers waiting to exit the car. I tried to be afraid for Jack's sake, and for my own, because if I was afraid, maybe I wasn't like . . . like the others.

We stepped out of the car into the biggest, grandest

SARAH ZETTEL

station I'd ever seen, even in the movies. It was built with a hundred different shades of marble, white and black and green and pink, all laid out in fine and fancy patterns. Everything was edged with gold, and the arched dome ceiling was aquamarine and filled with stars. Except for the tunnel the train had come through, there were only two exits, one marked NORTHBOUND TRAINS and the other SOUTHBOUND TRAINS.

The platform was crowded with people. Like the train passengers, they were all ages and all colors. They waved and shouted to the disembarking passengers. Couples embraced and kissed. Parents hugged their children and hoisted little ones up on their shoulders. Friends clasped hands and cried joyful tears. But there were cops too, in clean blue uniforms, who, all silent and solemn, linked arms with some of the passengers and walked them toward the stairs marked SOUTHBOUND.

Jack and I stared around. I had no idea what to do or where to go. Then I turned to see Daddy Joe coming down the stairs, with Morgan tucked under one arm. Morgan kicked and waved his fists, but this didn't seem to bother the porter at all.

"I . . . uh . . . Mr. Joe, what do we do?" I asked.

"Sorry. Not for me to say. I got to see this one delivered." Daddy Joe shook Morgan until his teeth rattled. "Besides, this young man's got somebody waiting on him."

"Jacob!"

She came pushing through the crowd. I recognized her

right off. She had Jack's blue eyes and the same brown hair, although hers was long and all in curls.

"Hannah!" Jack cried. "Hannah!"

The little girl leapt into Jack's arms, and he caught her and whirled her around so easily I knew they'd done it a thousand times before.

I grinned up at Daddy Joe. He touched his hat brim.

"Please," whispered Morgan from under the porter's arm. "Please, help me."

"You remember you said that," rumbled Daddy Joe. "Maybe next time it'll go better. 'Scuse me, Calliope."

Daddy Joe slung Morgan over his shoulder and marched away down the southbound stairs.

Jack hadn't noticed any of this, of course. He was on his knees in front of his little sister. "I'm sorry, Hannah. I'm so sorry. It was all my fault. Can you forgive me?"

But she leaned forward and rubbed her nose against his. "Silly!" she cried. "It wasn't your fault. Not ever. And I'm okay now."

"Are you really?"

She nodded. "Truly. And I do forgive you for not playing dolls with me."

Jack barked out a laugh, and the two of them hugged for a long time.

"I've been awful worried about you, though," said Hannah solemnly when she was finally able to pull away from her brother. "You wouldn't let go of me, and they were using it to hurt you." She laid her hand over his heart.

"You won't let them do that anymore, will you, Jacob? Please."

"I won't, Hannah. I promise. But . . ."

"But what?"

"I'm . . . I'm dead, aren't I?"

She laughed. "Not yet, Jacob. Not you."

They both turned to look at me. That huge, bustling station suddenly felt very small and very still. I reached my hand to the loose spot on my scalp and let it fall down again.

"Callie?" Jack whispered.

"That's up to her," said Hannah.

"What do you mean?" The words crawled awkwardly out of me.

Jack's little sister didn't have eyes in her face, but she didn't have empty holes either. Her eyes were like Baya's, filled with night and stars, and she was studying me, not hard, but kindly, like she just wanted to know me better. "Sometimes people who make it this far have to make a decision."

I looked from the northbound stairs to the southbound, and Hannah Hollander laughed hard.

"Not that kind of decision! That's made way before any of us get here. No. You've got to decide whether to go back or not."

The train was still behind me. I could hear the clink of cooling metal. The crowd had cleared out. The Hollands—Hollanders—and I stood alone on the platform.

"What about my grandparents, my mother's parents?"

"They weren't sure you'd want to see them, but they're

waiting for you that way." Hannah waved toward the north-bound stairs.

"My folks aren't here, are they?"

"Nope. They're still in the lands of the living."

"And Jack?"

Hannah's smile drooped slowly, and Jack took her hand. "Whatever you do, Callie, Jacob's got a long way to go yet."

But I didn't have to go so far. Not if I didn't want to.

I looked at Hannah and saw how she shone all happy. I felt a kind of peace settling around me. I thought about the way the faces of the people lit up as they climbed the stairs with their friends and family. I thought about seeing Grandma and Grandpa again, about being able to forgive and just be family, *real* family, without any schemes or tricks or traps.

But my parents weren't here. Mama and, yes, Papa were out in the wide, living worlds somewhere. Grandma and Grandpa couldn't help them. The king and queen of the Midnight Throne wouldn't help them. If I went up those stairs, the throne would go to Uncle Lorcan, and it would be like Mama and Papa didn't exist.

I had a choice to make, and I made it.

"I'm going back."

Hannah nodded solemnly. "It's going to be hard," she said. "That prophecy? It's still there. Both sides are going to want you for their own, and they are not going to give up easy."

"Neither am I," I said.

Hannah Hollander nodded, her brown curls bobbing. "You'd better take Jacob with you, then. You're gonna need him."

"Maybe . . . ," I began, but Jack shook his head.

"Oh, no. I'm seeing this through. How else am I gonna know how the story ends?"

There was a lot under those words. I'd go digging for it later.

Jack turned to his sister, his face creasing to hold back tears and get ready for good-bye. Little Hannah just went up on her tiptoes, wrapped her arms around him, and hugged him tight.

"It's okay, Jacob. I can come meet the train anytime."

"Thanks, Hannah."

"You take care of yourself, all right?" She looked him in the eyes with her midnight and stars.

"I will, I promise." He kissed her forehead, and she rubbed his nose. Then she spun around and ran up the northbound stairs. At the first landing, she turned and waved, and we both waved back.

Hannah whisked out of sight, and Jack lowered his hand. If the weight of the world had slipped from me when we boarded the train, I could see it rolled off Jack now. He'd been forgiven by his little sister, and I could see he'd forgiven himself too. Here, on the edge of all the worlds there were, something tight and hard had vanished from behind Jack Holland's eyes, and I was pretty sure it was gone for good.

He turned to me and took both my hands. "I got a wish, Callie. I wish you were better. I wish we were back in Kansas City."

We linked elbows and strolled away. I made the world key turn with a wave of my hand. It had never been this easy before, and I was sure it never would be again. But that was later.

Right now, a door opened in front of us, and we went through, walking easy and free all the way back to Kansas City.

Author's Note

No story springs to life in a vacuum. This one, however, has a longer history and more sources than much of what I've written before.

The story really started back when I was a kid listening to Woody Guthrie's Dust Bowl ballads while reading *The Wonderful Wizard of Oz* by L. Frank Baum. It came to life under the influence of *The Worst Hard Time* by Timothy Egan, *Riding the Rails: Teenagers on the Move During the Great Depression* by Errol Lincoln Uys, *Rising from the Rails: Pullman Porters and the Making of the Black Middle Class* by Larry Tye, and *Jazz* by Gary Giddins and Scott DeVeaux. Frequently, the most powerful influences for an author are novels, and two were very much in my mind as I worked on this book: *They Shoot Horses, Don't They?*, Horace McCoy's chilling story of dance marathons during the Depression, and *The Grapes of Wrath* by John Steinbeck. I also was able to draw on the eyewitness accounts collected by the Dust Bowl Oral History Project of the Ford County Historical Society (skyways.org/orgs/fordco /dustbowl/) and the writings and images compiled by Kansas State University (weru.ksu.edu/new_weru/multimedia /dustbowl/dustbowlpics.html), as well as *Farming the Dust*

Bowl: A First-Hand Account from Kansas by Lawrence Svobida, and of course the photographs taken by Dorothea Lange.

Oh, and just for the record—I did not make up the Fairyland amusement park in Kansas City. I found it in the book *Kansas City Jazz: From Ragtime to Bebop—A History* by Frank Driggs and Chuck Haddix. So thanks, gentlemen: you made me rewrite the entire second half of the story.

Suggested Playlist

Nothing tells the story of a time and place like music. So when the story for *Dust Girl* began to take shape, I went to the music of the 1930s, the Dust Bowl, and the Depression for insight and inspiration. Below is a partial list of songs and ballads I drew on to help Callie and Jack on their way.

"Dance a Little Longer," words by Woody Guthrie, music by Joel Rafael

"Do Re Mi," words and music by Woody Guthrie

"Drill, Ye Tarriers, Drill," attributed to Thomas Casey (lyrics) and Charles Connolly (music)

"Dust Bowl Refugee," words and music by Woody Guthrie

"Dust Pneumonia Blues," words and music by Woody Guthrie

"Going Down the Road Feelin' Bad," words and music by Woody Guthrie and Lee Hays

"Hard Travelin'," words and music by Woody Guthrie

"I Ain't Got No Home," words and music by Woody Guthrie

"Little Black Train," words and music adaptation by Woody Guthrie

"The Midnight Special" (traditional), sung by Huddie Ledbetter to John and Alan Lomax, 1934

"My Oklahoma Home (It Blowed Away)," words and music by Sis Cunningham

"Rock Island Line" (traditional), collected by John and Alan Lomax

"St. James Infirmary Blues" (traditional), recorded by multiple artists

"So Long, It's Been Good to Know Yuh," words and music by Woody Guthrie

"Take This Hammer" (traditional), collected by John and Alan Lomax

"This Land Is Your Land," words and music by Woody Guthrie

"This Train Is Bound for Glory," new words and music adaptation by Woody Guthrie

"Tom Joad," words and music by Woody Guthrie

"Vigilante Man," words and music by Woody Guthrie

About the Author

Sarah Zettel is an award-winning science fiction and fantasy author. She has written twenty novels and many short stories over the past seventeen years, in addition to practicing tai chi, learning to fiddle, marrying a rocket scientist, and raising a rapidly growing son. *Dust Girl* is her first novel for teens. Visit her online at sarahzettel.com.